· *Digging to Australia* ·

LESLEY GLAISTER

Minerva

A Minerva Paperback
DIGGING TO AUSTRALIA

First published in Great Britain 1992
by Martin Secker & Warburg Limited
This Minerva edition published 1993
by Mandarin Paperbacks
an imprint of Reed Consumer Books Ltd
Michelin House, 81 Fulham Road, London SW3 6RB
and Auckland, Melbourne, Singapore and Toronto

Reprinted 1993

A CIP catalogue record for this title
is available from the British Library
ISBN 0 7493 9864 7

Printed and bound in Great Britain
by Cox & Wyman Ltd, Reading, Berks

· Digging to Australia ·

Lesley Glaister is the author of
Honour Thy Father, which won a
Somerset Maugham and a Betty Trask
Award, and *Trick or Treat*.
She lives in Sheffield.

for Pete
with love

Empompey polleney,
pollenistic,
Empompey, polleney,
Academic,
So fa me,
Academic,
Poof, poof.

These are words to clap to with rapid slapping hands in a playground full of girls. They are words to chant so fast that they spill like glitter off the tongue, dazzling the girls who don't know. Mystifying the girls at the edges who lurk in doorways and long for the bell to go.

They are also a way of stopping thought. Not forgetting entirely, for that is impossible. But a means of jolting a memory off its track. A barrier of gibberish.

· Part One ·

· *One* ·

Mama told me, a very long time ago, that an ancestor of ours had been transported to Australia. The ancestor's name was Peggy, and all she'd done was steal a peacock. She was sent on a convict ship to Australia and never seen again. Fancy stealing a peacock. That's all that is known of Peggy. I don't even know whether the peacock was alive or dead. And that matters. Did she steal it for its beauty, or for her dinner?

We were standing in the kitchen and Mama was filling my hot-water bottle. My bare feet were cold against the floor.

'Where's Australia?' I asked.

She pointed at the floor. 'The other side of the world,' she said. 'As far away as you can get.'

I considered this. I already knew the world is like a ball. Bob had demonstrated with an orange how it moves around the sun. We used the orange for the sun and his globe for the earth. Of course, the scale was all wrong. To get the proportions right, he said, I would have had to carry the orange into the centre of town.

The globe was beautiful. It was an old heavy thing on a rickety stand. The land was all brown as mud and the pale sea netted with fine lines, meridians and tropics, things that had no meaning for me, although I liked the names. Sometimes I would spin the globe round and round so that it rattled and rocked, and then read the name of the place where my finger pointed when it had stopped: Madagascar, the Tropic of Capricorn, the Soloman Islands, Peru.

'What's it like, in Australia?' I asked.

'Topsy-turvy,' Mama said, screwing the lid on my bottle

and wiping it with a tea-towel. 'Their seasons are all upside-down. They eat their Christmas dinner on the beach.'

I went to bed that night thinking how glorious that must be, the crackers and the pudding and the holly against the gold and blue of sand and sea. I could just picture Peggy in some sort of long, old-fashioned dress but otherwise looking just like Mama, with the peacock strutting beside her on the shore, a purple paper crown upon her head.

One birthday – when I still believed my birthday was in June – Mama and Bob gave me a book. I was disappointed. I wasn't much of a one for books. Boring, I thought as I unwrapped it, although I looked pleased. Mama had made the wrapping paper herself, potato prints in powdery paint that came off on my fingers. On the flyleaf she had written, *To Jennifer, Happy Birthday, Love from Mama and Bob, June 1966.* The first *e* in Jennifer was altered, as if she'd started to write something else by mistake. I put the book on the shelf in my room and didn't look at it again for ages. It wasn't until I was ill, feverish and fretful and bored, that Mama began reading it to me. The book was *Alice in Wonderland*.

Mama sat on the edge of my bed reading. Her voice was monotonous and soothing. She paused periodically to wipe my face with a cool flannel. The room was cold, for Bob insisted that we keep a window open in every room in all weathers, except fog. This was extravagant because it meant keeping the stove roaring all winter to feed the radiators, but it was one of Bob's foibles. Our lives were ruled by Bob's foibles. I think this was a good one though, for we rarely suffered from colds. The lace curtain stirred slightly in the breeze. Mama shivered, but I burned. The sun shone coldly into the room, sharpening the edges of things so that they hurt my eyes. I kept them closed and listened to Mama, and her voice was something safe and solid to hold onto in the helter-skelter of my fever, something healthy.

'Starve a fever,' Bob proclaimed, and so I had not eaten for two days. Mama, who went along with Bob in most things, eventually sneaked me up a terrible nourishing drink – raw egg beaten into milk – and stood over me while I drank it, tears of disgust standing in my eyes. The story was silly, I thought, until she came to the part where Alice falls down the hole, and I had to open my eyes to stop myself from feeling as if I was tumbling downwards past cupboards and pictures and jars of marmalade on shelves. '*Down, down, down,*' Mama droned. '*Would the fall never end? "I wonder how many miles I've fallen by this time?" Alice said aloud. "I must be getting near the centre of the earth."*' I wondered if it was possible, not to fall of course, but to travel somewhere, through the earth, to get to Topsy-Turvy Land, the Antipathies, Alice called it, but I knew *that* couldn't be right.

Mama put the book down. 'All right?' she said. 'I'll have to stop now, it's time to cook Bob's dinner.' Mama had a gap where a tooth had fallen out. Not a front tooth, but one at the side that you could only see when she smiled. She rarely smiled properly because of this, especially in public, but sometimes she forgot. She smiled at me as I lay in bed though. I know because I saw the dark gap in her mouth and it gave me my idea. I would dig to Australia.

Down at the end of the garden, past the lawn and the vegetable plot and the fruit trees, was a patch that was mine. I had grown nasturtiums and radishes and marigolds but I was fed up with gardening, nothing turned out like it looked on the seed packet. I did like to be outside though. I liked activity and fresh air. I loved to dig.

When I was well enough to go downstairs wrapped in my dressing-gown, my legs weak and fuzzy, I had a look at Bob's globe. I put one finger on the tiny smudge that was Britain and reached my arm round to find the opposite side of the world. It wasn't quite Australia, it was a place in the Tasman Sea. The nearest speck of land was called Loyalty Island. But it was near enough. I don't think I really believed I could do it. Certainly I knew it wouldn't be easy or quick. I was prepared to take weeks, months even. Bob said it would be impossible, but that only spurred me on. If it had never been done before, then that was the best reason to try.

I had been excused the daily dozen while I was ill, but as soon as I was better Bob insisted that I join them again. It was a dull morning, a school morning. Bob took off his dressing-gown. Mama hastened to the curtain and twitched a gaping corner shut.

'Come along then,' Bob said. 'Breathe.' He began to inhale and exhale loudly, swinging his arms backwards and forwards in time with his breaths. He had his back to the fireplace, feet planted squarely apart. Bob was naked. His body was pink and plump beneath a curling grey fuzz. His chest made me think of gorilla breasts and his paunchy belly cast a discreet shadow on the soft giblets beneath.

Mama slipped out of her dressing-gown. She stood behind me, as always, so that I could not see her, only hear a rustle as the soft fabric crumpled on the floor.

'Come along, Jennifer,' Bob said. I never had the gumption to refuse, not then. I unbuttoned my pyjamas and took them off.

'Shoulders back,' Bob said and I stood up straight between them, aware of Bob's eyes on my naked front, and Mama's on my back. 'Now, breathe in . . . and . . . over and . . .' and we embarked upon the stretching, the toe-touching, the arm-circling and the ungainly joggling about on the spot. The open window sucked the curtain against it with a sad gasp and an oblong patch grew damp with rain. I wondered, as I always did, why it was called the daily dozen when there was never a dozen of anything as far as I could tell. This was another of Bob's foibles, this morning ordeal. I think it was his worst. No, the worst was the nakedness. We weren't allowed clothes for the exercises, that was bad enough, but what was even worse was that Bob wouldn't wear clothes at all in the house.

Mama and Bob had both been naturists once, they had met at a campsite where everyone frolicked naked in the sun. That's what they said, only all I could think of was brambles and goose pimples and rain. Mama had changed her mind gradually over the years. She thought bodies terribly boring, she confided to me once, when there were so many lovely clothes to wear. Mama went along with Bob in the mornings though, and I thought little about it. It was just what we did.

'And down and down and down and down,' Bob continued, breathless now, stretching one leg to the side and bending his knee like an archer so that his belly drooped almost to the floor. The grey curls on his chest were moist with sweat. 'And cease,' he said finally.

· Two ·

I had no proper friends at school, that was why I didn't like it. It wasn't because I was stupid that I never answered questions, it was because I was shy. I couldn't have friends like the popular girls because I didn't know how. It would have been all right if I'd been the same as them but I felt that I was different. I could never ask a friend round for a start, because Bob, being retired, was always there, and always quite bare. I couldn't let anyone else see his giblets and his great round woolly bottom, all creased from his chair. Word would have got round and they would never have stopped laughing. And he was an old man, all grey and done-for, not like the fathers I sometimes noticed dropping their daughters off at school, with black or brown hair and shirts and ties and cars. Bob wouldn't get a television either. Not everyone had one then, but the popular girls did, and they invited their best friends home for tea and *Blue Peter*. Everyone wanted to be friends with those girls. Bob said that televisions gave off gamma rays that rotted the brain. Instead we played games. The family that plays together stays together, he used to say, rubbing his hands and squelching his behind on his leather chair, and my heart would sink.

It was later that I started to dig the hole. It was a hot day marooned in the middle of the summer holidays, and I was twelve, already old enough to know that it was an impossible venture. But it was something to do. In the beginning the digging was easy. The soil was loose and I had got down a foot or more before it became really hard work. The soil grew darker and harder, packed solid, and there were stones, great knuckle-like flints and shards of slate that jolted the spade and refused to give. I had to get down and grub them out of the earth with my hands. There were worms threaded in the earth, and sometimes I sliced one into two flinching pieces with my spade. I was sorry to hurt them, but Bob said that both halves would live so that there'd be two worms instead of one. Mama said that that was nonsense and only the half with the head would live. And I still don't know whether either of them was right – or whether both halves die. There were centipedes too, and millepedes, and other grubs and scuttling creatures, and fine roots stretching from somewhere. I worked hard with my mind on another place, a place where I partly belonged because of Peggy the ancestor. I worked until there were blisters on my hands, thinking of buried treasure, ribbed caskets opening to spill gold doubloons and pearls. And soon I knew for sure that I would never get anywhere. Not this way. I had made a trench that I could stand in up to my waist, but that was nothing. Our garden backed onto a footpath, hidden from view by a high wooden fence, but we were above the footpath, so that even with all my digging I still hadn't reached the level of the ground behind. If I crouched in my trench I could get my head below the surface and breathe in the private smell of the earth, and feel the coldness. The soil was complicated, seen close to, not haphazard. It was an arrangement of filaments and pebbles and grains and damp-looking living things. It was a live thing itself, and that surprised me. I licked the earth and recognised the taste of potatoes.

Our back garden was surrounded by low walls but inside these Bob had built a high wood-slatted fence. Mama had insisted on this if Bob wanted to sunbathe naked. But there were knot-holes in the fence, and I used to press my eye against one at the bottom of the garden and watch people walking their dogs. Once I saw a boy and a girl kissing. I wasn't allowed to use the footpath by myself because it was so secluded. And, Mama warned me, there was danger in seclusion. Although I had given up the idea of Australia, or Wonderland, I still kept at my hole, partly because Bob was waiting for me to give up.

'Getting close?' he'd say, or, 'Through the earth's crust yet?'

One very hot afternoon I was messing about with the hole, digging and scraping listlessly, just waiting for tea-time, when I got down to some damp gravelly sand. It was grey, not at all like seaside sand although it was pretty in a clean, glistening way and it was surprisingly easy to dig. It was fun to dig after the stiffness of the earth, and so I carried on a bit longer just to see what would come next. I was digging very close to the fence, and suddenly to my surprise the sand began slipping away. I could hear it falling. There was a brick missing, two bricks, three, in the wall that supported the garden, and the sand and the soil gave way and fell down onto the footpath, leaving a space big enough to drop through. It wasn't far to jump and I stood on the footpath for a moment, scared and thrilled, looking up at the high walls and fences on our side, and the low gates and ramshackle sheds on the other. A marmalade cat which had fled when I landed crept back and rubbed itself against my legs. Its fur was quite hot from the sun. I didn't stay long that first time. It was enough that I had done it – got somewhere. I stood alone where I was forbidden to be until the cat sauntered off, and then I scrambled back up through the gap. I was very dirty, for the earth was still loose, but I could see how I could widen it so that I could get in and out more easily.

'I'm giving up my hole,' I announced at tea-time that day.

'Thank goodness for that,' Mama said. And Bob merely smirked.

· *Three* ·

Every day I slipped through the hole and walked on the
footpath. It was a game, the game of a lonely girl. And it
wasn't as dangerous as Mama and Bob thought. Nothing
ever happened to me. I hardly ever saw anyone. A woman
with a dog said hello sometimes, as if it was quite an
ordinary thing that I should be there. I discovered that
this path was part of a labyrinth that threaded between
and behind houses, that you could walk for miles this
secret way, and see into people's back gardens, see their
end-of-the-garden clutter – broken bikes and lawnmow-
ers, old window-frames and dead Christmas trees in pots.
On hot afternoons the paths were full of pollen and bees.
Poppies grew in one place, and I took some home for
Mama to make into ballerinas with crumpled scarlet skirts.
She asked me where I got them but I didn't say. I was
good at being vague.

Lots of cats lived on the paths. Most of them were sleek
pets with collars and little bells, playing at being wild but
never straying far from their saucers of milk. They had
their own territories though and sometimes I surprised
two cats, frozen into attitudes of defence, that would slink
off unwillingly at my approach, shooting threatening
looks over their shoulders at each other. I wanted a cat,
but Bob wouldn't have one in the house. What I wanted
most was a little white kitten with blue eyes. Mama said
that white cats were always deaf, that it was hereditary,
but she didn't know why.

One day I went further than usual. I followed the path
to a road, and although it was a busy road with shops, I
crossed it in order to follow the path further, where it
went between the post office and the first of a terrace of

houses. It was narrow and dirty and dustbin-cluttered. I didn't like it and wouldn't have gone far, if I hadn't spotted another cat, either half-grown or starved and stunted. Its fur was dirty and looked grey where it might really have been white. One ear was ragged and its eyes were rimmed with pus. It slunk away when it saw me and cowered as if it expected a kick. When I reached my hand out towards it, it fled. I followed it, and it was like following the flicker of a tiny pale shadow. I followed it as far as a cemetery and then I lost sight of it. The cemetery had the air of a forgotten place, no vases of flowers on graves, nothing pretty, except for the wild things – convolvulus, willow-herb, honeysuckle – that twined around the slumped gravestones. Long grass and weeds and brambles were tangled everywhere. The church cast a cold shadow; it made me shiver despite the heat. It made me remember that I should be in the garden where Mama and Bob thought I was, behind the hedge, reading *Alice in Wonderland* for the hundredth time. Out of the shadow, in a patch of sunlight, was one beautiful gravestone, a lofty white angel, only a little weatherbeaten. Her eyes were pure and blank and the end of her nose rubbed away. *Grace Clover* was the name I made out on the stone underneath, *Mercifully taken to the arms of the Lord, Dec. 24th 1868*. It didn't seem very merciful to me to let someone die on Christmas Eve.

At the far edge of the cemetery was a tangled hedge of briars and brambles. It was taller than me, taller than a man. It looked as if it would be impossible to get through. It looked as if it had been growing for a hundred years. It made me think of the Sleeping Beauty. The sun fell on the briars as the bees hummed and bobbed about the frail flat pink dishes of the flowers. I tried to see through the spaces between the leaves but the hedge was too dense. I walked about for a little longer, searching for the cat, thinking that I should get back home before I was missed, trying to read the words on the lichen-encrusted stones. Most of them were blunt lozenges, like old teeth, but some were carved into shapes. Apart from Grace Clover's angel there were other, stumpier angels, grizzled and grimed, there was a dove with something broken off in its beak, and a fat black chalice. I found a grave where three infants lay, the children of Hannah and Matthew Sparrow. They had all died at birth and never even been named. It was a stumpy little stone, not pretty at all, and the surface was flaking away. If I ever had babies and they died, I thought, I would choose a stone with elves and rabbits and have a nursery rhyme inscribed upon it.

And then I saw the cat again, poor skinny creature. It ran through the grass as if chased and disappeared through a small hole at the base of the hedge. I knelt down and looked where it had gone. Through the dense scratchiness I could see a bright patch of sunlight on concrete. The ground where I knelt was also concrete, an overgrown path. I pushed my hand in a little way. A thorn snagged the arm of my blouse and I snatched it free. And then I pushed my arm into the hedge, but it was too thick. I could not reach through to the other side. I lay on my stomach and I wriggled my way into the hedge. The buttons of my blouse scraped on the ground and I knew I would be filthy and that Mama would scold. For a second I thought I was stuck, the weight of the hedge pressed on my back and I panicked because nobody in the world knew where I was. But I could not go back, I could only go forward, so I forced myself on, screwing up my eyes against the batting leaves. A caterpillar, dislodged by my wriggling, fell in front of me. It was a strange colour, a sort of turquoise, a colour I had never seen in nature before. It reared up and seemed to look at me. We looked at each other for a moment and it seemed to satisfy its curiosity first and inched off in such a disdainful way that I almost laughed. Once it was out of the way so that I was sure I wouldn't squash it, I eased myself through and stood up and looked around me.

*

I blinked in the brightness of the space, a triangular space, absolutely light and hot. It must have been midday, for I recall no stretching of shadows. There were swings – one swing, rather – and four dangling chains, the ground hollowed between them where many feet had scuffed. There was a roundabout, old and splintery, traces of red paint still visible. There was a climbing frame, peaked like a witch's hat. The see-saw was just an iron stump.

There was no way in, other than the way I'd forced. The hedge of briars around me was high and thick. The air buzzed. I was in, but nobody else could come. The space under the hedge seemed to have healed behind me. The ground reflected the sun's white glare and beat its hotness onto my head.

The cat wasn't there. It must have squeezed its way out again as I struggled in after it. I don't know why I followed the cat. Because I wanted it, I suppose.

I put my foot on the roundabout and pushed. It would not give at first, not until I pushed with all my might, then it gave with a terrible harsh cry like a donkey's bray, and I could hear the pattering of stuff falling underneath, flakes of rusting iron, perhaps, or splinters. It moved only a little, then creaked to a stop.

I sat on the swing and held the warm chains. I swung backwards and forwards, just a little to begin with, shy of the emptiness. But, despite myself, my legs bent backwards and forwards more and more eagerly until I was swinging high, high enough to jolt the frame. I cut a cool slice through the air and my pigtail hung down behind me, grazing the ground with its end as I rushed forward, my head back, squinting through my lashes at the sun.

'Never look straight at the sun,' Bob had often advised, 'or you'll go blind.' Also, 'Never go out in the midday sun, not without a shady hat. Mad dogs and Englishmen go out in the midday sun. It addles the brain.' And he would know, I suppose, having been a desert rat.

But still, despite his advice, I swung in the midday sun and I trailed my hair in the dust and I dared to let the brightness into my eyes, so that when I stopped and stood up I felt myself stagger and my eyes dazzle with fuzzy coloured images. Addled.

You never knew with Bob whether what he said was nonsense. When I was a tiny girl I took it all in, sucked it all in like a sponge, truth and lies and the in-between things, because it isn't all black and white.

I squeezed my way back and my hair caught on a thorn, and I knelt on something sharp and hurt my knee. I looked round the graves once more but there was no sign of the cat. My hands were scratched and beaded with blood from the thorns. I licked the blood away as I hurried home, afraid, making up excuses for my absence. I didn't know how long I'd been gone but it felt like ages and ages. I was sure that I'd missed lunch, that they would have discovered my escape, that that would be the end of the game.

And I was right about the hole. Bob greeted me flushed and filthy, in a great state about the disappearance of half the garden.

'Subsidence,' he said grimly. 'That's *all* it is.' He had been mixing concrete, and he was so troubled by the subsidence that he didn't think to ask where I'd been. And neither did Mama. Apart from tutting at the state of my clothes, she said nothing. She was just washing the lettuce when I arrived in the kitchen. It seemed that less time had elapsed than I'd thought. 'Lay the table, dear,' she said, as if everything was perfectly ordinary, 'but for goodness' sake, wash your hands first.'

The playground was all mine. Not many children have one all to themselves, a real playground with a swing and a roundabout and a climbing frame. I visited the playground whenever I could, whenever it was fine. Now that there was no hole to drop through, I went round the corner to enter the secret network of pathways. I pilfered Bob's secateurs and clipped myself a passage through the briars, only a narrow space, not wide enough for anyone to see. I liked to clamber up the climbing frame and peer over the top of the hedge where there were, across a stretch of waste ground of perhaps ten yards, the backs of some houses – part of a new estate. They had small gardens, the beginnings of gardens, sparse newly seeded lawns, small shrubs, spindly trees, nothing established. The houses were pale brick, with pastel wooden panels, yellow and blue, bright in the sun. Sometimes I saw people going in and out of them. Two of the houses, next door to each other, had families with children. The women would stand in the gardens chatting over the fence, or throwing remarks over their shoulders as they pegged out washing on their revolving-umbrella affairs. The woman from the blue house was the one I saw most. She had two boys, very little, always dressed in identical clothes, who followed her in and out of the house like ducklings. It gave me a funny feeling, watching like that when they couldn't see me. Powerful. Sometimes the boys strayed off the path onto the grass and she slapped their legs and made them squeal. They were nothing to do with me and I didn't care about them, but I liked to watch.

Mama and Bob never missed me. Or they never said. I was always back in time for dinner or tea. It was always like the first time, that summer. However long I felt I'd been away I always got home at the right time. Bob was pleased with me for spending so much time in the fresh air, and he never kept track of me. He had converted part of the vanished garden into a pond and he spent long hours beside it, lying flat on his face, watching the golden fishes glide through the stroking fronds of weed.

Perhaps they knew I was wandering off and thought it was all right. Perhaps it *was* all right. After all, I wasn't a baby. Perhaps they trusted me. Perhaps they knew the secret way I went, threading through the pathways, but if they did they never said. But then they never said lots of things, things they should have said, omissions that amounted to lies.

· **Part Two** ·

· Four ·

Things changed, as things do. First the roses died. Fat vermilion hips took their place, reminding me of the sticky syrup Bob used to force down me every morning. The leaves began to fade and then to yellow and fall. I didn't like it. Each time I visited the playground it seemed less secret, less secure. Through the gaps I began to glimpse the gravestones: the dove, the chalice and the shape of the angel amongst the other blunt stubs. The hedge was still thick enough to hide me more or less. Only a determined observer could have seen me, and there was never anyone in the cemetery. All the dead were long forgotten. But still, I took care and wore my dull green school gaberdine mac and hid my crimson beret and gloves in my pocket.

Yellow leaves rotted squelchily on the concrete. It was a wet autumn. It rained every morning and turned still and misty each short afternoon. The seat of the swing was damp, the chains cold in my hands. They left a sickly iron smell, a brownness on my palms. It was strange to swing in the dusky after-school afternoons. I didn't swing so high, not high enough to churn the frame in the ground and cause the noisy jolting. Sad speckled thrushes sang in the hedge. Seagulls blown inland for the winter drifted above, grey as puffs of spume. The climbing frame was slippery, but I didn't need to climb so high to watch the people in the houses.

Mama and Bob never asked me where I went in the afternoons, but one day I came in quietly, not exactly planning to eavesdrop, but still, closing the door gently, taking off my wet shoes and pausing in the hall for a moment before I went to join them in the sitting room.

'Where *does* she get to?' I heard Bob asking Mama. There was no reply. I could picture Mama's face. She would be pressing her lips into a narrow line and frowning as she pinched folded paper into a crease. That was her origami time. She wouldn't answer until she'd finished the bit she was on. 'Are you going to tell her today?' Bob said, and his voice was unusually urgent. 'Don't tell her, Lilian. There's no need to tell her, let things lie, that'd be best.'

'There!' Mama said. She darted a look at Bob as I opened the door. 'Look, Jenny.' She held up a paper frog. 'And watch.' She did something to it that made its paper legs flex as if it was hopping. She laughed and then sighed and put it down.

'Eh?' said Bob, looking at Mama.

'Bob wants to know where you've been,' Mama said. 'Not that we mind you going out.'

'I've just been walking,' I replied. I wanted to ask, Tell her what?, but I couldn't. There was a nervous creeping feeling inside me. I did and I didn't want to know.

'She just walks,' Mama relayed to Bob.

'Alone?' Bob asked her.

'Yes,' I said.

'Christmas angels,' Mama announced. 'In silver and gold paper. A flock of them.'

'Throng, surely,' Bob said.

'Host,' I corrected.

'Whatever. Don't you think that would be lovely? Different anyway, for Christmas. Nearly tea-time,' she said, when we didn't reply.

I went upstairs and put on my slippers and washed my hands. There were tiny flecks of paint from the climbing frame between my fingers. I unplaited my hair and brushed the separate wriggling worms together. My hair had never been cut. It reached my thighs and was another thing that made me feel different at school. Nobody else had hair that went past her waist, and lots of them had it short. The popular girls had all had theirs cut short recently. Mine wasn't pretty hair, not a special colour or thick or curly, just thin and pale and straight. Not cutting it was another of Bob's foibles. Mama wasn't allowed to cut hers either, although she had had it bobbed as a girl. Mine had fine tapering ends like baby hair and was a terrible business to wash.

Before meals we always had to pause for a minute. It was a compromise. Because Bob didn't believe in God, we didn't say grace. At school we mumbled *For what we are about to receive may the Lord make us truly grateful Amen* as fast as we could and then tucked in, but at home we just left a gap where grace would have been. I grew up with it so it didn't strike me as strange until I was quite old. When I asked Mama the reason why, she said it was good manners not to pounce on the food like wild animals. And if there *was* a god he would see that although we didn't actually *believe*, at least we didn't take our food for granted. That's what she thought Bob thought. She couldn't remember properly. And even now I don't pounce on my food.

Once we'd started eating, there was a lot of unusual and nervous eye contact between Mama and Bob. And then Mama cleared her throat.

'It's your birthday next week,' she said. We were eating bloaters. I stopped mid-chew, my mouth clogged with the salty flesh.

'But . . .'

'I know.'

'But my birthday's in June!'

'You'll be thirteen on Thursday. Do shut your mouth when you're eating.' I swallowed painfully. Mama and Bob were both concentrating on their plates, extracting the hair-like bones from their fish.

'But Mama! My birthday's in June, it's not till June. Tell her, Bob!' Bob's eyes swivelled everywhere but at me. He dabbed at his mouth with his serviette. There were breadcrumbs caught in the fuzz on his chest.

'Another cup, I think, Lilian,' he said to Mama, pushing

his cup and saucer towards her. As Mama poured the tea, I noticed that her hand was trembling.

'Ready for a top-up, Jennifer?' she said.

'Is she all right?' I asked Bob. 'Has she gone mad?' I held onto the sides of my chair to keep me from toppling.

'There are things that you don't know. Many things.' Mama's voice was solemn and her forehead was stamped with a frown. She kept looking at Bob for support but he would not look back.

'Things best let lie if you ask me,' Bob mumbled.

'What things?' I demanded. 'That my birthday's in *November*?'

'I just wanted to prepare you. We'll say no more for now. Your birthday's next Thursday. Not another word till then. Get on with your bloater. Or a nice slice of malt loaf?' She held a plate of withered brown slices towards me.

I got up and stumbled from the room. My chair tipped over but I didn't go back and pick it up. I had the strange sensation as I lurched upstairs that the earth was tilting beneath me, a pole or an axis shifting, leaving me all askew, unsure of my bearings. A November girl. An autumn girl. And almost thirteen. That wasn't me, didn't feel like me. And why? From my bedroom I could hear them murmuring downstairs and I hated them. I hated them with their bloaters and their malt loaf and their secrets.

I pulled the net curtain back from my window and looked out at the dark massed bushes in the garden. There were blurred orange street-lamps in the distance, but no stars or moon. My breath misted the glass and I ran my finger through it, leaving a dripping trail. I watched the drips chasing each other down and gathering in a pool on the sill. I didn't belong, that was obvious. I wasn't who I thought I was. I'd always felt different, that's why I didn't have any proper friends. That's why I never got invited to a birthday party, or to watch television after school. That's why I hardly ever answered questions at school.

Miss Clarke asked a question and I knew the answer and nobody else did but I couldn't put up my hand. I couldn't single myself out. I would sit feeling dizzy, the answer leaping against my pursed lips, my hands heavy as cricket bats. Before I could force one into the air she'd tell us and I'd know that I'd been right and then everyone would learn the answer. But nobody would know that I'd known first.

Maybe the teachers knew what it was that was odd about me. Maybe everybody knew. I drew a miserable face on the window and tears rolled out of its eyes.

I got into bed with my clothes on and pulled the blankets over my head. I didn't sleep. It was too early and there was an awful gnawing inside me, a mixture of hatred and anxiety and curiosity – and a terrible taste of bloater in my mouth. Later, Mama knocked on my door. 'Are you all right, dear?' she asked. 'Would you like some cocoa?' I didn't answer. I heard her open the door a little and sigh into my room before closing it as gently as if I was ill.

· *Five* ·

I went to school the following morning without speaking to them again. I did the daily dozen sullenly, my eyes on the floor. I ate only a piece of toast for breakfast despite Bob's insistence on protein first thing. Breakfast was all heavy sighs and avoided eyes.

I slammed out of the house without a word. I looked back at the door and knew that behind it stood Mama, her hand outstretched, her goodbye frozen on her lips. I spoke to no one in the playground, but that wasn't unusual. All the popular girls giggled and skipped and linked arms and whispered secrets. I hung around by the door, twizzling the end of my long pigtail in my coat pocket, wishing the bell would go, wishing I hadn't come to school, that I'd dared to play truant instead. I could have gone to my playground and been properly alone. It was public solitude I detested. When at last the bell went and we filed in and sat at our desks, I saw that there was a new girl standing by Miss Clarke's desk. She was bigger than anyone else, with frizzy dark hair and a full-sized bosom.

'This is Bronwyn Broom,' Miss Clarke said when the fidgeting and rustling had ceased. 'She's joining us as from today. I want you all to be considerate and help her settle in, show her the ropes. Now. Let me see . . .' She eyed us all speculatively, skipping over the popular girls and letting her eyes rest on me and the empty half of the double desk that was mine. 'Yes, of course, Jennifer Maybee,' she said. 'I'll put Bronwyn next to you and you can help her find her way around. Sit down Bronwyn.'

Bronwyn came and sat beside me. I managed a sort of

smile but she just looked awkward and lumpish. She had olive skin, and thick black eyebrows like a man's.

'Jennifer will share her books with you for today,' Miss Clarke said. She was our form teacher and also took us for English and history. 'Now, where were we?' She opened her own book. We were reading a dreadfully long and tedious poem by William Wordsworth called 'The Prelude'. We were going round the class reading aloud, and some girls mumbled and some stumbled and the rest of us yawned. And when we'd read some of it we had to write a paraphrase. It had been going on for weeks.

I opened the book and pushed it into the middle of the desk. Bronwyn leant towards me and her hair tickled my cheek. She smelt faintly of sweat, but also of bacon, and I began to feel hungry. Bronwyn didn't look at me once for the whole double lesson. When it was her turn to read out loud, she faltered so badly, and made so many mistakes, that Miss Clarke let her off for the day, putting it down to nerves. I saw Bronwyn sneak a peppermint into her mouth, and then, to my surprise, she pushed one along the desk to me. It was warm from her pocket. I sucked it furtively as I wrote my paraphrase. When I'd finished my work, I looked at Bronwyn's exercise book and saw that she'd hardly started, that her writing was babyish and hardly even joined up and her spelling was hopeless.

When the break-time bell went we all slammed our books inside our desks and made for the door. Miss Clarke beckoned Bronwyn and me to her desk and bade me look after Bronwyn. 'Show her the lavatories and so on,' she said, and her eyes rested on me for a moment and I could see she was thinking that the responsibility would do me good. Bronwyn didn't say a word. She followed me out into the playground and we stood together by the wall, eating peppermints and shivering in the dampness, while the other girls paraded their friendships, arm in arm, or shouted the words of their clapping games so fast that I couldn't make them out, or dived around after a ball.

She stuck close beside me all day although we hardly spoke two words to each other. She even followed me into the toilets and waited right outside the door as if she thought I would try to escape. I wasn't talkative. And I was preoccupied, but she didn't seem bothered as long as she had someone to hang on to. At the end of the school day, when the final bell had gone and girls streamed eagerly out of the doors, she suddenly grasped me by my upper arm and looked at me intently. I was surprised by the paleness of her blue eyes in her olive face.

'Would you like to come to tea?' she asked.

I hesitated, thinking about Bob. If I went to tea with her then I'd have to return the invitation. And anyway, I didn't like her particularly.

'No thanks,' I said.

'Please,' she said; she wouldn't let go of my arm. I tried to pull it away. 'Please come.'

'No, sorry.' I managed to jerk my arm free. She looked as if she would cry. There was something in her eyes that I recognised. That filled me with a chilly dullness. It was the fear of rejection.

'Mum will kill me,' she said.

'Why?'

'She said I was to make friends.'

'Why should she kill you though? It's not your fault. You're a new girl. It's only your first day.'

She sniffed and then smiled. 'Well, not exactly kill me,' she admitted. She looked very different when she smiled, as if a light had been switched on inside her. 'But she'll be dis-app-oin-ted. She worries.'

Whenever she said a long word she broke it up, as if she was learning to spell it. It made me pity her. 'Oh all right then,' I said.

At once she changed. I thought she'd be grateful, but she was as cool as if *she* was doing *me* the favour. 'Would tomorrow be all right?'

'Fine,' I said, puzzled. She lived in the opposite direction to me and I watched her walk away. From the back she had a fed-up, matronly air, with her big splayed feet, like an exhausted washerwoman.

I didn't go straight home. I wandered along the main road looking into shop windows. Some of them were decorated for Christmas already. There were miniature snowmen and Christmas trees planted, as they had been every year since I could remember, amongst the gloves and stockings in the haberdashery. This was Mama's favourite shop, for it sold knitting wool and sequins, teddy bears' eyes and crochet hooks, all the sorts of things she needed for her hobbies.

I went into the newsagent's shop and looked at the Christmas cards, reading the soppy verses: *Though Christmas may, perhaps, provide new customs, fun and pleasure, The old sweet memories it brings our hearts will always treasure*, until the newsagent began to scowl suspiciously at me, and I went back outside and crossed the road and went down the footpath to the cemetery. I didn't like walking on the narrow slippery path in the dusk, and as I walked I repeated to myself the la-di-da Christmas verse. I didn't think I liked books or poetry, or words particularly except for communication, but I could tell that that was not good compared with some of 'The Prelude', not the same sort of thing at all. I'd found myself reluctantly entranced that morning by the part where the boy rows in his boat into the middle of a shining lake amongst mountains. *It was an act of stealth and troubled pleasure* were the words that had caught my attention, because they exactly described my feelings whenever I approached the playground.

The cemetery was so dark that I almost turned back, but I didn't want to go home yet. I wanted to be sure that Mama and Bob would worry. I wanted to pay them back. I fumbled to find my way through the hedge and pushed blindly into the spiky darkness and through into the playground. The street-lamp above the hedge bled its light into the darkening mist so that it wasn't completely black. I sat on the swing, my coat belted tightly around me, my arms linked round the chains that were too cold to grasp. Through the black twigs I could see the lights on in the houses. The woman with the two little boys came to the window. I climbed up the frame to see better. She stood gazing out for a moment before drawing the curtains. As she turned to the side I noticed that she looked bulky, as if she was pregnant. She drew the curtains, leaving no more than a hair's breadth of light. I shivered.

I climbed down and sat back on the swing. Water dripped from the swing-rail above me. A cold drop found its way down the collar of my coat. I swung backwards and forwards just a little, thinking about Bronwyn. I wasn't fooled. She was like me. She was an outsider too. Her eyes had been desperate when they looked into mine. She had no fondness for me, we were both oddities, that was all we had in common. We could, at best, be allies. The difference was that I was used to being alone, hardened to it. I'd given up looking for a best friend – but Bronwyn was needy. I could see it all. The idea of being alone in the playground was terrifying to her. I resented the way she had homed in on me, seen in me a fellow victim of exclusion. When I wasn't. Because I didn't care. I shook my head sitting there in the darkness as if I could shake her from me.

But even Bronwyn wasn't as odd as me. I thought of my approaching birthday and of the secrets I didn't know. I swung a little higher and the drops pattered from the frame and then I put my feet to the ground and stopped. Suddenly. I listened. I had a terrible crawling sensation that someone was near, watching me. In *my* place. I held my breath still in my lungs but there was no sound except for the dripping. I was sure I'd heard a movement, from the graveyard, a rustling and perhaps a footfall. But now all was still. I had the feeling that someone was on the other side of the hedge, motionless and waiting, holding their breath just as I held mine.

I grew colder as the drips ticked off the seconds. The noise became the memory of a noise, and then I began to wonder if it had been anything at all. I wanted to go home and warm up and have tea. It may have been my imagination, but had probably been a bird. It may even have been the little white cat. I stood up and went to the hedge. It was impossible to push through it without making a noise and I waited a bit longer, straining my ears for the slightest sound until I began to shiver. The darkness thickened around me. I pushed my way suddenly through the hedge, panicking, scratching my face on the wet thorns. Once through I stood still, my heart jumping. I looked around but there was nothing, just the looming angel shape and the dark stumps and the great black wall of the church. I picked my way out, not daring to look over my shoulder. And once I was out of the cemetery, I ran.

In the house there was the smell of baking. Not a welcome smell because I guessed it meant that Mama had started preparing for my birthday.

'She's home,' Bob said and I heard Mama rustling something away into the sideboard. I burst into the sitting room, without removing my shoes, hardly giving Mama time to close the sideboard door.

'What will I do in June?' I demanded. 'On my proper birthday?'

'You're all wet,' complained Bob. 'And what on earth have you done to your face? You're bleeding.'

I put my hand to my cheek, the place the thorn had scratched. 'What will I do?'

'Do take your shoes off,' Bob said, and to Mama, 'What *does* she get up to?'

'A cat scratched me,' I said.

'I thought you were going to be late for tea,' Mama remarked comfortably. 'It's quite dark. We drew the curtains half an hour ago. And don't fret about the birthday, dear.' She smiled blandly as if it was some trivial thing that was bothering me, a silly little worry. Something that would go away. 'And you'd better dab some TCP on that scratch,' she added.

I looked at their two grey heads, Mama's dark grey and Bob's almost white, and I began to sigh, but cut it off in my throat, recognising in it the timbre of Mama's sigh. 'I'm going out to tea tomorrow,' I said.

'Really? Oh how lovely. With a little friend?'

'Yes,' I said, thinking that Bronwyn was hardly little, and hardly even a friend.

Bob, as was his custom, had the *Guardian* crossword on his knee, and a blot of ink on his belly. 'Focal urban springs of gossip, Lilian? Ten letters. Put the kettle on would you?' he said, glancing at me. I went out and slammed the door and stomped as noisily as possible up the stairs, leaving the kettle cold in the cake-smelling kitchen.

From my room I heard Bob's voice niggling, and Mama going out into the kitchen and the tap running. I heard the bang of the oven door as she took something out and then the sound of the cutlery drawer opening as she set the table. They thought they could carry on the same. They thought they could throw a bombshell at me and just carry on exactly the same. A weak sickness rose in me that was partly hunger and partly helplessness. I couldn't even go to the playground so much now. Every day, after school, it would be a little bit darker. It wasn't the same in winter, anyway. It was nothing but a wet playground.

· Six ·

Bronwyn's house was one of a row of tall dim terraces. It was painted brown inside and out. The front door was at the side of the house, down a gloomy, cabbage-smelling passage. Inside, the floor was covered in brown and red patterned lino, worn thin and ridged over the floorboards. The light bulbs seemed miles above, dull yellow pears dangling shadeless, casting a wan flat light. Bronwyn's mother looked about half the size of Bronwyn, pale and hollow-chested. She held her hand out to me formally, as if I was important. 'So nice to meet you,' she said. 'Bronwyn's told me so much.' I wondered what, since she knew nothing about me at all.

I was disappointed to discover that the Brooms had no television set. Bronwyn ushered me upstairs to play until tea-time. It was bitterly cold in her room. There were no radiators, and although the window was closed we could still see our breath. There were shelves running right round the room, crammed with baby dolls. 'My coll-ec-tion,' she said proudly. The dolls were dressed in a dusty froth of lemon and pink and blue. 'I've been coll-ec-ting since I was born,' she said. 'Do you have a coll-ec-tion?'

'No,' I admitted.

'Sit down,' she said, and I sat on the stool in front of her dressing table. She flopped onto the rumpled candlewick of her bed.

'It must have been your mother who collected them for you when you were a baby,' I pointed out, but she ignored me.

'Shall I show you something?' she asked.

'If you want.'

'Promise you won't tell? Cross your heart and hope to die?'

'All right.' The lumpish look had gone from Bronwyn's face, her light eyes danced, she looked almost impish. She felt under the crumpled aertex vests in her open dressing-table drawer and pulled out a pack of cards.

'Is that all?' I said. We had cards at home.

'These are special,' she said. 'I nicked them.'

'What, stole?'

She nodded. 'From a club.'

'What sort of club?'

'A club where my mum works. Well she doesn't work there, it belongs to my uncle. We go there sometimes. Children aren't really allowed.'

'What kind of club?' I asked.

'A place where mostly men go. They smoke and drink and play cards.' She slipped the cards from the pack. 'Look at this!' The picture on the back of the card was of a blurry blonde woman with bare breasts. I took it and looked. The breasts didn't look as big as Bronwyn's own and seemed to lack nipples. 'And look at this!' A dark triangle could be seen in this one, and in another the bottom of a woman kneeling and looking over her shoulder as if ready to give someone a piggy-back. I looked at them without comment, Bronwyn's eyes fixed eagerly on my face. 'There's more,' she said. 'Look at the Jacks!' She held them behind her back, a teasing look on her face. 'Promise you won't tell?' I nodded. She handed me the Jacks. They were trouserless men wearing jesters' caps, standing in silly poses, their giblets no more than mysterious smudges. 'Aren't they foul?' Bronwyn squealed. Her face had gone very pink. She giggled, bringing her hands up to her mouth like the paws of an outsize squirrel.

I squeezed out a smile. 'Foul,' I agreed.

'Of course, I've never seen a real one. Have you?'

'No,' I lied. I got up and looked at the dolls. They were all sizes, some as tiny as my thumb, the biggest the size of a real baby. Their eyes were all open, wide and staring, except for the biggest doll's. One of its eyes was half closed as if frozen part-way through a wink.

'You've got no brothers then?' Bronwyn said, disappointed.

'No.' I started to pick one of the dolls up.

'Leave them be,' she said sharply. 'It took me ages to arrange them like that.' She put the cards back into the box, and the box into her drawer. 'Look at this,' she said, pulling out a grey and shapeless lump.

'What is it?'

'It's Puddy the Pig. I've had him years. He's made of sugar, very hard sugar. He used to be pink with a bit of string for a tail. I just chew a bit off now and then. Want some?'

I shook my head. Bronwyn's teeth grated against the sugar.

'Can I come to your house tomorrow?' she asked. 'So that you can show me your things. Can I stay for tea? Mum would like that. She gets upset if I don't have friends.'

'I don't know. I'll see. What shall we do? I'm freezing.'

'Dunno. Shall I tell you something . . .' She leant forward again, assuming a confidential expression.

'All right.'

'My dad's dead.' She sat back, making room for my reaction.

'Really?'

'Yes, that's why we've moved to this dump. That's why I've started at your school. I used to go to Moncrieff.'

'The posh school!' I looked at her with a new respect. I had never met a Moncrieff girl before. They wore brown felt hats with gold badges and I'd never thought they'd be so ordinary.

'When Daddy died we couldn't afford it any more. But I don't mind,' she added bravely.

'What did he die of?' I asked.

'Murder,' she said, opening her eyes so wide that the

blue swam in the white. I shuddered and felt a cold finger sliding down my spine.

'Murder,' I repeated.

'Yes.'

I sat with my mouth open as Bronwyn got up and stretched. She looked at herself in her dressing-table mirror. She picked up her brush and began to brush her hair. It crackled as the brush coursed through it and I almost expected sparks. Her hair was dark and massy but with reddish threads that held the light. She turned and smiled and with her hair glistening around her face; I saw that she was womanly. Probably enticing. 'I'm sex-mad,' she said. 'A nym-pho-man-iac.'

'What's that?'

'Sex-mad.'

'How do you know if you've never even *seen* a you-know-what?'

'I just know.'

'Oh.' I looked away. 'I'm not,' I said.

'Tea's ready!' called Bronwyn's mother.

Bronwyn pushed her hair behind her ears. I followed her downstairs.

'Who murdered him?' I asked.

She turned. 'Shut up,' she hissed. 'If you mention it you'll upset Mum. You must never mention it, ever.'

Before tea we folded our hands while Mrs Broom prayed. She thanked God not only for the food but for his goodness and mercy, and I watched her tired fervent face through the slits of my eyes and wondered how she could bring herself to thank him considering what had happened.

We had fish fingers and mashed potatoes once she'd finished, followed by treacle tart. Bronwyn ate heartily and her mother watched, her face clouded with love, as she picked at her own small plate of food – one fish finger and the merest dab of mash. And all the time she fiddled nervously with the strap of her apron, which she wore to the table, unlike Mama, who always tidied herself up before a meal. She asked me lots of questions about school, and although I disliked the place I described it as favourably as possible, since I supposed she was comparing it with Moncrieff. There was a little fluttering at her temple as she listened to me, and her hands darted and fidgeted. The end of her nose was very pink and damp and she kept sniffling as if she was getting, or recovering from, a cold. Several times she pulled off her wedding ring and slid it onto another finger and then put it back, and it made me sad to watch, because of her poor dead husband.

'What happened to your face?' she asked. I ran my finger down the crusty scab.

'Cat,' I said.

'Oh, have you got one?' Bronwyn said. 'I'd love a pussy, or a dog, but Mum's allergic.'

'Really?' I said politely. Bob's opinion was that allergies were all in the mind. 'It was a stray cat,' I explained. 'I'm not allowed one either.'

Straight after tea I put on my coat ready to leave. Bronwyn urged me to stay, but I refused, uneasy in the house, in the shadow of their grief, in the proprietorial watchfulness of Bronwyn's pale eyes. 'Can I come to tea tomorrow?' she asked.

'Bronwyn! You must wait to be invited,' scolded her mother.

'Not tomorrow,' I said to Mrs Broom. 'It's a bit difficult at the moment. My dad's ill, you see.'

'Nothing serious I hope?'

'No . . . but he needs peace and quiet.'

'Well you must come here whenever you like. Tell your mother. It's no trouble. We like a bit of company, don't we, Bron?'

It was only a white lie, that Bob was ill, not a proper one. It was a lie of politeness. And anyway, when I thought about it, Bob had seemed a bit off-colour lately.

· Seven ·

On the day that was supposed to be my birthday, we did our daily dozen as usual. I had some vain hope that they'd forgotten about the birthday. Bob's eyes flickered over me, a brief three-cornered glance, a check for progress. I felt like some sort of time-bomb. Thirteen now, about to go off. And indeed, there was a tender itchy swelling behind my nipples, and every day my school blouse seemed tighter under the arms.

At breakfast, I did my best to ignore the present beside my plate.

'Aren't you going to open it?' Mama said at last, clearing the eggy plates from the table. I spread marmalade on my toast. It was Bob's home-made stuff, with squares of peel the size of postage stamps, and pips.

'Cheer up,' Bob said. 'Birthday girl.'

'But I'm not,' I muttered, forcing a lump of toast past the lump in my throat.

'Open the card, at least,' Mama pleaded. I opened it. It was easier than refusing. I could not bear the bright row of their eyes across the table, watching and waiting. It was a home-made card with a dried pansy stuck on the front. Mama and Bob exchanged glances and Bob vanished behind his paper. A smaller envelope fell out of the card, an envelope with my name written on it in tiny cramped writing, no address or stamp.

'That is for you to read,' Mama said, unnecessarily.

I looked at Mama. She smiled and then busied herself with her toast. Bob flapped the paper and cleared his throat. I stood up. 'I'll take it upstairs to read,' I said. I could not bear to do so with Mama watching.

'What about your present?' she called after me, but I

didn't want it. I ran up the stairs into my room and closed the door behind me. I stood by the window with the letter in my hand. A bird was singing, a blackbird or a robin. I was scared to read the letter. I was being let in on a secret. It was the first important letter I'd ever received. I knew it must be important because of the anxiety in Mama's eyes and because it was old. The writing was unfamiliar. I could not read it at home, not even in the privacy of my own room. I couldn't read it with the attention of Mama and Bob fanning up from the dining room like radar waiting for some signal of my reaction.

I unplaited and brushed and replaited my hair, cleaned my teeth and went downstairs.

'I'm going,' I called from the front door, buttoning up my coat. Mama darted out from the dining room. She looked at me questioningly. 'All right?' she asked.

'Fine.' I was breezy. 'See you later.'

'Happy bir –' she began but I snapped off the word with a slam of the door.

It was a rusty day. Hydrangeas faded to old pink hung on the walls, cotoneaster berries glowed from hedges, the leaves of cherry trees blazed against the blue sky. I walked towards the school, and then turned. It wasn't to school I was going today. I had to be alone to read the letter, absolutely alone with nobody listening.

I skirted the long drenched grass of the cemetery. The angel met my eyes with interest, a little quirk beside her mouth. I pushed through the hedge in a scatter of raindrops and wrecked gossamer. Pools of milky sunlight glistened on the leafy ground. The lamp hadn't gone out and glared weakly against the sun. A bird had streaked a white dropping on the seat of my swing. I wiped it off with my handkerchief, and then I sat down, holding the envelope in my hand, my heart skittering in my chest. I could hardly bear to open it. I considered not doing so. Screwing it up and shoving it deep into the spikiness of the hedge. I was at a hinge-point in my life, a fork.

And then I slid my finger under the flap and tore it

open. Inside was a thin sheet of folded, lined paper. I smoothed it out, but did not at first read. I ran my fingers over it like a blind person, as if somehow I could soak the meaning up through my fingertips. The writing was extremely small. It was written untidily, as if by a person in a hurry, or in distress. I breathed in deeply, and then I read:

Dear Jenny,
You are only a baby in a pram. You are asleep. I'm sitting beside you in the kitchen. All I can see is a little patch of your fluffy hair and the curve of your cheek. When I have finished writing this I will go. I have my suitcase packed. I'll put my coat on and go and that is the last I'll see of you. Mum thinks it best that I disappear. I wanted you to grow up knowing the truth, but Mum thinks not. She thinks it would muddle you, that you should grow up innocent. You should be reading this on your thirteenth birthday. Mum thinks that by then you'll be old enough to understand. I don't know. I know nothing about children although I am your mother. I am eighteen. I'm going away. I've promised never to come back. I'm going, but replacing myself with you. That is the deal. I've promised Mum and Dad, and I don't break promises. Mum and Dad will bring you up as their own. I wonder whether you have guessed the truth, or whether they've already told you. It is useless to try to guess the future. I am a bad girl, a disappointment. I'm not strong. If I was I would take you. It will be hard for me to walk out of the door without you. It will tear me in half. There are sharp strings pulling from my womb and my breasts that bind us together. It will take all my strength to break them. I must be doing the right thing. Mum and Dad will give you a better start than I ever could. I've no money. I'm not a good person, not good enough for you. I am doing the best thing. The sensible thing. Don't hate me, Jenny. I will always think of you. Don't hate me, although I hate myself.
                                                                    Jacqueline

I folded the letter carefully and put it in my pocket. There was a stillness in the air, as if someone had stopped talking and was waiting for an answer. Of course I had known that Mama and Bob weren't my parents. They were too old. Anyone could see that. The funny thing was I'd always wanted a granny, and I'd had one all along. Only it wasn't funny. I sat on the swing for a long time, letting the knowledge percolate through me, like water through layers of sand. Jacqueline. My mother. Also, in a sense, my big sister. I felt nothing more than interest for a time. I waited for a feeling to arrive, dangling in time, there on the swing. All I felt, in the end, was cold. The cold seeped through my clothes and my skin, the complications of muscle and sinew and bone, until my blood, my heart itself, was cold.

I squeezed back through the hedge eventually and wandered around the cemetery. The sun made the angel glitter like sugar. I glanced at her and she shuddered. There were toadstools in the grass, a fat brown cluster which flaked when I kicked them, turned to pulp under my grinding feet. There were blackberries rotting in the hedge. The dark yew tree was studded with poisonous berries.

Small mysteries were explained. Although my name was Jennifer there had always been times when Mama would hesitate over my name, especially when she was calling me. 'Ja . . . Jennifer,' she'd say. I'd grown used to it. Now I thought about it, I was sure I could remember the whole name coming out, hanging inexplicably in the air. Strange that I hadn't thought it stranger. And Auntie May, who was really my great-great-aunt, always called me Jacqueline, but I had put that down to age.

I'd never called Mama and Bob Mum and Dad, or only when referring to them to outsiders. I think I once asked Mama why, and she said something vague about a family tradition, and I was satisfied.

'Grow up innocent,' the letter said. Ignorant, more like.

I looked up at the church, which was not used as a

church. There was no glass in its windows. They were clumsily bricked up, except for the arched spaces at the top. The walls were tall and dark grey, damp-looking, spattered with pigeon droppings. The knobbled spire rooted its way into the sky like some grubby vegetable. For the first time I walked right round it. I didn't like the church, I'd hurried past it before, taking as little notice as possible. The ground was spongy as if it might give, and I walked lightly. Old gravestones leant against one wall on the side I'd never been. Moss grew on their tops in luminous green cushions, softening the uneven edges. Behind the stones, against the wall, was a wedge of rustling shadow, the home I guessed of rats and spiders. I traced my finger over the almost-vanished inscription on one crumbling stone.

> With restless days and sleepless nights
> This weary frame was sore oppressed
> Till God the silver cord unloosed
> And gave the heavy laden rest.

I liked that: the image of a silver cord. It made me think of Jacqueline and the strings that she said bound us together and I thought that however far she'd stretched them they remained unbroken. The wet grass glinted in the pale sun; soaked strands of gossamer reflected light. It was as if the whole place was a web of silver cords holding everything in its place, delicate and precarious. The birds' music stopped and there was silence. Everything still. Everything balanced, glittering, motionless. Even the clouds paused in the sky. I held my breath and experienced a warm tide of meaning beyond words, of understanding that had nothing to do with thought. I was at once both happier and sadder than I'd ever been in my life. My heart seemed to stumble. And then, as if with a creak, the earth wheeled on. Birds resumed their singing, the grass began to nod with the weight of its wetness.

The leather of my shoes was sodden and my toes were numb. A shadow passed across the sun. I walked back towards the playground thinking of the long day ahead. It was only mid-morning and already my stomach growled for food. I paused to read the inscription on another stone. And then I heard whistling. Tuneless, human whistling. I looked all around me. There was no one. The whistling sounded odd. Distant and yet loud, as if echoing in a lofty space. The only place it could be coming from was the church. The great arched double doors were fastened with an outsize padlock and chain, but there was a gap between them and I pressed one eye against it and, squinting into the dimness, I saw I didn't know what. A huge stretching complex structure, struts and joints and spaces, which seemed almost to fill the interior of the church.

At first I couldn't see the man, but I could hear him whistling; the sound echoed in the great cavernous space above him. The tune was 'He Who Would Valiant Be'. As I watched, the man moved out of the darkness and stood for a moment where I could see him. He was a small man with a sharp face. He held a screwdriver. I noticed that the floor he was standing on was earth, that there was none of the paraphernalia you might expect to find in a church, no altar, no pews, not even a proper floor. The man moved around as if he was at home, stepping over the struts of the construction without a glance. He turned his back to me and bent to do something with his screwdriver. He continued whistling until he'd completed his task, then stood up. He remained motionless for a moment and then turned and looked directly at me, or directly at the gap between the doors. I stood hastily aside.

'If you wish to come in, come round the side,' he called. His voice was posh like a newsreader on the radio. I walked quickly towards the hedge, wishing to escape back into the privacy of the playground, but from behind me there was a sharp whistle, of the sort boys do through their fingers. I stopped and looked over my shoulder. He was outside now, watching me.

'Where are you scuttling off to?' he asked. 'And what were you doing spying on me like that? You could give a fellow quite a turn. Are you curious? Curiosity killed the cat, they say, but I won't do *you* any harm.'

I did not want him to watch my secret way into the playground, so I turned towards him. He didn't sound the dangerous type, and anyway, I felt reckless. The letter in my pocket had opened a chink in my life, offered me a new glimpse of myself. I had the feeling that I had stepped into a new world with different rules. Only I didn't know the rules.

The man was foxy with the rusty shadow of bristles on his sharply angled cheeks. But his eyes were not fox eyes, not narrow and sly. They weren't any colour I can name and they were blank. Not blindly and not stupidly blank, just open to what they saw, as if he did not see through a fence of judgements. He just saw. He gazed into my eyes, until I looked down, afraid of what he might see.

'What's your name?' he asked.

'Jacqueline,' I said without hesitation, surprising myself.

'A charming name. Are you known as Jacqui?'

'Always Jacqueline,' I said.

'From the French,' he observed. 'Were they hoping for a son, your parents?'

'Oh no, they wanted a girl. *She* did anyway.'

'Would you accept a cup of tea?' he asked. I nodded and followed him into the church through a narrow side door which I had failed to notice before. After the brightness outside, the interior of the church was dark. Shafts of light penetrated the gaps at the tops of the windows and fell in spots on the floor and the walls. It smelt of earth and wood-shavings and the ground was littered with these, like curls of gold where the light caught them.

'Why don't you switch the lights on?' I asked.

He chuckled. 'I light a candle or two in the evenings. No electricity, you see.'

'Are you here in the evenings then?' I shuddered at the

thought. It was so cold and unfriendly, so absolutely uncosy.

'I live here,' he said. 'A temporary measure, of course.' He struck a match and I saw that he had a small camping stove with a kettle balanced on the top. He picked it up and shook it. 'Enough for a couple of cups,' he announced. 'Have a biscuit.' He offered me a packet and I took one. They were the kind of biscuits that have a lattice of sugar on top. I nibbled at the edge, and then I stopped, a horrible thought occurring to me. I had been under the impression that I was alone when I came to the playground, completely alone with no one even near. And alone when I picked my way out between the graves.

'You're a solitary soul,' he said, just as if he could read my thoughts, 'wandering here at all hours.'

'Have you been watching me?'

'Not watching, no. By no means watching. But I've seen you. I've heard the swing. Frightened me out of my wits when I first heard it. Ghosts, I thought. Phantasms. Quite understandable given the setting, don't you think? Do you fear ghosts?'

'No such thing.'

'Ah . . . such simplicity,' he said, and I began to feel offended. 'But don't you feel it a mite unwise all the same?' he continued, 'to wander alone in such a very secluded spot? A young girl alone. Haven't your parents warned you?' I shook my head, although, of course, they had. They were always warning me. 'How old are you?' he asked. 'No!' he held up his hand, 'Allow me to hazard a guess. Thirteen, or fourteen?'

'Thirteen,' I said. 'Actually it's my thirteenth birthday.'

'No . . . is it really? Well then, many happy returns. Perhaps we should celebrate. And fortunately I have at hand the means.' He pulled a squat silver flask out of his pocket. 'Will you take a spot in your tea?'

'What is it?'

'Irish malt, a peerless tipple.'

'Whiskey?'

'That's it. Will you have a drop? To celebrate?'

'I've never . . . well all right then,' I decided. Jennifer might not have drunk whiskey in a church with a strange man, but Jacqueline did. The man sloshed a good drop into the two china teacups. He put another biscuit on the saucer for me. I sipped at it, wrinkling my nose at its manly smell. It was good and strong and tasted festive, Christmassy. It made me feel light-headed, and odd. The biscuit in the saucer had soaked up the slops and was soft on my tongue. 'Sherry trifle,' I said and my voice sounded loud and foolish.

'I beg your pardon?'

'It reminds me,' I said.

'Well, here's to you. Thirteen today, eh?' he looked at me as if I was the first girl ever to reach thirteen. As if I was unique.

There was quiet for a few moments but for the sounds of our sipping. I struggled to swallow silently but made a gulping sound. And then I grinned. 'What's the joke?' he asked, but I shook my head. I didn't want to say, it would have sounded ridiculous, but I was thinking of Alice and the cake and the little bottle and her obedient eating and drinking and all the growing and shrinking she did. I felt tiny now, as if I had shrunk. The roof of the church was miles above, impossibly far, as was the distance to the door. I shivered.

'What's that?' I asked, pointing to the wooden framework.

'You *would* laugh if I told you that,' he said. He unscrewed the top of the flask and tipped some whiskey straight down his throat, then he put it in his pocket. 'I see you're dressed for school,' he said.

'I . . .'

'It's perfectly all right. You don't have to make excuses to me. I wasn't much of a one for school myself when I was your age. *Has brains, lacks application,* that sort of thing. However, pleasant as this is, I must get on.' He pulled a long canvas bag out of the shadows and took

from it a large saw. He ran his thumb along its jagged
teeth. In the bag I could also see a hammer and a chisel. I
had the sudden thought that I was in danger. Or I would
have been in danger if this man had been dangerous.
Mama would have gone berserk if she could have seen
me. That thought gave me some satisfaction.

'Can I help?' I asked.

He looked at me for a moment, considering. 'I don't see
why not,' he decided. He gave me a pair of pliers and a
claw hammer. 'Go round looking for crooked nails,' he
said. 'Any nail that isn't strictly functional. Old wood,
you see. And extract them.'

'I'll try,' I said. 'And if I help you, will you tell me what
it's going to be?'

He didn't answer, but grinned and went off into the
gloom, and presently I heard him sawing. A spot of light
illuminated the top of his head. His hair was yellowish
brown, a tobacco colour. He whistled as he worked, but
breathlessly, as if all his energy was going into his arms.

I felt very peculiar. I may have been slightly drunk, and
I was chilled so that I couldn't feel my fingers and toes. I
wandered around, peering at the planks, which were old
and splintery. Now and then I found a nail and wrenched
it with the hammer and jiggled it with the pliers. Some
came out and some didn't. It didn't seem to matter. After
a while the smell of freshly sawn wood, the dust from it,
began to irritate my nose and I sneezed.

'God bless you!' he said. 'I'd forgotten you were there.
How are you getting on?'

'All right.'

'Methinks it's time for another cup of tea,' he said.
Methinks? I thought. He was invisible to me, across the
building, behind the chaos of wood, in the darkness.
'Would you mind awfully? There's water in a bottle.
Everything's there.'

I fumbled around and filled the kettle and lit the stove.
The blue flame wavered in the air and gave off a thin
streak of warmth before I put the kettle on top. I looked

inside the suitcase beside the stove. It was very neat –
shipshape, Bob would have said – all rows of things
arranged nicely, not how I'd thought it would be at all.
As well as cutlery and crockery there was a jar of marmalade, a loaf of bread, a china butter-dish, cut-glass salt and
pepper pots, a pot of anchovy paste and a wedge of a
cheese I did not know, threaded with veins of mould.
There were sausages too, wrapped in greaseproof paper.

'Where do you live?' I called. 'You must live somewhere, apart from here, I mean.'

'Around and about.'

'But you're not a tramp, and you're not a gypsy. Are
you?'   'Some of us defy classification,' he called back.
There was a crash as he dropped something. 'Bugger.'

'Oh.' The water began to bubble in the kettle. I fiddled
about, picking things up and examining them. I ran my
finger over the decorative crest on the handle of a knife. I
picked up the fat wad of sausages. 'It must be nearly
dinner-time,' I said hopefully.

He laughed, and I jumped because he had approached
silently and was close behind me. 'I tend to dine in the
evening, personally,' he said.

I flushed. 'I only call it dinner because that's what it's
called at school.'

'Oh don't mind me. You go ahead. The frying-pan's
there.' He indicated the wall and I noticed for the first
time that there were pots and pans hanging from nails,
and a picture too, a photograph of a boy dressed in a stiff
grown-up suit. I went closer and peered at it. The boy's
face was pinched and weak. He looked as if he was about
to open his blanched lips and whine.

'My grandfather,' the man said. 'Married my grandmother at eighteen and only lived to sire one child. A boy,
fortunately for the family name. My father. And then
snuffed it. A consumptive. To my grandmother's relief, I
imagine. He wasn't much fun by all accounts.' The boy's
eyes glistened resentfully.

I reached for the frying-pan. When the sausages began to sizzle, a wonderful sweet fatty smell rose and spread, incongruous in the mustiness. 'Sure you don't want any?' I asked.

'You've tempted me,' he said, and I put another couple of sausages in the pan. I sat on a box and poked at them until they curled and split. I felt very grown-up then, cooking for a man. The sausages were delicious eaten between clammy slices of bread. I licked my fingers and wiped my mouth on my sleeve, but noticed that he dabbed delicately at his own with a napkin. There was only one, in a silver ring. When he had finished he rolled it up and put it back in the ring, sausage fat and all.

'Not much as birthday parties go,' he said. 'Will you be having one this evening?'

'No,' I said. I shivered.

'You're cold,' he observed. 'If you care to look in that box you'll find a rug. Wrap yourself up in it while you drink your tea.' I stood up and opened the lid of the box and found a thick tartan rug inside, which I wrapped around myself, settling down once again on the box. The rug made me feel colder at first, the cold of the earth absorbed into its fibres, but gradually my own warmth crept into it and I began to feel sleepy.

'There was always a party, I remember,' he said. He had closed his eyes. 'With a conjuror, or a clown, and fifty or so children I'd never seen in my life before. Quite an ordeal.'

'Why?' I asked. 'I mean, why didn't you know the children?'

He didn't answer. He rubbed his head and then ran his hands over his cheeks. I could hear the grating of his bristly skin against his palms.

'What's your name?' I asked.

'My name? Must I have a name?'

'Of course you must!'

'Well then, let's say Johnny. Will that do?'

'Yes . . . I suppose so.'

'All your characters must have names.'

'What?'

'You said I must have a name. Why is that? No, let me guess. So you know what to call me. So you know how to think of me. So you know how to refer to me.'

'I suppose so.'

'But you won't do that last thing. You won't refer to me.' He stated it as a fact, not a question that required an answer. 'Now, more about you. You are the one who has come to me. Do you want or need something from me?'

'No.'

'I think you are mistaken. You sought me out.'

'No . . . I didn't know you were here.'

'Not consciously. But you did know.'

'I tried to go away, when I saw you . . . but you followed me out. *You* called *me*.'

'Only in obedience.'

'This is nonsense!' I stood up.

'Sit down a minute longer,' he said, and I did, but only because my legs were suddenly weak. He had splashed more whiskey in our tea. 'I've grown curious. You have aroused my curiosity. You don't add up.' He gazed at me with his clear eyes until my cheeks felt hot. 'Are you really not afraid of me? Not just a mite afraid? Not a smidgin? Perhaps you need to be afraid. Is that it?'

'No.'

'And it really is your birthday?'

'Well . . .'

'Ah ha . . . a lie?'

'No.'

'Well is it or isn't it? Surely the answer to that is in the nature of an absolute. A question that can be answered with a simple yes or no.'

'I've always believed my birthday to be on a different day. Now I know the truth.'

'Ah ha. Result, methinks, confusion. Lost sense of identity. Yes?'

'I suppose that's what it is,' I agreed, reluctantly. 'Lost something, anyway.' He leant back and stretched.

'I honestly wasn't looking for you, or for anyone,' I said. 'I was just wandering around outside, just being alone, when I heard you whistling.'

'Must endeavour to refrain from that,' he said.

'Just before I heard you whistling, I had a funny sort of experience,' I said, remembering.

'Which was . . .'

'I was reading something on a gravestone, one of the old ones that aren't even on graves any more.'

'An enigma, those. Don't belong.'

'There was something about . . . loosening a silver cord or something . . .'

'I've seen it.'

'And as I was reading it something happened . . . everything went . . . oh, I can't explain it.'

'Try.'

'Well, as if everything held together. As if I could see how everything held together, only very precariously, like some sort of balance. As if it all made a sort of sense.'

'And you felt what? Joy?'

'Something like joy, only not as simple,' I said. Johnny was looking at me intently.

'Epiphany,' he said. 'Have you read Joyce?'

'Who?'

'James Joyce. No I don't suppose you have yet. You must. Read *Portrait of the Artist as a Young Man*, for a start. There's a moment in there. Epiphany.'

I thought the word sounded holy, like something from a church service. 'It had nothing to do with God,' I said.

'Did it not?'

'No, it was the world. Just the world.'

'A wild angel appeared to him . . .'

'No angels. No nothing. Anyway there's no such thing.'

'As?'

'Angels. Or God. Or ghosts.'

He laughed. 'I'll tell you what. Borrow the book.' He bent down to reach it. He was like a sort of conjuror. The church was like a conjuror's cave. Cosy now, despite the cavernous cold of it. There seemed to be endless things concealed in the shadows. I saw now a bookcase, just a low thing. He drew a small volume out and dropped it on my lap. I leafed through. It was damp. The print was tiny and dense, impossible to read in the poor light.

'I may not read it,' I said.

He shrugged. 'That's of no relevance to me. Take it or leave it. Now I really must get on.' He had switched away from me and I was disappointed. The strange conversation had been exhilarating. I always knew exactly what Mama and Bob would say next. I liked the surprise of Johnny's utterances, the not-quite-sureness of whether he made sense, or whether I quite understood. And now it had come to an end. I decided to take the book, so that at least I'd have an excuse to return. It just fitted into my coat pocket. 'Work to do. Dark soon,' he said. 'You'd better be getting home.'

'But it can't be that time . . .' I stood up and let the rug drop from my shoulders. And all at once the chilliness closed round me. 'I'll come back soon to see you,' I promised.

'Not too soon,' he replied, and disappeared almost immediately into the gloom. I opened the narrow side door and stepped out into the chill afternoon. Johnny was right. Time had passed, more time outside the church than within. And if I dawdled now, I would be home at the right time.

· Eight ·

At tea-time I opened my present. It was a white jewellery box. When I opened the lid I saw that there was a ballerina inside the mirrored top, twirling on one toe to a tune which Mama said was called 'The Dance of the Sugar-Plum Fairy'. It wasn't something I particularly wanted, or didn't want. 'Thank you,' I said. Mama showed me the little key at the back to wind up the music when it ran down.

'Now show her the secret compartment,' said Bob.

'See if you can find it,' Mama urged. I ran my fingers over the smooth wood. The inside was padded and lined with red velveteen. 'Press,' Mama said.

'Press where?' I pressed my fingers methodically on the spongy interior until I felt a little space in the padding, and then the inside of the box slid gently forward revealing a shallow drawer in which there was another present.

'Cunning, what?' said Bob proudly.

'Open it then,' Mama said. I unwrapped a gold charm bracelet with one charm, a golden wishbone, attached to it. 'Every birthday and Christmas from now on we'll add to that,' she said. 'And by the time you're twenty-one . . .' She sighed pleasurably at the thought; and then her eyes anxiously sought mine for an answering sign of pleasure or gratitude. I closed the box, putting an end to the music, and the dizziness of the dancer.

I fastened the bracelet on my wrist.

'Thank you,' I said. 'I'll look after it.'

'I should jolly well hope so,' Bob remarked. 'Eighteen-carat that is.'

'There,' Mama said. 'Now we'd better eat our tea.' She

had baked my favourite food, bacon-and-egg flan and a marble cake, each slice a swirl of brown and yellow and pink. Everything was all right. I was careful and controlled. Everything was all right as long as I could keep edges around what I was feeling. If I thought of this day as just a day and not as part of a year that had been turned upside-down, then it would be all right. Sense of identity, I thought as I chewed. The afternoon with Johnny was hard to credit in the hard-edged electric light with the fat cake in the middle of the table. The golden wishbone tickled my wrist. Mama lit the thirteen candles on the cake and they sang to me, Bob's voice a low grumble beneath Mama's tremulous piping.

'By the way,' Mama said, as I got up to leave the table, 'a girl called round this afternoon.' She spoke as if this was the most natural thing in the world, as if girls called round every day.

'A girl?'

'I think it must have been Bronwyn. A big girl.'

'Oh.'

'Yes. She called to see if you were all right, since you weren't at school today.'

'Oh.' I steadied myself on the back of the chair.

'Ask her where she was, then,' Bob asked.

All at once I felt the careful edges dissolving. 'You may well ask,' I said, and my voice was cold. I left the room, walking carefully as if the floor was unsafe.

'Jennifer!' Mama said, 'wait. We're not angry. I'm sure you can explain . . .'

I stopped half-way up the stairs. 'Explain!' I shouted. 'Explain! You still haven't explained about my birthday.' There was a silence. 'Well?' I felt something now. I felt what I should have felt in the morning when I read Jacqueline's letter, I felt rage. It gripped me by the scruff of my neck and shook me so that my voice came out in jagged pieces. 'Tell me why? Why did you lie?'

Mama came out of the dining room and looked up the stairs at me. Her hair was quite grey. She was an old woman. I hated her for her age and her wrinkles and the snaky veins on the backs of her hands. Suddenly they seemed deliberate, as if to prove how old she was, that she couldn't possibly have been my mother, lying old grandmother that she was.

When she spoke, she did so quietly. 'Jacqueline's birthday is in June,' she said. 'Midsummer's day.'

'But that's mine.'

'No. It's Jacqueline's. When she went we decided to keep the occasion. We thought it would be easier.'

'Easier!' I gasped. 'Easier? Easier for who?'

'Stupid,' she said, 'we can see that now but . . .'

I ran upstairs and slammed the door so hard that the whole house flinched. I flung myself down on my bed and wept into the bedspread. I made as much noise as I could, gulping and gasping and sobbing until my shoulders ached and my nose and eyes stung. I'd never cried like that before, with every bit of me. Although it couldn't have been every bit, because there was enough left over to be aware that Mama and Bob were listening, and there was even a bit of me that enjoyed the abandon, that looked on with interest at what I could do.

When I'd worn myself out with crying, I lay in a blank state, my shoulders convulsing, my cheeks itching from the drying tears. I knew they'd be relieved downstairs, I knew Bob would be saying things like, 'I'm glad she's got *that* out of her system.' And then they'd carry on as usual. And sure enough, after a pause, I heard a buzz of voices, then the washing-up being done, then the radio.

I did not join in with the daily dozen in the morning. Bob sent Mama upstairs to call me, and then he called me himself, but I remained curled up in the warmth of my bed. Mama came up eventually, but I turned my face away.

'Aren't you well?' she asked. 'Can I get you something? Some aspirin?' This was a sure sign that she was worried, because Bob didn't go along with aspirin. I wondered if he knew she'd offered it. I didn't answer and she left the room eventually, sighing. I heard a short muffled argument downstairs, and then a silence, and then the rhythmic lumping and thumping sounds of the exercises, and Bob's barked instructions. The muscles in my arms and legs twitched in response, so well trained were they, so obedient. So obedient no more.

Bob would not speak to me at breakfast-time, and I would not speak to Mama. I ate my boiled egg and bread and Marmite and drank my tea with my eyes fixed on the brown bakelite cruet in the middle of the table. Then I got up and left the room. As soon as I'd gone they started fretting in burrowing undertones. They made me want to laugh. They were so simple. My shoes were warped and stiff after their soaking and subsequent drying-out on the stove. I should have stuffed them with newspaper. Bob usually did it for me, but he'd neglected to this time, or maybe just forgotten. The pinching of the stiff leather against my toes seemed somehow fitting. I would have left the house without a word, but Mama darted out into the hall with a folded piece of paper in her hand. 'A note,' she said, 'for Miss Clarke, excusing you for yesterday.' I took it. 'Jenny,' she began, putting her hand on my sleeve, 'I know it's been a shock . . .'

'Ha!' I said and snatched my arm away. I went out and slammed the door. It was a foggy day. The first of my new life.

· Nine ·

Bronwyn was waiting for me outside the school gates. 'I never thought you'd be the type to bunk off,' she said. 'You'll be in for it, today.'

'No I won't,' I said. 'Mama wrote me a note.'

'Your mum?'

'My grandmother.'

'Why do you call her that?'

I shrugged.

'What does it say?'

'Read it if you like,' I said. Mama had a special way of folding notes that saved using an envelope, she folded and tucked them into a neat square. I unfolded it and held it out to her. She read it, frowning, her lips moving. 'You lucky thing,' she said. 'I wish my granny lived with us. Mum would never cover up for me like that.'

I put the note in my pocket. She linked her arm through mine and we walked into the playground. It was awkward, I couldn't walk quite in step with her. I saw the popular girls smirking to each other as we walked past. Bronwyn was oblivious. I let her hold onto me but my own arm hung limply. She wanted me to go to tea again, and I said I would. I didn't mind going. It was better than being at home.

Miss Clarke said she'd decided to give Wordsworth a rest for a week or two. 'I propose a change this morning. I want you all to write a poem for Christmas.' There were faint groans. 'Christmas is the theme,' she said, 'but try to be original. Try not to rhyme "holly" with "jolly", for instance.'

'Does it have to rhyme?' someone asked.

'No, free verse if you prefer. But don't forget rhythm.'

'Does it have to be religious?'

'No, no. Look, take an image . . . something associated with Christmas. A robin, for instance. A poem about a robin would be fine. You needn't mention Christmas as long as there's a seasonal theme. And, I've a little prize tucked away for the winner . . .' She beamed round at us, and then set to concentrating on something on her desk.

The classroom was warm and brightly lit. The fog pressed itself against the windows. There was the smell of girls and woolly jumpers, and someone was sucking Parma Violets. Bronwyn muttered under her breath. I couldn't concentrate. I stared out into the nothingness of the fog until my eyes hurt with having nothing to focus on. I tried to remember the stupid Christmas-card rhyme. I tried to think of the warm things about Christmas that keep it rooted to the earth, cakes and puddings and blazing logs, but my mind was strange that day. I'd stopped believing in God when something terrible had happened. A mountain of coal waste had slipped down onto a school in Wales and killed the children. Either there was no God, I reasoned after that, or God was a terrible thing. In Bob's newspaper I'd seen the faces of two people whose children had been killed, and whenever I tried to think about God after that, whenever I saw the picture-book God with his flowing beard and cornflower eyes, I saw the grainy twisted grief of the parents superimposed. No, I tried not to believe in God but there was something that was playing in my mind, something above the density of plum pudding, beyond the warmth of the flame. The nearest I could get to it was the idea of angels. Not Mama's host of paper angels, not the blank eyes of the stone angel, not a Christmas-card angel lit like a birthday candle with a halo of light. It was easier to say what the angels in my head were not than what they were.

The scrabbly sounds of writing and crossing-out and sighing filled the room. Bronwyn kept trying to attract my attention but I took no notice. Miss Clarke was hunched over something on her desk, frowning and chewing her nails, and suddenly I remembered a dream. I had to force it back into my head, screw my brain into a recognition of it before it was snatched away again like a wisp of chiffon and gone for ever. The feeling of the dream remained once the substance had gone, and I took up my pen and wrote a poem:

> Angels flopped from the sky
> And hunched upon white gravel
> Gnawing, anxiously, their feathered wing-tips.

> They sought hay and warm breath
> – a messiah. But there was nothing.
> No star, even, to point the way.

> Lost angels rose and clanked
> and scattered black shadow-feathers
> on what seemed to be white gravel. Or snow.

It wasn't Christmassy of course. I was puzzled by it, but it did catch the feeling my dream had left, like the negative of a Christmas card, a bit of dark brought out into the light. I called it 'Lost Angels'. It was the first proper poem I'd ever written.

It didn't win the competition. Miss Clarke didn't mention it, or call on me to stand up and read it out like some of them. And I was grateful. I would have died of shame to have had everyone staring at me, and listening to my dream, as much as if they peeled off my clothes and looked at my naked skin. Bronwyn wasn't called upon to read hers either, but I sneaked a look. She'd written four lines entitled 'Stockings'. Susan Carter, the first girl in the class to boast a colour television, won the prize, a chocolate snowman, for her poem about a fairy on top of a Christmas tree.

At the end of the day, Miss Clarke called me to her desk and waited, before she spoke, until we were alone.

Bronwyn waited outside the closed door, peering nosily through the glass panel.

'About your poem, dear,' Miss Clarke said. 'I was very . . . well, rather taken aback . . .' She left me room to speak, which I didn't take. 'Are you all right? Quite happy I mean?'

'Yes Miss,' I said.

Her pink face was crumpled with concern. 'It's not that it's bad,' she said, 'it's just that it's a little unusual . . . rather a bleak vision for a child before Christmas . . .'

'It was from a dream,' I said.

'Ah . . .' Miss Clarke sighed with relief. 'A dream. Dreams are funny things. Best take no notice. Think about something nice instead. And by the way, always remember there must be a verb in every sentence. "Or snow" isn't one because it hasn't got a . . .'

'Verb.'

'Good girl. You won't go far wrong if you remember that. Now run along.' I went towards the door. 'And if you do have a problem . . . some thingummy at home . . . you can always talk to me, or one of the other teachers. You do know that.'

'Thanks Miss,' I said.

'What was that all about?' Bronwyn demanded the moment I was outside. 'Was it because you skipped off yesterday?'

'No. She just thought my poem was a bit . . .'

'Weird,' supplied Bronwyn. 'Come on. Will you walk home with me?'

'All right,' I agreed, since I was in no hurry to see Mama and Bob. The fog and the gathering darkness had combined into a brownish soup. We dawdled back to Bronwyn's house, stopping to look in the window of a corner shop at the boxes of chocolates with bows on the lids.

'My dad used to buy Mum boxes like that,' Bronwyn sighed.

'Tell me about your dad,' I said.

'I don't like to talk about him,' she said.

'Go on.'

'Are you my best friend?'

'I suppose so.'

'Will you keep it a secret, anything I tell you? Cross your heart and hope to die?'

'Of course I will. Who would I tell?'

'You must never mention Dad in front of Mum,' Bronwyn said.

'I know, you told me.'

'She gets terribly upset. Her hair went grey overnight when she heard the news. She's quite young really.' Bronwyn's voice had become throaty and confidential. 'I've never told anyone before. Not the details.'

'When was it?' We resumed our walk, and I let her take my arm.

'*I* know,' she said, and she got hold of my plait and put it round her shoulder like a scarf so that we were tied together. I had to walk in step with her because otherwise it pulled but I let her do it because I wanted to know. I'd never known anyone with a murdered parent before. Or anyone dead at all. 'It was about six months ago,' she began. 'In the spring. He was an ae-ro-plane pilot you know. We were quite rich then. He was always giving me presents. He gave me most of my dolls. He was handsome, with dark hair and eyes and a mole on his cheek, just here.' She touched the skin beside her mouth. 'And then one day he didn't come home. The police came instead. They told us he'd been murdered by gangsters.'

'Gangsters!'

'In A-me-ri-ca,' she confirmed solemnly. I looked at her face. It was sad and excited and I quite understood. I was almost envious.

'But why?' I asked.

'Nobody ever found out,' she said. 'I don't suppose they ever will now.'

'How did they know it was gangsters then?'

'I expect he said something with his dying breath.'

'You poor thing,' I said, wincing as she stumbled and tugged my hair.

'It *was* terrible. A trau-ma-tic event, Mum said. He was *so* handsome. I miss him lots. And we used to be so rich. I hate the house we live in now. Our other house was posh with two bathrooms and thick carpets and Mum was happier. Her hair went grey overnight.'

'I know,' I said, wondering if this was really possible.

'You must never say a word about this to anyone. Promise? Swear it on the Bible?'

'Yes,' I said. When we reached the corner of Bronwyn's street we parted. I walked back alone and as I walked I contemplated the terrible glamour of her father's death, and the terrible coming down in the world, which is what Bob would have called it.

· *Ten* ·

There were still three weeks to go until Christmas and I wasn't in the mood for shopping. But it was what we did, Mama and I, every year, part of the lengthy ritual that was Christmas. We'd go into town on a bus and I'd choose my present – always clothing – and she'd give me five shillings to buy presents for herself and Bob and Auntie May. This year I wasn't ready, although the occasion was approaching just the same. I'd signed my name on all the cards Mama sent to relatives we never saw. I'd stirred the pudding mixture and shut my eyes and tried to think of a wish. Bob gave me an advent calendar but I wouldn't open the doors until he reminded me. We had a small tussle of wills each morning. He couldn't bear the day's door to remain shut, yet he could hardly open it himself. He kept nodding towards the advent calendar, a manger scene with a knowing donkey in the foreground, and clearing his throat and remarking on the date, finally asking, 'What have we today, Jennifer?' And I would say, 'Oh no, I forgot,' then prise the thing open with my thumbnail and say sarcastically, 'Oooh it's a cracker!' or whatever it was.

'Last time I bother with one of those,' he grumbled one morning to Mama. 'Waste of money.'

'Well, she's growing up,' Mama said wistfully. 'Bound to happen, after all.'

'Growing up! Is that what you call it?' Bob retorted. 'Sheer bloody-mindedness if you ask my opinion. Wants bringing down a peg or two. Wants a clipped ear.'

'Now, now,' soothed Mama absent-mindedly.

'I am *here*,' I reminded them. 'You talk as if I wasn't.'

*

Mama and I sat on the top deck of the bus that carried us into town. The bus creaked and swayed along the main road past the church, the derelict expanse of graveyard and the briar hedge which bounded one side.

'What church is that?' I asked. 'I've never seen anyone going to it.'

She looked pleased that I had spoken to her. 'It's not a church really,' she said.

'What do you mean? Of course it's a church!'

'It's never been . . . made holy . . . what's the word . . . consecrated.'

'Why not?'

'I'm not sure, dear. You'll have to ask Bob. He's the one with the memory.'

'So it isn't holy?'

'Oh no. No more holy than any other old building, or empty house. Wouldn't be surprised if they pulled it down. Rather an eyesore, don't you think?'

We went into the Co-op's big department store to choose my present. Mama wanted me to have a special dress for Christmas. She chose a scarlet one with a zip up the front. 'So festive,' she said. But I didn't want a dress. I wanted a jumper, a tight black jumper with a polo neck. I held it up to me and liked the way the blackness made me look so pale. I decided, seeing my reflection in the shop mirror, that I would cut my hair. I looked too much a child with the long pigtail hanging over my shoulder.

'It's a waste buying a jumper,' Mama complained. 'I could knit you one like that in no time.' But she bought it all the same, and then we went into the café for a cup of coffee. This was the tradition. Once we'd finished, she'd give me my money and hover discreetly by the lift while I made my purchases and then we'd go home together with our arms full of parcels, moaning that our feet were killing us, so that Bob would serve us lunch.

I drank my coffee black, which was horrible but sophisticated, and we ate mince pies as we always did, and

Mama remarked that though she said it as shouldn't, the pies weren't a patch on her own. The café was decorated for Christmas with bits of cotton wool stuck on the windows. I scalded my mouth on my coffee. Mama smiled at me so that I could see the place where her tooth was missing. Mincemeat glistened on her lips.

'Why don't you go straight home?' I said. 'I'll do my shopping and get a later bus.' Mama looked hurt. 'I'm quite old enough. Thirteen, remember.'

'I know, but we *always* go home together. Bob's baking us some potatoes.'

'So? I'll be back later.'

'I don't know . . .' Mama took another bite of her mince pie. I detested the way her jaw moved when she chewed, as if she was something mechanical. I could see the sinews in her neck standing out like strings. 'Well all right then,' she sighed, 'but don't be too long.' When she walked away I noticed that there was a thread trailing from the hem of her coat. Among the bright mirrored surfaces of the shop she looked tatty and aged, bending with the weight of her shopping bag. I looked around to see if anyone was staring at her. She looked so completely wrong, so out of place. I'd never seen it before. It was a relief to be alone. I tucked my plait inside my coat and pulled the collar up and went into the perfumed cloud of the cosmetics department.

I bought Mama some bath salts in a glass swan, Auntie May a tiny bottle of eau-de-Cologne, and Bob a handkerchief with a horse printed on it. This left me one and sixpence with which to buy a maroon lipstick, a packet of five cigarettes and some matches. I caught the bus but got off it two stops early and walked to the cemetery. I walked straight past the church and pushed through into the playground. I hadn't been there for ages, but it was just as I'd left it. I felt a sense of relief at being in my private place. I wanted badly to be alone, just because I liked being alone. And also so that I could learn to smoke.

I sat on my swing and unscrewed the lipstick and drew

a pair of greasy perfumed lips upon my own, and then I put a cigarette between them. I was immediately glamorous. The first lungful of hot smoke made me choke and my eyes run, but I persevered. I smoked right down as far as I could go and squashed the lipstick-stained butt into the ground. And then I sat and dangled on the swing, feeling sick and giddy. This was me: a teenager, a smoker who didn't know her own mother. These were thrilling things. I had drunk whiskey alone with a strange man. I had a friend whose father had been murdered by gangsters. My life was opening up like some exotic flower. As the mild air revived me I began to swing, feeling the childish drag of my plait. The swing jolted and rattled as I flew through the air. I watched the stumpy vegetable spire sway and I could see that indeed it was not holy, had never been holy. The church was a failure, a sham.

I climbed up the frame and peered over at the new houses. The kitchen light was on and the woman was standing at the sink working, her head bowed. The little boys were outside with their father, wearing wellington boots. It was like a picture from a reading book. It was the sort of family you could believe in. I could feel Mama and Bob's fretting stretching out all the way from home. They would wait a certain length of time for my return, but eat lunch without me in the end. 'No sense letting good food go to waste,' Bob would say. And after lunch Mama would wrap my jumper so that I could pretend surprise on Christmas morning, and Bob would settle to his crossword. And it would be all as normal, except that I wouldn't be there. And I would have spoilt the day for Mama, with her Christmas traditions. Because for those I needed to be twelve and a half with a birthday to look forward to in June. I needed to be hoodwinked.

I climbed down and pushed my way back out through the hedge. I hesitated outside the church. I had almost decided not to visit Johnny today. He had said I shouldn't go too soon, and I was ashamed that I hadn't got far with the book. I had read only the beginning which was about a baby called Stephen wetting the bed. *When you wet the bed, first it is warm then it gets cold. His mother put on an oilsheet. That had a queer smell.* I was shocked to read that. I didn't know it was possible to have such an ordinary sordid thing in a book, the sort of thing you never talk about. But it caused me to remember the times that I used to wake with my nightdress soaked and the sheets all sticking to me, and how it was always Bob who'd come to me, and never say a word. He'd peel away the wet sheet and flip over the mattress which had a permanent peppery wee-wee smell and put on a clean sheet. He'd pull my nightdress over my head and I'd shiver till he put on a dry one. This was all done silently as if it wasn't real. As if speaking might make it real. I never liked to look at Bob in the middle of the night. His eyes were slitty as if he didn't want to open them quite, and his giblets were swollen.

I stopped by the angel for a moment. Today it was just a lump of stone. I listened for Johnny's whistling, or for the sound of him working, but it was quiet inside the church. I decided just to peep inside. I went to the side door and turned the handle. At first, as before, I could hardly see a thing in the gloom, just the grey bubbles of light falling through the tops of the windows and the long slab of light stretching from the door. I stood for a moment squinting into the darkness, and then Johnny's voice said, 'Remind me to put a lock on that blessed door will you? Come in if you're coming.'

I stepped inside and closed the door behind me, shutting out most of the light. 'Sorry,' I said. 'I didn't really mean to disturb you, I was just passing.'

'Just passing!' he scoffed.

'I *was*. I've just been to my . . .'

'To your swings and roundabout? Little girls must have their fun.' His voice had a different sound, a hard sound, slow and cold.

'I'll go,' I said. 'I'm sorry.' It was peculiar talking to the darkness. I still couldn't see him.

'No,' he said. 'Wait. You might as well make yourself useful now that you're here. Make me a cup of tea, will you?' I heard a rustling sound and then saw him rise. He'd been lying in the deep shadow under a blanket. 'Excuse me,' he said and lurched past me to the door. He was wearing many clothes, including a black woollen hat.

I put down my shopping and lit the flame under the kettle. I looked hopefully in his suitcase for sausages, for my stomach was growling. He came back inside doing up his trousers. 'What I could do with is a proper breakfast,' he said, as if he was reading my mind. 'A full English breakfast, as they say, I believe, in the catering trade. Bacon and sausages. The whole caboodle. Although strictly speaking, I suppose the hour for breakfasting has passed. I'm a mite tardy this morning.'

'What have you got?'

'Bread and cheese. I wasn't expecting a guest for luncheon.'

'You haven't got one,' I said. 'I told you, I was just passing. I can have lunch at home.'

'Suit yourself,' he said. He cut chunks off a loaf and ate them standing up with pieces of cheese. He handed some to me.

'Well just a little then,' I said. The cheese was pungent with soft threads of mould. I didn't like it much although I couldn't help eating because I was hungry, and also because I was nervous. The bread was both damp and stale.

The kettle boiled, and I made the tea, watching out of the corner of my eye as he shaved. He lit a candle and then set up a round mirror with a china stand on top of his box. He added a splash of hot water from the kettle to his basin of cold water and tested it with a fingertip. He knelt before the mirror, put a white towel round his shoulders and lathered his face with a soapy brush before sliding a silver blade over his cheeks and chin. I winced as he stretched his neck back and slid the blade up his throat from his Adam's apple to his jaw. I noticed the curved sharpness of his fingernails, manicured nails, perfect little blades themselves. There was the faintest soapy scraping sound and then the dabbling as he dipped the blade in the water before wiping it clean on the towel between strokes. I had never seen anyone except Bob shave before, and he used an electric razor that buzzed like a demented bee. It was an intimate thing to see, the deftness and delicacy with which Johnny shaved, touching himself tenderly, almost lovingly. Finally he splashed his face with water and rubbed it with the towel. Then he smiled at me, pink and shining.

'That's better,' he said. 'Almost human again now.' I handed him his tea. He looked closely at me for the first time. His eyes had a colour that day, a smoky grey, but they were strange and blank and piercing. 'What have you done to yourself?'

'What do you mean?'

'Look.' He gestured to the mirror. I knelt down and glimpsed my reflection. I'd forgotten all about the lipstick. It was smudged and smeared round my mouth like dried blood. 'Not much of an improvement if you don't mind me saying,' he said. Then, 'Come here.'

I stood up and went towards him. He dipped the corner of his towel in the soapy water and wiped my lips, his hand cupped behind my head. He pressed so hard that it hurt slightly, and I could taste the soap between my lips. A new feeling ran like a warmth from my mouth right down into my belly, a yearning that had started when I saw the way he touched his own face.

'Where's the lipstick?' he asked. I took it out of my pocket and gave it to him. He unscrewed the top and wound up the solid greasy tongue then he licked it over my lips, moving it precisely round the contours of my mouth. 'Now look.' I stooped and saw my face, just the same, a child's pale face but with the voluptuous lips of a woman. I smiled at myself and then at him, and it was a smile with a different meaning.

He watched me for a moment, and then turned away.

'It'll take you a few years to grow into those lips,' he said. 'You'd better watch it till then. Now run off home to your mother.'

'Can't I help you?' I asked.

'Not today.' He began tidying up his things, went to the door and flung the soapy water away so that it made a long grey arc in the air before sploshing over a gravestone.

'Did you know that this isn't a real church?' I asked him.

'What do you mean "real"?'

'Not consecrated.'

'What difference does that make? So some pompous fool hasn't muttered magic spells in it, that's all. Makes no odds to me. It's still bricks and mortar. Still a roof.'

'But that's *all* it is. It's no more than a house, or a warehouse. It's not holy.' I licked my slippery lips, I wanted him to look at me, but he kept his eyes turned away.

'I didn't think you believed in anything.'

'I don't.'

'Then what does "holy" mean for Christ's sake?'

'It's what other people believe in,' I said. He gave an exasperated laugh. 'I wrote a poem at school,' I said, willing him to look at me, wanting him to take me seriously. 'A good poem about angels, but not holy angels.'

He stood looking out of the door with his back to me. 'What kind of angels?' he asked.

'Just creatures from the sky.'

'What manner of creatures from the sky?'

'Something like rooks and something like women.'

He stood aside from the door and looked at me at last, but obliquely. 'Are you a poet then?'

'I mean to be,' I said, though it was the first time the thought had even entered my head. I wanted to interest him.

'You should know that angels are hermaphrodites,' he said.

'What's that?'

'Both man and woman.'

'Like snails?'

'You should wipe that muck off your face until you've grown up a bit,' Johnny said, his voice harsh. 'And I don't want to see you like that again. You're a child, you're supposed to be a child.' He pushed past me quite violently and began slamming things into his suitcase.

'I'd better be going,' I said.

'If you know what's good for you.'

'I'll return your book another day,' I said, nearing the door.

'Book? Oh . . .' his voice trailed away vaguely, as if I had already gone, and I picked up my shopping bag and walked home. He had changed. The way he spoke had changed. As if he was acting before, or maybe not. Maybe the harsher Johnny was real. There was a little tremor inside me, a fluttering, not unpleasant, a frisson of fear. As I left the church behind I felt something else too. I felt disappointed, as if someone had snatched something away from under my nose.

· *Eleven* ·

'Jennifer!' Mama darted out into the hall to meet me. 'Oh . . .' She stopped when she saw my lips and made a little fretting sound in her throat.

'I'll just take my presents upstairs,' I said.

'I'll find you some wrapping paper presently,' she called after me.

From my bedroom I could tell they were talking about the lipstick. I crept down the stairs. 'Her mother all over again,' I thought I heard Bob say, and I smiled. Serve them right, I thought. They didn't say anything about it to me at all. I ate my potato – withered from being kept hot for so long – standing up in the kitchen. And then I went into the sitting room and slumped into a chair. Bob didn't look up from his crossword. I felt strange and wild and scornful.

'Would you like to help me?' Mama asked. She had sheets of coloured paper spread out all over the table and the carpet.

'Help you do what?'

'I'm making a nativity scene.'

'Whatever for?'

'For Christmas, a decoration.'

'No one's going to see it. What's the point?'

'There's us, and Auntie May. Do try and get rid of that expression Ja . . . Jennifer, you'll age so badly if you cultivate a frown.' Her voice had taken on a sharp edge, but when I flicked a look at her, she forced the corners of her mouth into an upward curve. 'My goodness you smell of smoke. It's a scandal the way they smoke on the buses.' She switched her attention to Bob. 'Jennifer was asking about the church in the old cemetery,' she said. 'I'm right in thinking it never was a proper church, aren't I? I said to Jenny that she must ask you, that you're the one with the memory.'

Bob cleared his throat. 'That's an interesting question,' he began, and my heart sank, for this signalled a lecture. 'The land was originally consecrated in the 1830s but there was subsequently a problem with the consecration of the building itself, which I believe I'm right in saying was never ultimately completed.'

'OK,' I said.

'But as I was going on to say . . .'

'It doesn't matter. That's all I wanted to know.'

'Jennifer . . . there's no need to be rude. Bob was only trying to . . .'

'I *know*.'

'Off the rails,' muttered Bob. He went back to his crossword, trying to work out an anagram on the margin of the page. Mama bent her head over her piece of folded paper. 'Did Jacqueline help you with your origami?' I asked.

Bob made a sound as if he'd been winded, rustled his newspaper fiercely, and tapped his pen several times on the arm of his chair. Mama pressed her lips together until they were white before replying: 'I hadn't taken it up then. She crocheted though, lovely crochet, so I dare say she would have done.'

I looked at the sideboard with its set of crocheted mats, one long oval and two smaller circles. 'Yes,' Mama answered my unasked question. 'Jacqueline did those.' I got up and examined the mats for the first time. They had always been there, but I'd never taken any notice before. They were made of a cream-coloured silky thread, patterns like flowers linked together on a fine mesh. I could never imagine myself doing anything like that, anything so delicate.

I sat down again. There was a fragile silence and then the triumphant sound of Bob filling in an answer. Then he cleared his throat and said, 'Old copper receptacle of certain friars? Lilian. What do you think?'

'Stars are simple,' Mama said to me. 'Watch.' She began to fold and pinch and crease a sheet of paper, turning it over and demonstrating the technique. Her fingers were quick and clever, as Jacqueline's must have been. She must have sat just where I was sitting, between Mama and Bob, conjuring with her crochet hook.

I tried to fold a star, but I was never any good at fiddly things. My folds and creases were ill-defined, I could never manage a sharp crease. But I made a few second-rate attempts. Mama snipped at a piece of paper. 'I'm cheating now,' she confided. 'In true origami you never use scissors, it's all in the folding. It's thought of as art in Japan, you know.'

I looked at Bob's legs and feet. His calves were hairy and webbed with purple lines and the soft protuberances of varicose veins, and marked as if splashed with the stains of ancient bruises. His feet were long and warped, the toenails curved and yellow, thick as horn. On each of his toes was a patch of straggly hair, getting less as his toes got smaller until on each of the little toes there were only one or two. I had taken to staring at him sometimes, a bit of him at a time, though never looking quite at his giblets. I knew my scrutiny made him uncomfortable. He'd flick me a puzzled, wounded look now and then, and shuffle uneasily, and I was glad. He was hurt that I would no longer take part in the daily dozen. They no longer even called me. I'd wait in the mornings for the thumping to cease before I got out of bed. Now, he ignored me, hiding himself behind the newspaper.

'Twins sit clad in tatters. Eight letters,' he said. 'Any idea, Lilian?'

'Why doesn't he get dressed?' I asked Mama. There was another silence and in the silence I experienced a strange creeping sensation, almost as if I was growing, growing as big as Alice squashed into the rabbit's house, so big that I could not take seriously these manikins with their puzzles and their folded paper. Bob got up suddenly and knocked the table with his clumsy foot and the paper donkey Mama had just completed fell to the floor and was trodden underfoot as he left the room. He banged the door as he went out, causing the clock to emit a timid chime.

Mama picked up her ruined donkey and tried to smooth it out. She said not a word but looked at me reproachfully.

'Well why doesn't he?' I insisted. 'Doesn't he know how . . . how grotesque he looks?' I shouted to be sure that Bob would hear me, wherever he was skulking.

She picked up another piece of paper and began folding. I stood up. I felt as if I was looking down on her from some immense height, dwarfish thing that she was, pinching the paper with her bony fingers into tiny folds, sharp enough to slice her skin.

'I'm going out,' I said.

'Where?'

'Don't know. Might go to Bronwyn's.' I went out quickly, grabbing my coat as I went. I was frightened of the anger swirling inside me like rubbish in a gale. I was frightened to let it out. I ran down the road. It was a cold afternoon, darkening already. I thought longingly of the playground. I could not go there now, because of the darkness, and because of Johnny, who might well be mad. That would explain why he lived in the church although he was not an ordinary tramp, but a well-read man who shaved with a silver blade. I paused to light a cigarette, cupping my hand round the flame of the match, and drawing the smoke deep into my lungs. I imagined my lungs revealed like the lungs on the diagram in the science room at school, two pink, spongy embryonic wings, filling now with tobacco smoke, fading to grey. Johnny didn't smoke, at least I had never seen him smoke, but he did drink a lot of whiskey so that his innards would be stained brown. All the innocent baby pink of our lungs and curled intestines was gone to brown and grey like Mama's hair or the bruisy stains on Bob's shins.

Under the street-lamps my own skin was grey. I splayed my fingers, grey skin over grey bones. My great body shrunk around me like a shrinking coat and a brightness fled from me as I scurried smokily along.

I went to Bronwyn's house for want of anything better to do. I thought again of the playground, but the creature who had swung in the sparkling sunshine was a stranger to me now. Bronwyn opened the door and drew me inside. 'I was so *bored*,' she exclaimed. 'You must have read my mind.'

'I was just passing,' I said.

'You're wearing lipstick!' she said admiringly, and touched it with her finger. 'Have you brought it with you? Can I have some?' She led me upstairs to her room, sat in front of her mirror and held out her hand for the lipstick. I watched the way her eyes became dreamy as her lips darkened. When she'd finished, she blotted her mouth expertly on a handkerchief and held the blurry butterfly shape up for me to see. Then she turned and pouted. She fluffed out her hair and blew kisses at me, and then at herself in the mirror, until the greyness inside me let up a bit and I smiled, and even felt the first tickly edge of a laugh.

'*I* know!' she said. She took off her cardigan and then unbuttoned her blouse so that I could see her big grey brassière. Then she pressed her elbows against the sides of her breasts so that they rose into a shadowy crease and paraded round the room like that, waggling her hips and tossing her head and blowing maroon kisses into the air.

'Oh I'd love to do it,' she sighed, suddenly flopping down onto the bed with her skirt all up exposing her solid mottled thighs.

'What?'

'*It*.'

I had a book at home which Mama had given me about pond life. The centre pages showed the life-cycle of the frog: first the spawn, then the tadpoles, then the tiny frogs. But before the spawn there was fertilisation. This took three hours, I thought, three hours of cold froggy embrace, clammy frog sex-organs jammed crampily together. It sounded terrible, but I knew it couldn't be, for if it was where would the temptation be?

'Angels are hermaphrodites,' I told her.

'Are what?'

'Both man and woman.'

'Don't be daft!'

'They are.'

'How can they be? I don't believe you!' She giggled. 'Go on then, draw one.' She gave me a pencil and opened the back of an exercise book.

'I can't,' I said, and then I giggled too, just as if I had changed into a child again. I drew wings and an angelic face and breasts.

'And a penis,' Bronwyn ordered. 'Go on, draw a penis.'

I drew a little dangly thing. 'That's no good,' she said. 'Do a bigger one.'

'Do it yourself.'

'*I* can't draw! Go on . . .'

I did another version, more explicit than angelic, and she brought her hands up to her mouth and shrieked with glee: 'Like a horse!'

'Bronwyn . . .' Mrs Broom's voice sounded from downstairs. 'What are you up to up there?'

'Jenny's here,' Bronwyn replied. 'We'll be down in a minute.' She took a last look at the angels and then closed the book. She fastened her blouse and we went down into the warm baking-smell of the kitchen.

'Hello dear,' Mrs Broom said, 'I didn't realise you were here.' She looked at my lips and then Bronwyn's. There was a little fluttering at her temple. 'Be good girls and go and wash that off.'

'In a minute, Mum,' Bronwyn said. 'No one's going to see.' Mrs Broom shifted from one foot to the other and wrung her hands together as if there was something terrible in the room with us, not just four smears of coloured grease. 'Jennifer's going to help me ice the buns,' Bronwyn persuaded.

'Oh all right then.' Mrs Broom turned away from our faces and back to her work. There were long strips of white pastry spread out on the table. She took handfuls of pink sausage-meat between her palms and rolled them with a licking sound into long pieces like skinned snakes. Then she flipped the pastry over and stuck it down with beaten egg and chopped it into little pieces.

'That's a lot of sausage rolls,' I said.

'It's for the bazaar. The church Christmas bazaar. Monday evening. One hundred. And Bronwyn's in charge of the buns.'

The buns sat in rows on the side, each in its own fluted paper case. 'I'll put the icing on and you can sprinkle on the hundreds and thousands,' Bronwyn said, and we set to work on the buns while the sausage rolls were baking. It was cosy in the kitchen with the sausagey smell emanating from the oven, and the stickiness of glacé icing to lick off our fingers.

'Don't do them all the same,' Mrs Broom said. 'Put some cherries on some of them.'

'Why don't you come to the bazaar?' Bronwyn asked me. 'After school on Monday?'

'I don't know . . .'

'Go on . . .' Bronwyn urged. 'It'll be fun.'

'I'm not sure,' I said.

'You'd be most welcome,' Bronwyn's mother said, as she took the first batch of sausage rolls from the oven, little golden brown bundles, the meat stretched out from each end with the heat. I eyed them greedily.

'Go on then,' Mrs Broom said, and held the tray out to me, and I took one and tossed it up and down until it was cool enough to eat.

'Don't burn your mouth! We're getting the baking done today because tomorrow's Sunday,' Mrs Broom explained.

'Day of rest,' explained Bronwyn and mimed a pious prayer behind her mother's back.

'Are your family church-goers?' Mrs Broom asked.

'No . . . not really . . .'

'That seems a shame.' Her eyes lingered again on our painted mouths. 'Now, be good girls and wash that stuff off your faces.' I tensed, expecting an argument, but Bronwyn meekly led the way upstairs to the chilly bathroom where we both scrubbed at our lips with coarse coal-tar-smelling flannels. I thought about Johnny as I rubbed and tasted the soap.

'What was that word again?' she asked. 'Her . . .'

'Maphrodite. Do you always do what she says?'

'Her-ma-phro-dite,' she repeated thoughtfully. And then, 'Well . . . since Dad . . . she gets upset so easily. You'll come to the bazaar? Go on.' She clutched my sleeve in her pleading way. The skin around her mouth was pink from the scrubbing.

'Might as well,' I said.

· Twelve ·

There was a thief at school. Miss Clarke's face was grave.
She stood before us waiting for the culprit to speak up.
Someone had stolen money from her desk. It was one of
us. It could only have been one of us, she said, and until
the culprit revealed herself, we would all suffer. Miss
Clarke's eyes were very small. She looked at us each in
turn. The silence was terrible. In the distance we could
hear the rumble of the rest of the school proceeding as
usual. I thought about the money. I wondered how
anyone could steal money from Miss Clarke's desk, how
anyone would dare. I shifted uneasily. Someone had a
cold and every time she drew her breath to cough or
sneeze we all tensed as if she was drawing her breath to
confess.

'I am disappointed,' Miss Clarke said. 'Deeply disappointed.' She left a long pause for this to sink in. 'I've
given the thief a chance. If she'd put her hand up then,
then that would have been the end of it. All over and
forgotten and a lesson learnt.' She looked at her watch.
'We'll wait in silence until the bell goes.'

I wondered what would happen when the bell did go.
Perhaps she would call the headmistress. There was the
sound of a netball bouncing outside, and a shout, and the
drone of an aeroplane passing overhead.

Somewhere in the room there was a thief. The word
made me think of masks and sacks of swag and windows
lolling open; of men with scars and stubble. But this room
was full of girls in bottle green. One of us was a thief, and
also a liar, and also, a coward. Someone was squirming
and scared. Stealing is taking what doesn't belong. I
thought of the Great Train Robbery and how I used to

scan the hedgerows for the loot, how I'd thought of buried treasure when I dug my hole. Digging to Australia. Australia was where they used to send thieves. Peggy was a thief, a peacock thief, and she sailed to Australia on a convict ship and was never heard of again. But everyone takes things that don't belong to them. There was the Christmas money I'd spent on myself, there was the smoke and the greasy taste of the lipstick. I began to squirm. Someone in the room was a thief. I thought about Johnny and wondered who he really was and why he was in the church and what he was building. I thought that Mama and Bob were thieves in a way. They'd stolen the truth from me and ruined everything. They'd given it back when it was too late. I couldn't forgive and forget. Everyone's jersey was bottle green. The popular girls, the lucky ones, even Bronwyn, had smooth-knit shop jerseys in the regulation shade. Some of us had home-made affairs in not-*quite*-the-right-shade of green, cardigans with peculiar buttons, or cable patterns, or saggy fronts. Mama had knitted mine in a fancy basket stitch. 'Just that little bit different,' she'd said proudly, stupidly, because she didn't understand. The point was to be the same as everyone else, not to stand out. Everything about me had to be that little bit different, and now I knew that I was different all the way through.

'This is getting tiresome,' Miss Clarke said. 'A waste of everybody's time. I don't know what's become of the spirit of Christmas.'

A daring girl put up her hand, and everyone held their breath, but she only wanted to go to the lavatory.

'All right. Those of you that need to can go. But one at a time. And straight back here until we get this matter resolved.'

The tension eased as one by one girls traipsed in and out. There was some muttering and scribbling of notes. Bronwyn passed me a peppermint under the desk. I thought about the money in Miss Clarke's desk. She kept it in a Gold Leaf tobacco tin. I'd seen it, we'd all seen it. It would have been simple to take it. The desk was never locked. Stupid Miss Clarke to be so trusting. I imagined how easy it would have been to steal it. I could imagine doing it myself. I couldn't blame the thief. I imagined sliding open the drawer and taking the tin. I imagined the weight of it in my hand. I felt a creeping sense of guilt. I could have done it. It was in me to do it. I could be the thief. I began, against all the evidence, to wonder if it *had* been me. Bronwyn nudged me but I ignored her. It wasn't as simple as innocent or guilty, not nearly as simple as that. Someone had actually taken the money and knew it and there might have been others that knew. But lots of us could have done it. Lots of us might have stolen, or might steal in the future. Miss Clarke looked at her watch. It was nearly time for the bell to ring. I wondered whether we'd sit there right through break or whether she would fetch the headmistress, or even the police. I thought of Peggy eating her Christmas dinner on the beach, with her purple paper crown, and then of the Queen of Wonderland shouting, 'Off with her head!' The judge and the jury in that book turned out to be nothing more than playing cards in the end, flying up at Alice like dead leaves at the end of her dream.

Miss Clarke had been sitting with her hands flat upon the desk in front of her, examining each of us in turn. Her face was not angry so much as sad. I could smell Bronwyn's sweat. I considered owning up, just to put an end to this waiting. But that would have been no good, for in the future I would never have known whether I had been guilty or not. Miss Clarke opened her handbag eventually to take out her handkerchief, and I saw her start and flush before she closed it again. The bell went. 'All right,' she said. 'Off you go. We'll forget the matter for now.' We looked at each other, puzzled, disappointed as well as relieved, and we were abnormally subdued as we filed out of the room. I looked at Miss Clarke's face before I went out. She was very pink, as if she was the guilty one.

It might have been that the money was in her bag all along. But she wasn't going to own up. Oh no. For it wasn't as simple as innocent or guilty. It wasn't as simple as that.

· *Thirteen* ·

It was mostly old women who organised the Christmas bazaar. Some of them were less than old, like Mrs Broom, but all of them were dipped in the same greyness. Bronwyn and I were the only young people. We went straight from school, still in our uniforms, and were immediately absorbed into the preparations. I was given the task of tacking red and green crêpe paper onto the fronts of trestle tables to hide the legs, and Bronwyn pumped up balloons. While they worked, some of the old women sang a chorus called 'The Wise Man Built his House Upon a Rock', while others bickered about the layout of the hall.

The large cake-and-refreshment stall was Mrs Broom's. It took pride of place at the far end of the hall, a cluster of chairs and tables in front of it. There were also stalls selling picture frames and knitted hats and matinée jackets, a second-hand book stall, a Christmas-card stall, a bran-tub, a raffle to win an iced Christmas cake and various other games. There was a wiggly electric wire that you had to pass a loop down without touching it. If you touched it it buzzed, if you didn't you got double your money back. I had a go before the doors were open, but buzzed at the first bend. Near our refreshment stall, in the back corner of the hall, behind a tall clothes-horse draped with yards of crêpe paper and tinsel, was Father Christmas' Grotto.

I quite enjoyed the excitement and bustle. Everyone was friendly, and the chilly hall warmed up as we worked. For the first time I felt Christmassy.

Mrs Broom switched on the tea urn. There were giant teapots and gallons of milk and a mountain of sugar lumps. Bronwyn and I arranged the buns and the sausage rolls, along with several varieties of mince pie contributed by others, on tin trays lined with doilies. And then, just as the urn began to bubble and steam, the pastor arrived to bless our efforts. He was a stout man with a shiny pink face and a fluff of sparse grey hair standing surprised on his head. He moved around the hall, beaming at everyone and everything and patting the odd hand, and he led us all in a prayer, beseeching the Lord to make our efforts fruitful. And then we sang 'O Little Town of Bethlehem' to get us in the mood. The doors were opened and a surprising number of people flocked in. It grew very noisy and it was hot work filling and emptying the heavy teapots, dodging the urn's erratic gushes of steam, washing cups and collecting money.

'Want to visit Father Christmas?' Mrs Broom asked me during a lull towards the end.

I looked at the disorderly queue of children waiting beside the grotto. I hadn't seen Father Christmas arrive. I shook my head. I was too big for Father Christmas, too old to be taken in by cotton wool and fancy dress, but Bronwyn spoke for me. 'Yes let's, Jenny. Give us sixpence each, Mum.'

'What's the point?' I asked Bronwyn as we stood at the back of the queue.

'What do you mean, point?' she said. 'Why does there have to be a point?'

'Who is it?'

'Wait and *see*.'

I went in before Bronwyn, feeling foolish – as much a fraud as Father Christmas himself – masquerading as a child. He was sitting in the shadows and his hood and coat did not look red, but brown, or even green, an earth colour. His beard was long, but thin and straggly and grey. It was a real beard, and his face was real. A thin, pinched nose, no rosy fatness, barely even a smile. I couldn't see his eyes, so deep in the shadow were they and shadowed further by his hood.

He said nothing. The crêpe-paper screen blotted out the light and warmth and even most of the noise from the hall. Beside him on the floor was a sack. I stood awkwardly waiting.

'You don't believe in me,' he said wearily.

'Of course not,' I replied, trying to force a laugh into my voice.

I could feel him staring at me but I couldn't bring myself to meet his hidden eyes. 'Here we are then,' he sighed eventually, holding out a package, 'put your sixpence in the box.' I took the oblong package from him. It felt cold, as if the sack was damp. 'Merry Christmas,' he added dismally.

Outside the grotto it was bright and noisy and warm. I put my gift, unopened, into my coat pocket and went back to help Mrs Broom. When Bronwyn came back she was pink and giggly. 'Isn't he great?' she said. 'I always see him, every year.'

'Who is he?'

'Father Christmas, of course. Who else?' Inside her package was a string of white popper beads. She put them on and they looked ridiculous against the collar and tie of her school uniform.

'What did you get?' she asked.

'I'm opening it later,' I said, and turned away from her to wash some cups. There was a sudden rush of customers, people having a final cup of tea before they went out into the cold. My feet were tired, and I scalded my wrist on a spurt of steam from the urn. All the sausage rolls were sold and most of the buns and mince pies. The tin of money was brimming. People began to drift away, leaving yards of tatty crêpe paper and a scatter of litter and crumbs.

I went to unfasten the tinsel from Father Christmas' Grotto. He had gone already, leaving not a trace. The corner was still very cold. I rolled the tinsel up neatly and then screwed the crêpe paper into big balls. Bronwyn came over to help. 'What's up?' she asked.

'Nothing,' I said. 'I'd better go home now.'

'Why don't you come home with us? We could have some cocoa or something.'

'No, I'd better be going.'

I said goodbye to Mrs Broom and some of the other helpers. Mrs Broom had piles of coins in front of her and was trying to add up on paper how much profit we'd made. 'Thanks for your help, dear,' she said. 'Have you enjoyed yourself?'

'Yes,' I said.

'Good. I've been meaning to ask if you'd like to join Sunday school with Bronwyn?'

I shook my head. The pastor returned and I had the feeling that there was going to be another prayer so I put on my coat. 'See you tomorrow,' Bronwyn called after me as I left.

It was a clear night and the stars were like nail-heads hammered into the sky; the frosty path rang underfoot as I walked. I put my hand in my pocket for my gloves and found the present. I stopped beneath a street-lamp to unwrap it. The Christmas paper was printed with crackers and puddings. Beneath it was a layer of brown paper and inside that was a box. Inside the box was nothing – and I was not surprised.

I stood still for a moment and it was as if I was standing on something very fragile, like a skin of ice stretched above a dark space, a hole that was not a passage to Wonderland or sunshine, but just space, just nothing. I screwed up the wrapping paper and flung it into a hedge. There was a contraction in my throat as if I was going to cry, but the moment passed and instead I felt a frosty smile spreading across my face. For he was a joker, the one who had given me nothing as a gift, a joker and a fake, and I recognised that in him. My laughter made silly plumes in the lamplight. I flung the empty box into someone's hedge and ran home, clattering my feet. I ran home to Mama and Bob.

*

Bronwyn said it was a mistake. She said that lots of other children had been given empty boxes. It was just a mistake, she said. It should have been beads for the girls and water pistols for the boys. Complaints had been made, she said, but I didn't hear anyone complaining. I was there all the time and I didn't hear. And Bronwyn got *her* beads.

I sat with Mama and Bob and I tried to make it all right again. I kept my eyes off Bob's body and I answered Mama when she asked me questions. I told her about the bazaar, about the tea and the cakes and the raffle, but I didn't mention Father Christmas. When I was very small, noticing that Father Christmas didn't come to Mama and Bob, I'd asked Mama when he would stop coming to me. 'When you're thirteen,' she'd said, and that had seemed a safe time away when I was six or seven, a never-never time. But now I was plunged into being thirteen and had to suppose that he wouldn't come again. I felt cheated out of knowing that the previous Christmas had been the last, but I didn't mind too much otherwise. For the past two or three years I'd been awake when Bob tiptoed into my room and replaced my empty stocking with a full one. I had glimpsed the suppressed excitement on his face in the light shining in from the landing as he crept out with a sort of exaggerated tiptoe. I had remained awake then for ages, prodding with my toe the lumpy weight that lay across the foot of my bed, curious, but tired too, and unwilling to spoil the surprise before Christmas Day began.

That evening as I sat between Mama and Bob, I tried to regress. Mama was knitting, Bob had a book and I tried to pretend that everything was cosy and normal, to return to the self I had been before my glimpse of the greyness that lay behind everything. Before it had infected my soul.

I said, 'Do you remember the year Auntie May ruined the pudding?' and Mama laughed at the memory. Auntie May was old – senile, Bob said – but Mama would click her teeth at him when he said it. One year Auntie May had poured methylated spirits over the pudding to make a flame, and it had flamed all right, so fiercely that we couldn't put it out and we had all flapped uselessly around until eventually Bob had the presence of mind to smother it with custard. And then we couldn't eat it because of the terrible scorched methylated taste. I had been given the job of dissecting the shrunken relic on Boxing Day to rescue the silver threepence before we took it to the park to feed to the ducks.

'And it sank!' Mama remembered, 'before the ducks could even try it! It sank like a stone.'

'A blessing in disguise for the ducks,' Bob remarked.

'Is she coming this year?' I asked.

Mama paused to count her stitches, her glasses balanced on the end of her nose, her lips moving soundlessly. 'Sixty-eight,' she finished, 'thank heavens for that. Of course she'll be here.'

'More gaga than ever,' Bob muttered.

'It wouldn't be Christmas without Auntie May,' Mama said.

'It will be have to be, sooner or later,' Bob pointed out. 'She's had a good innings.'

I was quiet. Auntie May had always called me Jacqueline, and nobody took any notice. She only came to our house once or twice a year, always on Christmas Day, and sometimes at Easter too. She couldn't walk more than a step or two and had to be fetched by taxi from the old people's home where she lived. Mama visited her often, as I had done when I'd been younger, but that habit had fallen off. She had always called me Jacqueline and looked at me blankly when I corrected her, and said, 'Oh yes . . .' in her trailing way and then continued to call me Jacqueline, or else nothing at all.

Auntie May was Mama's great-aunt and she was a hundred and one. She'd always looked the same to me, tiny, with a lizard face, long scaly hoods to her cloudy eyes and fingers warped into claws. Her voice when it came had a prehistoric sound, dry and gravelly, even when I bent my ear to her lips, very far away, like a radio tuned to another century. Auntie May had always been as old as you can get in my eyes, and Mama and Bob considerably younger. Not young, but about half-way along the line of life – middle-aged. But Mama was old now, a grandmother, nudging Auntie May off the end of the line in order to take her place. I looked resentfully at Mama's greyness.

'Time for bed said Sleepy Head,' Bob yawned. 'Are you going to join us for the daily dozen in the morning, Jennifer?' I flinched. I thought they realised that I'd finished with all that. I hadn't thought they'd ask again. Mama pushed her needles through her squeaky wool while they waited for my reply.

'I don't like it,' I whispered. I felt precarious. I wanted to hold onto what I had and not be pushed. The memory of our flapping flesh and flailing limbs all incongruous and naked amongst the curtains and the flowery cushions frightened me. I wanted us to be normal. It was bad enough the way Bob went on. That was almost too much to bear without the rest of us . . . I looked gratefully at Mama's woollen skirt and stockings and slippers. If only we didn't have to be naked, I wanted to say, but I couldn't. I didn't want an argument. I wanted us to be safe. So I sat dumbly, misery clogged in my throat, until they gave up waiting for an answer.

I sat up in bed and read some of Johnny's book so that I would have something to say when I returned it. There were pages about a political argument over Christmas dinner. I didn't understand the politics but I could just picture the family sitting round the table, and the great red fire, and the ivy twined round the chandelier. I could almost smell the aroma of warm ham and celery and turkey, all steamy and fragrant in the Christmas glow, and I thought the argument was a shame. It was a shame when things had to change, when people had to realise things. It made me sad. It made me sad that I couldn't properly look forward to Christmas ever again. I could and would pretend, and sometimes I might even believe my own pretence but it was only a thin skin, only a wrapping like the jolly paper on the empty box. Mama and Bob were terribly easy to fool. I only had to smile once or twice, make some light-hearted remark and they would believe that everything was all right again. But then perhaps it was, for them. I put the book under my pillow and switched off my lamp. 'Jacqueline,' I whispered into the dark. 'Mother . . . Mum.' I thought 'mum' a dull sort of a word, a numb sound. I would never call her that. If I ever got the chance, I decided, I would call her Jacqueline.

· Fourteen ·

Saturday was a mild sunny day. The dazzling kind of day when the moss on walls and paths is brilliant green and the bare shafts of twigs gleam golden in the bushes. Flowers still bloomed in gardens, late roses, geraniums even, still scarlet in their pots. Midges danced between the gravestones. I went to my playground. I had Johnny's book in my pocket ready to return, but first of all I wanted to be alone. Birds thrilled in the unseasonal warmth. I sat on my swing, and swung gently to and fro, adding the faint squeak to the song of the birds. The sky was a tender blue, flushed to a wintery pink round its rim. When the sun set it would be cold, but for now it was mild and it was beautiful. A blackbird, his beak bright as a buttercup, snatched a morsel from the ground, hopped on his delicate feet and then flung himself upwards with a little feathery burr.

Something had happened at home that morning. Bob had appeared at the breakfast table clad decently in trousers. Only he wasn't decent, he looked more naked than ever, somehow, with his too-tight khaki trousers biting into his paunch. I had heard, late into the night, the buzz of conversation between Mama and Bob, the result of which must have been the decision to forgo his nakedness in my presence. I said not a word about it, and neither did they. Otherwise, Bob had been as usual, except for the sheepish look on his face when he asked me to pass him the milk or the marmalade. I could tell that he wanted me to say something, or to make some sign of approval, but I said nothing. What was there to say? I remained quiet but I experienced an exhilarating shock of power. I had caused this change of a life-long habit simply by sulking and staring, and all he wanted in return was my pleasure. I would not acknowledge the difference.

I took Johnny's book from my pocket, but I did not read. The sun danced too brightly on the pages, it made my eyes smart. I climbed the frame and peered over at the houses. The pregnant woman was standing in her garden wearing a dressing-gown and wellington boots. She was doing nothing, just standing, staring straight ahead. As I watched, she began to run her hands over her belly, as if exploring. She pressed first the top of the great bulge and then ran her hands round underneath, and her mouth was moving as if she was talking to the baby inside her. The upstairs curtains of the house were drawn and I wondered if someone was ill, one of the boys, or the husband. There was a Christmas tree in a pot outside the back door, ready to be taken in and decorated. It was still two weeks until Christmas and I knew that Christmas in this house would be fine, that the children would believe in Father Christmas, and that they would have a magical time. Looking at the pregnant woman made me think about Jacqueline, and how I, once, had been curled like a fat bud inside her. She might have another child, or several by now. I might have brothers and sisters some-where, preparing for Christmas, unaware of my existence. I even imagined for a moment that that was Jacqueline, standing there, so dreamily pregnant in her garden, and that she was thinking about her stranger-daughter, dreaming about how it might have been if she had kept me. I looked harder, more critically. No. This was an ordinary woman. Nice, but not striking. Jacqueline, I knew, would be tall with high cheekbones and dark hair, and she wouldn't be living in an ordinary place like this. She couldn't be living so close to me, so close that we might have bumped into each other on the street.

All at once, the woman's eyes focused on me and for a fraction of a second our eyes met. She turned quickly and went back into her house. I was far away, only a distant figure peering over a hedge, over a gap of wasteland. I represented no danger. But almost immediately the upstairs curtains parted, and the husband looked out, the woman behind him, pointing at me. I climbed down. I had meant no harm.

I sat back on the swing. Now that I had been seen, the place was spoilt. I waited glumly to see what I would do next, grinding the cigarette end I'd left there the time before into the ground with the toe of my shoe, and then I heard a movement in the hedge, a frenzy of rustling and shaking that was more violent than any bird or animal might make. I tensed, waiting to see who or what might appear. And of course it was Johnny, with thorns tangled in his hair, who emerged, accompanied by many tiny ripping sounds.

'Good morning,' he said, just as if he'd stepped through a door into a drawing room. I looked away, angry with him for entering my place. In the brightness and warmth of summer it had been mine, with the pink and green and the golden buzz of the bees. But now winter had stripped the briars and sent the bees to sleep and made it cold and so often dark that I was losing the feeling that it was mine. And now hostile eyes had seen me, and Johnny himself had penetrated my place like a rude shout finally destroying a fading dream.

'It's been some time,' he said. 'It's nice to see you back.'

'I'm not here to see you.' I looked at my feet and at the ground, anywhere but at him.

'You're offended,' he said. 'I was out of sorts when you called before. Accept my profoundest apologies. Up and down like a bloody see-saw, I'm afraid.' He looked around, but of course there was no see-saw, just the iron stump.

'You didn't offend me,' I said. 'I *was* surprised though. You were so different.'

'Well, aren't we all, from time to time?' he said. 'Aren't you?' He pushed the roundabout round and round, causing the terrible dry screeching sound. I put my hands over my ears.

'Shush!' I shouted.

'Let me push you round, Jacqueline,' he said, and I was taken by surprise. I had forgotten who I was supposed to be.

'No.' The roundabout grated to a stop.

'This place is redolent with the past,' Johnny remarked. 'High jinks. Think of all the children . . .' His finger traced the carved initials still visible on the surviving remnants of paint on the frame of the swing.

'None lately,' I said. 'Except for me.'

'No. And not for some time. That hedge didn't grow overnight. Mysterious, methinks.'

'Like your church,' I said, 'that isn't really a church. That's strange too.'

'Makes no odds.'

'I was thinking, there must have been a church, a real church, there once. What about the old gravestone?'

'Till God the silver string unloosed . . .'

'Silver cord, yes.'

'It will have been moved from somewhere else.'

'But why should anyone want to move an old gravestone?'

Johnny shrugged. 'People do things for their own reasons. Or for no reason at all.'

'Anyway,' I said, 'it isn't a holy place now.'

'Holy place,' Johnny mused. 'Holey places graveyards. Get it?' But I would not smile. 'Lacks sense of humour,' he noted.

'I don't want you here,' I said, and the feeling of power which Bob had triggered in me that morning glowed under my ribs and made me brave. 'Get out.'

He gave a surprised laugh. 'That's nice! After all my hospitality to you! What's brought this on?'

I knew I was being unfair. I shrugged and I felt my face grow thin and sullen. 'I didn't invite you,' I mumbled. 'It's my place, that's all.'

'Ah, but it isn't, is it?' Johnny said. I tossed my head back and began to swing. 'It isn't really yours any more than the church is really mine. We borrow them, such places, such spaces, in the same way that we borrow our bodies.'

'Borrow our bodies?'

'Yes. Bodies are puppets, just puppets, machines . . .'

I swung higher and higher in an effort to dodge the possible truth of this, and the frame clanked and swayed.

'And when you've worn it out, or someone's wrecked it, you bugger off somewhere else,' he shouted. 'The only thing that's truly yours you cannot see.'

'What are you on about?' I mocked. The frame jolted violently.

'Watch it,' Johnny warned. 'Stop. Look, the ground is coming up. It's cracking.' I slowed down and put my feet to the ground and saw that around the base of the swing there were indeed fresh cracks in the concrete.

'It wouldn't fall down, would it?' I asked.

'Don't ask me. *I* wouldn't risk it, though.' He smiled at me and I met his eyes for the first time and they forced a smile from me.

'I've brought your book back,' I said.

'Did you enjoy it?'

'Some, bits of it . . . I found it difficult, but I like it, what I read of it. The way it's written.'

'Well you would.'

'Would I?'

'With your poetic soul.'

'Oh yes . . .'

'Do finish it. It deserves to be finished. My intention is to remain in the immediate vicinity for an indefinite span which may indeed exceed the quarter. That should allow you ample time to digest such a slim volume.'

I laughed. 'You do talk funny sometimes,' I said.

'Do talk funny,' he repeated, 'there's grammar for you.'

'Well you do.'

'I like to exercise my vocabulary,' he conceded. 'And

you're not the first to remark that I employ, upon occasion, a somewhat idiosyncratic, not to say eccentric, idiolect.' He grinned broadly, and I was reminded of a clever little dog sitting up to be patted.

'But you don't always talk like that,' I said.

'I don't *always* do anything.'

'And when you go, where will you go?' I asked.

He turned away. 'I'm about to put the kettle on,' he said. 'Can I interest you in a little refreshment?'

'Won't you tell me what it is?' I asked, walking all round the wooden structure. 'Go on. I won't tell. Who would I tell?'

'Can you not see what it is?'

I squinted at it from all angles, and racked my brains, but had no idea. It was an enormous thing, a kind of scaffolding or framework.

'Look at it without preconception of possibility,' he said.

'Pardon?' I said. But I quite understood him. I closed my eyes and opened them again and let myself see whatever was there, and suddenly I could see it was wings. It was so obviously a pair of wings that I couldn't understand why I hadn't been able to see it before. I was standing at one wing-tip and recognised now that the structure was symmetrical, joined in the centre. Each wing was hinged and jointed in several places so that it would flex and flap like a bird's, rather than than stick out stiffly like the wing of a plane.

'Well, it looks like wings,' I said, feeling ridiculous.

'Absolutely!' he exclaimed. 'What perspicacity she shows.'

'What?'

'Wings. For the purpose of flight.' He looked pleased, no, more, as if he was suppressing pleasure or glee.

'Really? Truly?'

'Unfinished of course.'

'But will it be possible? For you to fly?'

'Daedalus did it. Do you know your Greek myths? And his son – Icarus – but he flew too close to the sun, youthful high spirits . . .'

'And what happened?'

'He fell into the sea with an almighty splash, like a great fried fowl.'

'And Daedalus?'

'He made a safe landing. A brilliant man, Daedalus. He accepted no impossibility.'

'Like you?'

Johnny laughed, pleased. 'They're not complete, of course. Once I've completed the basework I'll have to cover them.'

'With feathers?' I suggested.

He furrowed his brow at me as if this *was* ridiculous. 'Feathers my foot! No, silk. I have silk. A parachute. I'll be like a butterfly, a bloody butterfly. No, a moth, soft as a moth.' I looked back at the heavy splintery wood. 'You're sceptical,' he said, and I thought that I was more than that. 'Look at this,' he said and bent down and from somewhere in the shadows, behind his suitcase, he pulled a stream of what looked like water flowing upwards into his hands. He pulled until his arms were full and it billowed to his feet.

'Beautiful,' I breathed.

'Come outside,' he said. He walked towards the door, the stuff trailing behind him like a bridal veil. Outside in the sunshine he flung it up, brushed off the clinging wood-shavings and spread it out, a thin glistening skin through which the gravestones jutted like bones. 'Go over there.' He indicated the other side of it and I obeyed and then between us we lifted and lowered the silk, in unison at first, the silk gasping against the air, and then we got out of time and flapped it crazily so that it billowed and rippled like moonlit water in a storm. I shouted with laughter.

'See, it almost has a life of its own,' Johnny said,

laughing too. He gathered it up into his arms. I followed him back into the church and watched as he made the tea.

'I still don't see how you're going to fly,' I said. 'You could float with the silk maybe, but the whole thing together will weigh a ton.' I put my hand on a wooden strut. A shaft of sunlight struck it, making a brass nail-head gleam in the centre of an odd streak of red paint. He lifted his eyebrows at me. 'In fact,' I dared to say, 'I think you're potty.'

'Perhaps,' he agreed, regarding me with blank eyes, and now I was not sure whether they were mad or wise.

'Where did you say you were from?' I asked.

He smiled. 'You're wondering if I've escaped from the loony bin now, aren't you?' He added sugar to his tea and stirred the spoon round and round in his cup making an irritating repetitive clink. 'Or perhaps I'm an outlaw, an escaped convict. What do you say to that?'

'I had an ancestor who *was* a convict,' I said, and I felt proud.

'Oh yes?'

'She was called Peggy and she stole a peacock and she was transported to Australia.'

'A poacher then.'

'No . . . I think it was more of a pet,' I said, hesitantly, realising how much of what I knew was my own invention.

'She went on a ship you say? To Botany Bay?'

'Is that in Australia?'

Johnny held his finger up to silence me. He put his cup down and turned away. He slicked his hair back from his brow and turned back, stepped into a spot of yellow light, put one foot on his box, cupped his hand over his ear and began to sing in a curious nasal voice, as if he had troublesome adenoids.

> '*Come, all you daring poachers, that wander void of care,*
> *That walk out on a moonlight night, with your dog, your gun, your snare;*

· 99 ·

> The harmless hare and pheasant – or peacock – you have
>   at your command,
> Not thinking of your last career upon Van Diemen's
>   Land.
>
> 'There was poor Jock Brown from Glasgow and Auntie
>   Peggy too,
> They were daring poachers the country well did know;
> The keeper caught them hunting all with their guns in
>   hand,
> They were fourteen years transported into Van Diemen's
>   Land.
>
> 'The very day we landed upon that fateful shore
> The settlers gathered round us, full forty score or more;
> They herded us like cattle, they sold us out of hand,
> They yoked us to the plough, my boys, to plough Van
>   Diemen's Land.'

I had laughed all the way through the song at the serious way Johnny included Peggy in the song, but I stopped when he had finished, picturing Peggy with her paper crown on her head, bent under the weight of the yoke, the furrows of the earth stretching red behind her.

'They built Australia. Made it what it is. All those mad bad people. You'd think it would have turned out worse,' Johnny said, sitting down on his box.

'Although there were people there already, weren't there?'

'Aborigines, yes.'

'I wonder what they thought when the convicts arrived?'

'I doubt if anyone thought to ask. And by the way, for the sake of accuracy I must point out that Van Diemen's Land is in Tasmania, not Australia itself.'

'More directly underneath than Australia if you look at the globe,' I said.

'Is that so?'

I looked hard at Johnny. He had changed again. All the fun had suddenly gone from him and he actually seemed smaller, his shoulders narrow, his voice flat. He had finished with me. I couldn't get used to it: the sudden way he changed. He went to the door and flung the dregs from his cup out into the grass. 'Must get on, while there's still a bit of light.'

I put my cup down beside his suitcase, and looked at the picture of his miserable grandfather, held for an instant by the pale gleam in his eyes. I wondered if insanity ran in the family.

Mad as a hatter, I thought.

Johnny began getting out his tools, ready to work. 'Are you, perchance, referring to me?' he said.

I winced, startled to find that I'd spoken. 'No, not really. I was thinking about the Mad Hatter's tea party,' I explained. 'You know, in *Alice in Wonderland*. With the dormouse.'

'Weren't they *all* mad, in Wonderland?' Johnny said. 'Wasn't that the point?'

I considered. They were certainly illogical. 'All except Alice,' I said.

'And they would have thought she was mad, you can depend upon it,' Johnny said. 'Now hop it.'

'What I *don't* quite see,' I said, 'is how you're going to get the wings out, even if you could fly with them. They won't fit through the door, you know.' I went to the door and looked back into the gloom.

Johnny had already started planing a piece of wood. I wasn't sure whether he'd heard me. 'By the way,' he called, pausing for a moment. 'I'd like to see some of your poetry.'

'All right,' I said. 'Cheerio.' I went outside to find the brightness already fading, the sun hidden behind the dark spire. Far above me an aeroplane scratched a pink weal on the wintry sky. I trailed slowly home worrying about poetry, wondering whether one poem would do, or whether he'd expect sheaves of them.

In bed that night I thought about Johnny and his wings. I tried to imagine him soaring or gliding. I tried to picture the silken moth that he thought he would be. But all I could see was the rough splintery wood, more like floorboards than wingbones. All I could picture was him plummeting and crashing. It was a grand idea, I could see that. But it was quite mad.

· Fifteen ·

'Only a week till Christmas,' Bronwyn said, linking her arm through mine. 'Only two more days of school. Aren't you excited?'

'Of course,' I said, and I *was* trying to be excited. The house was crammed now, with fragile folding things, angels and stars and reindeer, even a Father Christmas, all papery and frail. Mama had spilt a packet of glitter and it had gone everywhere so that we trod it into the carpets and found it in our hair. Even my porridge had sparkled that morning. We didn't have a tree yet. Our household tradition demanded that Bob got dressed, late on Christmas Eve, and went out to buy a Christmas tree. We decorated it, all together, after tea, and then ate mince pies and even sang carols, sometimes, until it was my bedtime. And then there was the business with the Christmas stocking, and leaving a glass of sherry for Father Christmas and a carrot for the reindeer. Mama had decided that I could have a stocking this year, but it was to be the last. And in the morning, as always, Auntie May would be fetched after breakfast by Bob, who would look strangely formal in a collar and tie, and then there'd be the presents and the feasting and the crackers – and the games.

I was trying hard to be excited, but there was a dullness over it all for me, like a darkish film. Perhaps I had courted it at first, what with my anger with Mama and Bob, what with their lies. I had wanted to feel separate, to see them as foolish little people, to see them and all they did as trivial. But now I wanted to go back. I wanted to peel away the film and see everything in bright simple colours again. I wanted Father Christmas to be red and white and jolly and make-believe; not dismal and greenish and – quite possibly – real. I wanted to retreat from the fright I had given myself, to step off the thin ice onto solid ground that I could never, ever fall through.

'You must come round over Christmas,' Bronwyn said. 'Mum insists. Not on *the* day, we have all my boring cousins over then. But after Christmas. You could even stay the night. Would you like that? Oooh, you've got glitter on your nose.' Bronwyn licked her finger and pressed it on the end of my nose to remove the sparkle. 'Would you be allowed to?'

'I could always ask,' I said.

On the penultimate evening of the school term, the carol service was held in the school hall. We had already had one service for the rest of the school, this one was for parents and the public. I was in the choir, and I sat at the front of the stage, conscious of the way my rough knees poked out from under my skirt. At the back of the hall, behind the rustling rows of the audience, was the tall Christmas tree. Candy-bright lights glistened amongst the darkness of its boughs. I loved to sing, but I was nervous with all the eyes, watching. Bronwyn was there, with her mother, and Mama and Bob sat just behind them, and then there were the parents of the popular girls, in their smart clothes with their styled hair and make-up. Mama looked terribly old and wispy beside them. I was angry with her. She could at least have put on a bit of lipstick, or a hat to cover the greyness of her hair. Bob wore his Christmas collar and tie and looked all wrong too, seedy and shiny-faced. Everyone else was talking, and looking round and acting naturally, but Mama and Bob sat in silence, looking humble, staring down into their laps, or searching me for my eyes. But I would not look back at them. I stared straight over the tops of their heads at the Christmas tree, thinking that not long ago it had been a wild live thing, with roots fanning far down into the earth. I wondered what it would think, if it could think, of the way its roots had been lopped off and the stump stuffed into a decorated dustbin, of the irritating prickle of the lights. I was ashamed to look at Mama and Bob, and I was afraid to look at Bronwyn, for fear that she would make me laugh.

At last the headteacher made her speech, and the audience settled down. The girls with the loudest, clearest voices read the lesson, a few verses each, and at first I couldn't concentrate, my mind flocked with irrelevancies, silly awarenesses, but once the choir had sung a carol and then everyone had risen for 'Once In Royal David's City' and shuffled back into their seats, I forgot myself and listened to the popular girl called Susan, who was in my class, reading:

'And there were in the same country shepherds abiding in the field, keeping watch over their flock by night. And, lo, the angel of the Lord came upon them, and the glory of the Lord shone about them, and they were sore afraid. And the angel said unto them, Fear not: for behold, I bring you good tidings of great joy, which shall be to all people. For unto you is born this day in the city of David a Saviour which is Christ the Lord. And this shall be a sign unto you: ye shall find the babe wrapped in swaddling clothes lying in a manger. And suddenly there was with the angel a multitude of the heavenly host praising God and saying, Glory to God in the highest, and on earth peace, goodwill toward men.'

And as I listened I felt a lump in my throat because they were beautiful words. The star on top of the tree was there to represent the star that guided the three wise men to Bethlehem, Miss Clarke said. And I thought of a hot star in the sky and imagined the enormous faith it must have taken to believe it meant anything at all. And as the words trailed away and Susan sat down, someone whispered, 'Well done' to her and I had to swallow back the tears that nearly welled up for the dull sense of loss inside me, the nostalgia for something I never even knew I had.

All the parents and all the school seemed suddenly so sweet and trusting and childish that I could hardly bear it. And the tree was dark behind them all. Not a Christian thing. It had a pagan dignity, and even the silly jolliness of the decorations, the trivial sparkle of the lights, could not take that away.

The choir sang some carols by Benjamin Britten, clever things that I loved, and then everyone rose for 'O Come all ye Faithful'. And I was all voice. All the complicated feelings inside me flooded out in great waves, and despite my efforts my eyes were wet when a silvery voice sang the first 'O come let us adore him,' and I could hardly contain myself, hardly wait for the great loud powerful rush at the end when all the voices in the hall would rise together. I felt hot in my belly, churned up, excited and disturbed. In my ears I heard a feathery beating and it was Johnny's face I saw and Johnny's clear eyes between the muscular angel wings. And then it was time for the final prayer and I saw Mama pretending to pray, her head bowed, but I saw that Bob at least was not being a hypocrite. He was looking at me, his head erect amongst all the bowed and mumbling heads. I smiled at him – the first time I'd smiled at him for weeks – but there was no response and I realised that he was not looking at me at all. Just staring straight ahead, his eyes unfocused, bored by all the ritual passion.

After the service, as I went to find Mama and Bob, Susan caught my arm. 'I like your voice,' she said. 'I could hear you above everyone else. You should have had a solo.' I thought at first she was mocking, that I'd been foolish, that I'd sung too loudly and made myself a laughing-stock. I looked round for her friends who would be ready to laugh. But there was nobody in particular there, just a jumble of people putting on their coats.

'Thanks,' I said.

Her father claimed her then, and I looked enviously after them as they left. He was a smart man in a suit with a silky tie and he put his hand gently on her shoulder to guide her through the crush.

I found Mama and Bob further down the corridor, in a shabby huddle with Bronwyn and her mother. Bronwyn caught hold of me, and pulled me a little way away. 'That went on for ever,' she complained. 'Were you all right? I thought you were going to cry.'

'Don't be daft,' I said. 'Why should I?'

'My mum's asking if you can come to tea on Boxing Day,' she said. 'Would you like to . . . we'll have a special tea. I hate Boxing Day normally, it's such a let-down, but if you were coming round . . .'

'Jenny,' Mama said, smiling over at me. 'That was beautiful. I do like to hear a carol or two at Christmas. Of course, there's always the radio, but it's not the same, is it?' She looked at Mrs Broom.

'I wish my Bronwyn could sing,' Mrs Broom said, looking fondly at her daughter. 'She's like a foghorn. No ear at all.'

Bronwyn grinned.

'Would you like to stay with Mrs Broom and Bronwyn for a night?' Mama asked me. 'It might be rather fun.'

I looked at Bob. I was surprised that he was in agreement. He usually liked us all to be together, and Christmas was one of his favourite times. He was busy studying a collage on the wall and gave me no sign either way. 'All right,' I said.

'Jennifer!' Mama warned.

'I'd love to. Thank you for inviting me,' I said to Mrs Broom.

'That's that settled then, God willing,' she said. 'Come along, Bronwyn.' She took Bronwyn's hand. 'Merry Christmas, and we'll see you on Boxing Day.' They walked away together, holding hands although Bronwyn was half a head taller and from the back it looked as if she was the mother and Mrs Broom the child.

'Off we go then,' Bob said, relieved to see them go, for he was never easy in company. 'We thought a surprise was in order, didn't we Lilian? We thought a nice bag of chips would round off the evening.'

For once we didn't rush the food home to be reheated in the oven and eaten properly at the table, but wandered along eating the chips out of the newspaper, hot and golden and gorgeous, and as I licked the grease and vinegar off my fingers I was almost happy for a moment, happy in a simple physical way, relaxed in the amicable silence as we concentrated on our chips. And I was puzzled and surprised by Susan's friendliness. That was an extra gift. I had always thought her tiny neatness intimidating. She had frothy red curls cropped short in a way I longed for, and a nose so small that the shadow her profile cast on the classroom wall was almost flat. I had always been excluded from the shared secrets and unexplained laughter which I saw behind her marbly green eyes. But not tonight. I breathed pleasurably and my breath was a soft white blossom of joy. But then as soon as I became conscious of my happiness, I was seized again by the terrible fear. It was like a fear of falling off, or through something into nothing. Or perhaps it was a fear of happiness, a fear of being taken *in* by happiness. It was a sort of fierce nostalgia for the present.

Bob and Mama murmured to each other about how chips always tasted better out of a newspaper and I dropped behind, my mouth full, counting the Christmas trees that dazzled from between curtains all the way down the street. Then I stopped and looked up into the sky at the tiny faraway stars that had no meaning, outside their own existence, pointing the way to nowhere. I stood, my head tilted back, staring upwards through millions of years until I was dizzy. I felt as if I was falling into the blackness. A sliver of moon hung frostily, a tilted smile – or frown, depending on which way you looked at it.

'Come along, Jennifer,' Mama called, and I saw that they were waiting for me at the corner, and I hurried to catch them up.

'Mrs Broom seems nice,' Mama said.

'A nice type,' agreed Bob. 'That Bronwyn's a big girl for her age. My goodness she is,' he added with relish.

'It must be difficult for Betty – Mrs Broom,' Mama mused.

'What must be?' I asked.

'Being alone with a child while her husband's . . . you know . . . absent. I must say, I was surprised by the way she came out with it, just like that.'

'She probably thought we knew,' Bob said. 'That's my impression of the matter. She probably assumes Jennifer's told us. She probably assumes Jennifer talks to us.'

I didn't reply. I'd finished my chips and dropped back again in order to lick the vinegary salt, and the tiny crispy bits of batter that had been in with the chips, from the paper before screwing it up into a ball.

'But she does seem nice, all the same,' Mama continued. 'And it's good for Jennifer to have a friend at last. I don't think we need worry about . . .'

'About what?' I called.

'Influences,' Mama said.

'It's not *their* fault,' I said. 'I feel sorry for them.'

'And so do I,' soothed Mama. 'That's just what I mean. Most families have a skeleton of some sort . . .' she tailed off uneasily, 'and as I say they do *seem* a very nice type.'

I lay in bed that night thinking about what Mama had said. It seemed a terribly cruel way to put it – every family has a skeleton. It made me imagine poor Mr Broom just bones – handsome bones – in a long box under the frozen earth. Although whether it was English or American earth, I didn't know. The carol tunes still beat in my ears as I drifted off to sleep.

I dreamt that night that the church had wings, branched and flapping, extending from its roof. It flapped as if it meant to take off while Johnny watched, smiling and whittling away at a stick and whistling 'Waltzing Matilda' – although only in a dream could a person both smile and whistle at the same time. Then I was in a house and on the floor was a locked box that I knew I must open. I had to find the key. Bob was in a corner, in a playpen, wearing a nappy. The key was hanging on a hook out of my reach. Something suddenly crashed to the floor and I picked it up and saw that it was the church, tiny now like a sparrow. It had a broken wing. I fed it on crumbs of sponge cake and wrapped it in my school beret. Mama said that cake would kill it, it must have worms. Johnny said she's right, that she's a wise woman and used to be a dancer. Johnny reached me down the key but it was soft and sticky like toffee and melted in the keyhole.

On the last afternoon of term we had a party in the classroom, with fizzy lemonade and crisps and mince pies followed by a general-knowledge quiz. Susan was the captain of one team. She had to pick her team and I slumped into my chair, certain that I would only be chosen last, or possibly next to last, before Bronwyn. When Susan said my name straight after the names of the popular girls it gave me a jolt. A sharp pleasurable shock. I was chosen. And before many others. I felt envious eyes on me as I crossed the classroom to take my place in her team and just for a moment the air was full of sparkles and the only darkness was the scowling of Bronwyn's eyebrows. Because Susan chose me, I was able to answer questions. 'Who wrote *Alice in Wonderland*?' was one question and of course I knew that better than anything. And it felt like a sign, a good omen.

After the quiz I was shy of Susan, but she said, 'Happy Christmas, see you next term,' and I waved and watched her go, admiring her little ankles and the way she walked – as if she was just on the verge of dancing.

I turned round to find Bronwyn waiting behind me. 'What's up with you?' I asked, knowing perfectly well why she frowned.

'Nothing,' she said, and I let her walk beside me, and even tuck her arm in mine, although I was contemplating the beginning of a miracle and didn't listen to a word she said.

· *Sixteen* ·

On the morning of Christmas Eve, Bob brought the cardboard box of Christmas decorations down from the loft. It was my job to sort through them, dust them off and untangle the lights, before Bob tested them. I'd always relished that job. Every year I'd find that I'd forgotten quite how many baubles there were, and how pretty. I loved the string of lights. They were ancient – lethal, Bob said – and always caused trouble. Every lamp was different. My favourites were sugared like fruit pastilles, some were shaped like old-fashioned coach-lamps, some were like tiny apples and oranges and pineapples, and some were plain bright orbs of colour. There was only one of the originals left, a tiny electric candle with a little clear wisp of glass that lit up like a flame. However carefully they had been packed away on the previous Twelfth Night, they were always tangled up by the following Christmas Eve, as if they'd been snuggling together in the box. One of the glass baubles had broken in the bottom, and the shards glittered dangerously. There were almost too many decorations for one tree, what with all the paper things Mama made, and the gold- and silver-paper-covered chocolates that Bob always produced with a flourish as the finishing touch. The finishing touch before the fairy, that is, for the fairy was always last.

For the first time I wondered what the fairy meant. It didn't have the same significance as a star. The Christmas-tree fairy had been one of my favourite things in the world when I was small. I took her carefully out of her shoebox. She was a true fairy, not an angel, *definitely* not a hermaphrodite. She was dressed in a white and silver ballgown, fringed with tinsel. Around her waist was a girdle of pearls and she wore a circlet of the same, like an expensive halo, around her golden head. Her wings were made of chiffon sewn with sequins into a spiral pattern. She held a glittery wand, tipped with a starburst of tinsel, like a puff of magic. She was the same fairy we'd had every year since I could remember, and yet every year I'd thought she looked as fresh and new as if she'd just been made. Mama said it was Christmas magic, but this year I could see that her bare shoulders were slightly faded and her stiff hair was caked with dust.

'Did you dress the fairy?' I called through to Mama who was doing something with stuffing in the kitchen.

'Partly,' she replied, and I knew why only partly, because Jacqueline had done the rest. The almost invisible stitches on the wings, the sequinned pattern had been done by my mother's hand. I stroked the fairy with my finger, and blew the dust from her hair. She had a serene smile upon her face, and her eyes with their painted spot of blue gazed mysteriously past me into the distance. I carefully replaced her in the box to await her moment.

'I think I'll go for a walk,' I said, going into the kitchen.

'Get me some bacon would you? Streaky,' Mama said, nodding towards her purse on the table. 'And get yourself a bottle of pop if you'd like some.'

I took some money from the purse and then went back and looked at the decorations. I was thinking of Johnny alone in the church. I picked up a few of the lesser baubles – they would never be missed – and pulled a handful of Lametta from its box and stuffed it all in my satchel. I took a copy of my poem and folded it inside a Christmas card.

'See you later,' I called.

'Don't be too long, Ja . . . Jennifer,' Mama called. 'We've still got to ice the cake, remember.' I went out, pulling a face, imagining Mama flinching in the kitchen at the old slip.

*

I walked past the shops, gazing into the windows. They were almost all decorated: lights winked, snowmen and Father Christmases grinned. It was a grey, undistinguished day with not a hint of snow. It wasn't even cold. I crossed the main road and went towards the cemetery the back way, up the narrow path. I more often walked along the road now, which was longer, but in the daylight I still used the pathway. The gound was damp and slippery, and there was a broken cider-bottle on the ground, and piles of rubbish. A cat licked a discarded chop bone. I looked out for the little white cat. I had not seen it since the first time when it had led me to the playground. I feared it might be dead, it had looked so thin and neglected.

When I reached the cemetery, I broke a branch off the yew tree and decorated it with the baubles and Lametta. It looked pretty, but out of place amongst the damp gravestones. I knocked on Johnny's door. There was no reply immediately, but after I'd knocked again I heard his voice and I opened the door and went in holding the decorated branch before me. As usual, I could not see him.

'I've brought you a present,' I said.

There was quiet for a moment, and then a woman's voice said, 'Who the hell?'

'It's perfectly all right. Hello Jacqueline,' Johnny said as he stood up. His hair was dishevelled and his face was flushed. 'It's my young friend,' he explained to the woman beside him, who was gradually becoming distinguishable from the shadows.

'Jacqueline meet Mary, Mary, Jacqueline,' he said, as if we were at a dinner party. I could not shake hands for she was still crumpled into the shadows and my hands were full of the branch. I felt silly. 'Mary's an old friend,' he said to me.

'Not so much of the old, if you don't mind,' she said.

Johnny came forward and took the branch from me. 'Happy Christmas,' I said, foolishly.

'Benevolence personified,' he said, and I could not tell whether mockery was intended. The woman stood up. Her hair was dark and short and standing on end. She was slightly taller than Johnny, and she held his arm very firmly.

'Well, I'd better be going,' I said. 'I only wanted to say . . .'

'Happy Christmas.' Johnny smiled, and forced me to look into his eyes.

'Yes. Well, goodbye.' I started to go, my face burning with embarrassment.

'No, no, no,' he said, 'you can't go yet. Stay for a drink, a Christmas toast. She must stay, mustn't she Mary.' I could tell by his voice that he'd had several Christmas toasts already.

Mary, quite plainly, was not so sure, but she shrugged good-naturedly.

'Look, I'll put this here.' He propped the branch against the wall. 'Doesn't it look splendid? Pulchritudinous in the extreme.'

'Pardon?'

'Don't worry about him, darling. He's swallowed the bleeding dictionary,' Mary said, and then turned to Johnny. 'Isn't she a bit young?'

'For what?'

'For a drink.'

'A little drop never harmed anyone.' Johnny took three glasses that I'd never seen before from his case and poured some whiskey into each.

'You should be flattered,' Mary said. 'We've been drinking from the bottle until you came along.'

'Ah well, Jacqueline's a poet,' Johnny said.

'I'm not really . . .'

'What's that got to do . . .' objected Mary and I together.

'Here's to us all. Season's greetings,' said Johnny, and lifted his glass. He swallowed his drink all in one go but

· 114 ·

my throat closed at the hot strength of it. I'd preferred it diluted in a cup of tea. It made me choke and splutter.

'Give her some water in it, for Jesus' sake,' said Mary.

Johnny did as she advised, and they both watched me while I got myself under control. My face was burning hot and I was thankful for the shadows.

'Mary's come to give me my Christmas present,' Johnny said.

'Oh, what's that?' I asked politely.

'A good screw,' Johnny said. Mary blurted out a laugh, but I didn't know what he meant.

'And a pair of boots,' Mary said. 'Show her, Ray.'

'Not so elegant, but good quality. Mary's no scrimshanks.' Johnny did a little dance, lifting them up in turn for me to see. They were the sort of boots that builders wear.

'They look nice and strong,' I said. 'Is Ray another name for you?'

'Ha!' Mary said. 'What did he tell you he called himself?'

'Johnny,' I said.

She laughed. 'Well that's original. I'll give him that. Johnny!'

'What's in a name?' Johnny objected. 'The concept of the name . . .'

'Oh bugger your concepts,' Mary said. 'I wouldn't give you tuppence for your concepts. All hot air he is,' she said to me. 'All hot air and verbal diarrhoea.' She sat down on the pile of blankets with her legs drawn up so that I could see the blue-white glimmer of the inside of her thighs. 'Sit down.' I sat obediently on the box. 'How did you come to know Raymond . . . Johnny?' She grinned and ran her hand through her hair. She had a mischievous face, a lot younger than Johnny's.

'I heard him whistling,' I said, 'I looked in . . .'

'Hmmm. Fancy a rum truffle?' She rummaged under the blankets and brought out a paper bag and took from it a sweet the size of a golf ball covered in chocolate vermicelli. I bit into it and the vermicelli pattered to the ground.

'Well just you watch out for him,' Mary said, as if he wasn't there. 'A nice girl like you. How old are you?'

'Thirteen,' I said, and she sighed.

Johnny took a swig from the bottle and grinned at me. 'You might as well use your glass now you've dirtied it,' Mary said. She leant towards me: 'The places I've been, the places I've had to go to catch up with him,' she complained.

'How do you find him?'

'He sends a card now and then . . . thinks I'll drop everything and come running.'

'Which you do,' Johnny said, and staggered.

'Sit down, for Jesus' sake,' Mary said. 'Which I do, *sometimes*. When I'm not otherwise engaged.'

'Are you married?' I asked. 'To each other, I mean.' The question sounded impertinent even to me.

'Married!' Mary hooted. 'Marry this old sod?'

'She'd do it in an instant if I asked her,' Johnny said.

'Not if you went down on your bended knees,' Mary said.

Johnny knelt unsteadily before her. 'I hereby solemnly request your hand in the holy estate of matrimony,' he said. 'Or the estate of holy matrimony.'

Mary pushed him over with her toe. 'Sod off,' she said, and though she smiled, she looked upset.

'Are you staying here for Christmas?' I asked Mary, to change the subject.

'No fear. I'm just passing. I'm staying with family, for a proper Christmas. I'm taking Raymond with me for a day or two,' she said.

I looked at Johnny, surprised, but he just sat up and shrugged as if it was out of his hands.

'Has he told you what he's up to here?' Mary said. She gestured at the wings.

'Flying,' I said.

'Flying?' she laughed. 'Flying! That's rich!'

Johnny seemed to wink at me and then he rubbed his face vigorously with his long sharp fingers. He needed a shave. I wished Mary would go away, and that he would shave so that I could watch him, and hear the sudsy scraping, and smell the soap. I wanted to be alone with him so that I could give him my poem. I couldn't possibly with Mary there. She would laugh in the same way she laughed at Johnny's grand ideas which were nothing but a joke to her, a folly. She was a woman without imagination, I could see that. I thought I understood Johnny better thar her, that she didn't appreciate him. And Raymond was quite the wrong name for him, it didn't suit at all.

'It *might* work,' I said.

'Ha, he'll no more fly than *I* will.'

'I don't see how he's going to get the wings out,' I admitted. 'But I'm sure he will.'

'All will be revealed,' said Johnny patiently.

It was cold in the church, there wasn't the cosiness that sometimes surrounded Johnny and me when there was just the two of us. The whiskey hadn't warmed me. I felt blundery and huge, my fingers like bananas. I took my cigarettes out of my pocket and offered Mary one. Johnny tutted.

'You're never smoking at your age?' Mary said, helping herself from the packet. 'Filthy habit. If you were mine I'd smack your arse.'

'I've only just taken it up,' I said, 'but I don't like it much. I'll probably be giving up when I've finished the packet. Might as well use them up.'

'Give them here,' Johnny demanded. I did so. He held the packet in his hand for a moment and whispered a word of the abracadabra sort, and passed it behind his back, and returned it to me. I looked inside. The cigarettes were gone.

'But where?' I said. I couldn't believe it. There had definitely been two cigarettes inside a moment before, and now there were none. Nothing but the tobacco smell and a couple of ginger flecks.

'Ah ha,' he said.

'Conjuring tricks,' said Mary disparagingly, lighting her own cigarette. She breathed the smoke deep into her lungs and then opened and closed her mouth like a fish, letting the smoke out in rings.

I watched the rings grow pale and loose and finally dissolve as they rose into the darkness. 'I'd better go,' I said, standing up. I felt dizzy and huge, towering over them. Neither replied. 'Happy Christmas, then,' I said. 'Will I see you after?'

'You mind out for him,' Mary advised. 'Can't trust him as far as you can throw him.'

Johnny winked. 'Compliments of the season,' he murmured. I left them both on the floor beside the Christmas branch and went outside to find that it had started to rain. The whiskey burned inside me and made me clumsy and liable to stumble. Before I left the cemetery I stopped beside the angel. There were greenish bird droppings dribbled over one of its eyes. 'Happy Christmas,' I whispered, feeling foolish. There was no glimmer of a reply, just the rain dripping steadily off the stone scallops of the wings. I was glad that the cigarettes had gone, even the taste of Mary's smoke had got inside my mouth and made me feel wretched, but I did wonder how Johnny had done it, and whether he would make them reappear later as a present for Mary. I put my hand in my bag and felt the envelope with the poem inside, still there. I'd have to wait until after Christmas to give it to him, when we were alone again.

I left the cemetery to walk along the road rather than the slimy pathway in the rain, and I heard the clatter of running feet behind me. Mary caught me up. I waited while she leant against a wall to get her breath back. She pressed one hand into her side. 'Stitch,' she gasped. Her hair was wet and there was orange make-up on her face, I could see in the daylight, and a smear of darkness under her eyes. 'Stay away,' she said when she'd recovered. 'I'm telling you, seriously, he's not one to mess with. I don't know . . . I'm not sure or even *I* wouldn't be here, but we've been through thick and thin together, Ray and I. Years. I've never been sure.'

'Of what?' I asked. 'I don't know what you mean.'

She sighed. 'Nor do I, darling, that's the trouble. But look, better safe than sorry, eh? I wouldn't bother only you're a nice kid.'

'But what . . .'

'I'm off,' she said. 'I'm bleeding drowning out here. Remember . . .' and she hurried away, head down against the rain, wobbling in her high-heeled shoes, her bare legs spattered with mud.

On the way home, I remembered Mama's bacon and stopped at the butcher's and joined the queue that stretched right outside under the dripping awning. In the butcher's window, between the birds and the slabs of steak, was a flock-covered Father Christmas faded to the colour of dried blood. People came out with huge turkeys under their arms, and the dimply white of the turkey skin reminded me of Mary's thighs, and I thought that she was jealous of me, that's why she warned me to keep away, and the thought made me grin.

· *Seventeen* ·

For the first time I noticed the female smell of the stocking Mama gave me to put on the end of my bed. It was a cast-off of her own. It lay across my bedspread like a sloughed snake skin. I kept my face turned to the wall when Bob crept in. My mouth was dry and my head pounded. Mama had allowed me a tiny glass of sherry after we'd decorated the tree, when I was not yet thoroughly over the whiskey. I heard the rustling creak of the packed stocking as Bob replaced the empty one, and I breathed as smoothly and easily as a sleeping person. He stood still for a moment, watching me, and I even stirred slightly as if in a dream.

When he'd gone and closed my door, I turned and looked at the luminous face of my alarm clock. It was half-past twelve. I reached for the stocking, and in the tiny amount of light that seeped round the edges of my door from the landing, I pulled everything out. There was a chocolate snowman just like the one Susan had won for her poem; a new toothbrush; a flannel and a bar of soap; three pairs of knickers; some chocolate money; and a tangerine. They were all, but for the chocolates, things they would have bought me anyway. I prised open a few chocolate coins and ate them, feeling obscurely cheated. And then I pushed everything to the end of my bed, lay down and slept soundly until morning.

After breakfast Bob, fully clothed and looking uncomfortably festive in a new red tie, went out to telephone for a taxi, in order to collect Auntie May. I helped Mama wash the breakfast things, and then, while she peeled the potatoes and put the turkey in the oven, I went and stood by the Christmas tree. I switched on the lights. Bob had tinkered with them late into the night and now they twinkled obediently, reflecting themselves in the glass baubles and the shimmering Lametta. I put my face close to a large green bauble and saw my tiny contorted reflection receding from a huge blunt snout. It opened its mouth to me, like some monstrosity rising through water. I stood quickly back.

The tree looked perfect, like a picture on a Christmas card. It was dark green and healthy, bristling with life. Bob had planted it in a red bucket, and then we'd draped it in its finery so that every branch dripped with sparkles. The fairy was tied to the pointed branch at the top. Bob had arranged the lights so that a red one was behind her and made her wings glow a rosy pink. She gazed serenely across the room like a person in her element. I sent a thought to Jacqueline then, wherever she was, celebrating Christmas somewhere in the world with her own finely stitched fairy on the top of her own tree.

Under the tree were the presents that we'd open when Auntie May arrived. They were all wrapped in the same garish paper. The rest of the room was crammed with paper angels and stars. They crowded the windowsills, jostled with Christmas cards on the mantelpiece and dangled from the ceiling on bits of black cotton. On a low table was Mama's nativity scene, crumpled donkey and all. It was absurd. It was sweet. It was beautiful in its own way. My own feelings jostled inside me. I could not bear the frailty of all that paper folded with such maddening care, or the fragility of the whole festivity. I wanted to stamp on it and smash it and scorn it – and I wanted to believe in and be a part of it. I wanted to swallow it all in one great gullible gulp.

Bob carried Auntie May into the sitting room and settled her down in his own armchair. Just as I had grown bigger during the year, she had grown smaller, and her feet dangled in the air. She regarded me brightly with her sunken hooded eyes. The dry little nut of her skull was visible through her sparse puff of colourless hair. Her eyebrows were reduced to three or four hairs each, but these were long and stuck out like twisted wires. Round her mouth were whiskers. She had no teeth left in her mouth, which had shrunk to nothing but a little moist bud.

'Hello, Auntie May. Happy Christmas,' I said, bending to kiss her cheek. Bob was pulling a face and screwing his finger into the side of his head to Mama, who ignored him.

'Auntie May . . .' Mama sat on the arm of the chair and hugged her with quite genuine love.

Auntie May stared at me. 'The girl's changed.' She squeezed the words out in her rustling distant voice.

'Thirteen now. A teenager,' Mama said. She turned her face to May as she spoke so that May could read her lips, for she had grown very deaf.

'Now. Let the festivities commence,' Bob said, rubbing his hands. 'Sherry, Lilian? May? A glass of pop, Jenny?'

When I had been younger, the way we used to open presents would drive me to distraction. It was my job to distribute them and then we opened them slowly, in turn, everyone watching and admiring each present and passing it round for general inspection. It was a lengthy process, and ridiculous, at least from Mama's point of view, since she had chosen and wrapped almost everything. The procedure took even longer this year because Auntie May kept drifting off, not to sleep, but to some place beyond us, and it was with great difficulty that we kept her engaged with the task.

'Auntie May!' bellowed Bob. 'A torch from Lilian to me – look – a good 'un.' He clicked it on and off. 'Bright beam – normal beam – and off. Thank you, Lilian. Just the thing. Most useful.'

Mama smiled and unwrapped the present she had chosen for herself from Bob, a book about macramé and a ball of string. Auntie May was passed the string to admire and she held it in her hand and looked, puzzled, at me. 'Anyone for tennis,' she said, or something like, and Bob laughed as if it was a joke.

I unwrapped my black jersey and ran upstairs to put it on and model it. 'You're filling out,' Bob remarked, and Mama called it 'chic'. I had some peach-blossom bath cubes from Auntie May that I distinctly remembered giving her the year before. 'Thank you,' I said. She looked at me through the little slits of her eyes and nodded.

Mama and Bob opened and exclaimed over their presents from me, and Bob blew his nose on the handkerchief there and then to express his approval.

'Another little present for Jenny,' Mama said. She was on her knees before the tree. I held my breath thinking, just for a moment, that Jacqueline had remembered me. Mama burrowed beneath the tree and came out with a miniature parcel. 'Almost got lost it's so tiny.' The paper was the same, and I knew at once what this would be: another charm for my bracelet. It was a little golden book. 'Open it,' Mama said eagerly. I pressed the tiny clasp with my finger and a little concertina strip of miniature photographs fell out. Views of Paris.

'Lovely,' I said. Disappointment lodged in my gullet, as big and fragile as an egg. There was the Eiffel Tower and the Arc de Triomphe and Versailles – all pictures I recognised from the posters on the walls of the geography room at school.

'You'll be able to jingle now,' Mama said, 'if you fasten it on beside the wishbone.'

Auntie May chuckled for no apparent reason. We all paused to look at her. Mama helped her open her present from herself and Bob – a pair of slippers. She eased Auntie May's narrow black shoes off and replaced them with the blue fluffy slippers. They were far too big and slipped off her dangling feet at once. 'I can change them,' Mama said sadly, looking at the bent and wizened twigs that were Auntie May's feet.

I thought I wouldn't be able to eat the lunch that Mama

had worked so hard to prepare, but I found my appetite growing as I ate, and loaded my plate with tender white breast-meat and thick gravy and more and more potatoes. It was Bob who didn't eat much, which was unlike him, and Mama kept urging him to eat until he grew annoyed. Mama fed Auntie May little chopped-up titbits. She opened her mouth wide to receive the forkfuls and made me think of a bright-eyed baby bird in a nest. We pulled the crackers and read the silly mottoes and wore paper crowns to eat the pudding. Auntie May's crown was far too big and kept falling down to sit round her neck like a collar until Mama fixed it on with sticky tape.

After lunch we sat, sated, round the fire. Bob twiddled the knobs of the radio and we listened to the crackly voice of the Queen and then Bob and Auntie May nodded off and Mama knelt on the floor and tied some lengths of string to the back of a kitchen chair and began experimenting with her macramé. 'I think I'm going to get on famously with this,' she said. 'Would you like a belt? Or I could make a bell-pull.'

'Whatever for?' I asked. I watched her fingers busying away until I dropped off to sleep myself. I was awoken a short time later by a paper angel falling from the ceiling onto my lap. Mama had completed several inches of her work.

'Criss-cross diagonal cording,' she said eagerly, as soon as I opened my eyes. 'And look at this – a flat-knot-button. I need some beads. I could make a wall hanging. Curtains even . . .'

'I'll make some tea,' I said. In the kitchen, gazing into the cavity of the half-devoured turkey, I thought about Johnny and the sort of Christmas he'd be having with Mary and her family or, perhaps, all on his own in the church with only the little branch to remind him that it was Christmas at all. It had been a surprise – a shock – to find that he had a girlfriend. I'd thought of him as a man alone. The kind of woman Mary was surprised me too, an ordinary woman who made fun of him and bossed him about. I couldn't imagine what he saw in her, but supposed it must be sex-appeal. I picked a shred of meat from the carcass. I was restless. Bob had started to snore, I could hear him from the kitchen. It was too hot and stuffy in the house.

'I think I'll go out for a walk,' I whispered to Mama, round the sitting-room door. She looked up at me over her glasses, surprised, keeping her finger on an instruction in her book. 'All right?'

'All right,' she said. 'Would you like me to come?' It was a sacrifice for her to offer now that she had begun her macramé.

'No,' I said. 'I won't be long. Just a bit of fresh air. I'll make the tea when I get back.' She nodded, relieved, and went back to her knots.

I liked to walk around the streets in the afternoons when it was dark enough for lights to be on, but not quite time to draw the curtains. I liked the houses without net curtains best, where as I dawdled past I could most clearly glimpse the family tableaux. Many were centred round the television and, by pausing and straining my eyes and ears, I caught a snatch of circus, a spangled leap and a roar of applause. Tree lights winked. It was the very day. Pudding-heavy families slumped all along the streets, behind the lighted glass. I saw a slumbering man with his paper crown over his eyes, I saw a boy batting a shuttlecock, I saw a woman with a tray of tea. A car drew up beside me and a family spilt out with squawks of excitement and armfuls of parcels, and I bent to tie my shoelace while the door of a house opened and they were welcomed and swallowed into a hallway full of light and balloons. I didn't need to go to the playground and climb the frame to know that the family in the blue house would be having a picture-book Christmas. I forced my feet to walk away from the church and back home.

Bob had woken up and was in the kitchen pouring out

the tea. 'Got rid of the cobwebs?' he asked. I thought he looked pale and noticed that his hand shook.

'I was going to do that,' I said. 'Are you all right?'

'Don't *you* start fussing,' he said.

After a cup of tea it was time for a game. Bob was the enthusiast. Mama played along loyally and I joined in because I had little choice if I wasn't to wreck Christmas altogether. I never longed for a television set more than on Christmas afternoons. I thought enviously of the families all along the road slumped in companionable quiet in front of their screens. We started harmlessly with Twenty Questions. Bob was a stickler for the rules, and invented more and more as the game progressed, 'To keep us on our toes,' he said. He employed the bird-shaped whistle he had found inside his cracker, and gave a sharp peep on it whenever there was an infringement. There was never any suggestion that anyone else should take this umpire's role. He invented the rule that there should be no umming or erring and that each question must be answered within five seconds – four beats of his fist on the arm of the sofa and then, on the count of five, a fierce pointing of his finger at the victim to demand the answer.

Auntie May was at a complete loss, and had to be left out. She sent me a mischievous look, and I grinned back at her. You never knew with Auntie May how much she was taking in. She had been always laughing and teasing as a young woman, Mama said, and even now her old eyes glinted with fun whenever Bob raised his whistle to his lips. The first game passed successfully enough. It was always like this. We started with harmless rule-bound games where you won or lost – there was no prize for winning other than relief, for, as the level of the brandy bottle crept down, Bob became increasingly scornful of the loser. Dumb Crambo and Consequences followed, and I actually found myself enjoying the latter. Then Mama and I made the tea: turkey-and-stuffing sandwiches, picalilli and Christmas cake. After tea there was a pause for washing up and digestion, and then, as I had feared, Bob announced Village Life.

This was a game he'd invented himself. It had so many rules that nobody except Bob could possibly remember them, or tell whether he was changing them as he went along. I was the postman this year and my sack of Christmas mail had been stolen and the point of the game was to discover who had stolen it and where it was. This was all done with dice and a laboriously drawn and much folded and smudged map, matchsticks stuck into plasticine and scraps of paper – secret notes which had to be written in code – and each turn could take twenty minutes. Every now and then Bob would order Mama or me out of the room so that a confidential discussion could take place. Bob was, as always, the detective. He picked up one of Mama's knitting needles, a thin whippy one, and waved it as he ordered us about and waited in the panic-stricken pauses for us to take our turns. Mama and I looked at each other askance. Auntie May made an enigmatic sound in the throat. Bob drew the needle through the air and a shadow passed my eyes and I seemed to see him loom and just for a moment I cringed and screwed shut my eyes, certain that he was going to whip me. But when I looked up he was sitting in his chair with the needle in his lap, not even looking in my direction.

Mama looked at me curiously. 'Let's stop this and play Scrabble,' she pleaded to Bob. I saw her eyes wander towards her macramé.

'But we're on the track now!' Bob objected. 'Don't you *care* who did it?'

Mama raised her eyebrows at me, and I looked at Auntie May, who nodded. 'Home,' she said, looking across at the clock.

'Yes, Bob, it's time you got Auntie May back,' said Mama and her face showed a mixture of relief that the game was over and sadness that it was time to say goodbye to Auntie May. Bob reluctantly agreed, and we never did discover who had stolen the mail, and Bob said this was because *someone* had gone wrong somewhere, looking darkly at Mama, whose face was quite blank as she helped Auntie May on with her coat.

I was glad when the day was over. I helped Mama clear up and then went up to my room, where the Christmas-stocking presents still lay on my unmade bed. I put on my pyjamas and sat in the midst of the tangle eating my tangerine. Christmas day was gone and the dread had proved unfounded. It had been no worse than usual. I picked up Johnny's book and read about Stephen breaking his glasses and then getting unfairly pandied for it. I thought 'pandied' a funny word for something painful, if was too much like panda, or candied, a sweet and cuddly word. Mama came hesitantly into my room.

'What are you reading?' she asked. I showed her. 'I haven't seen that before,' she said.

'I borrowed it from a friend,' I said.

'Ah . . .' She sat down on the edge of my bed. 'Enjoyed yourself?' she asked.

'Yes,' I said.

'I know Bob's a bit . . . but that's families for you. And he's good at heart. You must know that. Not bad as fathers go.'

'Except that he's not my father.' I tried to shift away from her weight on the edge of my bed. Irritation welled up. The day had been all right, I had kept it under control but now it was over and she had to follow me into my room, she had to push a bit further. 'There's no need to pretend, Mama, I'm not a baby.'

'No,' she sighed. 'Of course you're not. That's very true.'

'You can't say *very* true,' I quibbled. 'It's either true or not true.'

'I suppose so.' She sat there for some moments, clearing her throat and sighing.

'Well?' I said at last. I was cramped by her presence, unable to move or think, unable to rest.

'There's another present,' she said. She looked down and fiddled with the fringed edge of my bedspread. 'I didn't want to give it you earlier with Auntie May there – and Bob – and everything. I didn't know what to do. I didn't want to upset you – upset everyone – upset Christmas.'

She waited for me to speak, and when I found my voice it was very cold and clear. 'From her? From Jacqueline?'

'Yes dear. You were so upset about the letter I didn't want to risk . . .'

'Where is it then?'

'I'll fetch it.' She hurried out of the room and came back with a parcel wrapped in different paper, not Mama's paper. It was dark green with tiny silver holly leaves, expensive, tasteful paper – exactly the kind of paper I'd have expected Jacqueline to choose. On a matching label were the words, written in green ink, in an elegant hand, a grown-up sophisticated version of the writing in her letter: *To Jennifer, With Love at Christmas, Jacqueline.* That was all. I read it and read it, but there was no more to it than that. Still, there was love, and she had remembered. I stared so long at the label that Mama began to fidget.

'Aren't you going to open it?'

'I'd rather be alone,' I said, not looking up, not trusting myself to look away from the parcel.

'All right, Jenny. You can show us in the morning.' Her voice was flat. 'Night, night,' she said, and I muttered some reply, and she hovered for a moment as if about to kiss me, or say something else, and then went out, closing the door behind her with a disappointed click.

I got out of bed and took the nail scissors from my manicure set, and carefully, very carefully, so as not to tear the paper even slightly, I snipped the parcel open. Inside was a box, and even without the comforting weight of it I would have known that *this* box could not, would not, be empty. I smoothed and folded the paper and put it and the label in the secret compartment of my trinket box. I made myself wait for a moment, watching the ballerina pirouette to the ice-cream jingle of the tune. My heart was beating so that it hurt. It mattered what was in the box. It mattered more than anything had mattered since I could remember. Eventually I opened the flap on top of the box. Inside, well packed with screwed-up tissue paper, was a squat black camera. It wasn't new, there were scratches on it and other signs of wear. It was all the more precious for this. I cherished the hope that it had been Jacqueline's own. She had given me not something shop-bought and meaningless, but something of her own, something that was, perhaps, precious to *her*. I searched through the box and unscrewed every piece of tissue paper, but there was nothing else, no message, no photograph, which was what I craved. But the camera was a sign that I was important, that I lived in her mind just as she lived in mine.

I lay down on my back with the camera on my chest and pulled the blankets over me. I had never had a camera, never taken a photograph in my life. Mama and Bob didn't go in for photography. I realised, for the first time, that there wasn't a photograph in the house: no albums, no framed portraits, no pictures of me as a baby, no pictures of Jacqueline. It was good to have something of hers weighing down on my chest, pressing over my heart, pinning me down. I drifted off to sleep contentedly, but woke later in the grip of a nightmare, sweating. Johnny was kneeling on my chest, pressing his knees against me until I thought my ribs would cave in and I would die. But it was only the camera. My pyjama top was soaked with sweat where it had pressed. I moved the camera to the floor beside my bed, turned over and lay with my hand upon it, waiting for sleep to return.

· *Eighteen* ·

'Well?' asked Mama, at breakfast, when it became clear I wasn't going to offer any information.

'Well what?'

'What was it? The present.'

Bob slurped the dregs of his tea and tapped his cup to indicate to Mama that he wanted some more.

'Well?' he repeated.

'A camera,' I said.

Mama poured the tea. 'Yes,' she said, 'of course.'

'What do you mean?'

'She had a camera from us for her birthday one year. Was it her thirteenth, Bob? She took it up as a hobby. Photography. She was very keen.' This was the most Mama had ever said about Jaqueline. I was possessed by a desire to know more.

'Expensive business,' grumbled Bob.

'Perhaps she still is keen,' I said.

'Well yes,' Mama agreed.

'What did you call her?' I asked. 'Jacqueline, or Jacqui? What did she look like? Do I look like her? Haven't you got any photographs? What happened to all hers?'

'Twenty Questions all over again,' Bob said.

I looked at Mama, waiting for a reply, and saw that her eyes were very bright and her lips were trembling. She got up and left the room.

'Lilian . . .' Bob called after her, but we could hear her fleeing up the stairs and the bathroom door banging shut. Bob raised his eyebrows at me.

'Sleeping dogs,' he said, 'best let lie.'

'Lie,' I said, 'yes, that's what you've done to me. I only want to know the truth.'

'Don't be ridiculous,' Bob said and he looked right at me, hard into my eyes, in a way he hadn't done for months. 'What's truth got to do with it? Look at you, sitting there radiating self-pity. You've been fed and clothed and loved. *Indulged*. It could have been a lot worse considering. We don't expect gratitude, but do you realise what your behaviour is doing to Mama? And now that girl is sending presents to the house, deliberately provoking, stirring up . . . We should never have let the cat out of the bag. I told Lilian . . . And never a word to *us*. Presents for *you*, yes . . . but never a word to Lilian, her own mother. It'll break her heart.'

I was cold. Bob never said so much. His face was pale and his fingers shook as he lifted his cup to his lips. There were drops of sweat on his upper lip, and a red weal on his neck where the collar of his shirt had dug in yesterday. It was true I hadn't thought about Mama's feelings. She and Bob together seemed nothing but a barrier that kept me from the truth, from my mother, and from my real self.

'So she didn't send you anything?'

We could hear Mama's footsteps on the stairs. Bob returned his cup to his saucer and his eyes slid away. I was relieved to see him return to his old vague self. 'Not a sausage,' he said. Mama came in then, and caught the end of the conversation.

'Well, we wouldn't expect . . .' she said, in her normal bright voice. 'Now, more toast anyone?'

'No thanks, Lilian,' Bob said. 'Sit down and have another cup of tea, there's a girl.'

'I will have more tea,' Mama said. 'It's still Christmas after all.' She poured herself a cup and sat down. 'Auntie May looked well, didn't you think?'

'Yes she did,' I agreed.

'For her age,' Bob said. 'This'll be her last Christmas though, you mark my words. She's had a good innings.'

'You always say that. And anyway it won't be. She'll go on for years and years.' I said, to try and cheer Mama up, but also because I hoped it was true. I liked Auntie May and the dinosaur gleam in her ancient eyes. I liked to see her perched on Bob's chair, her feet dangling, her little head nodding, beside the Christmas tree.

'You're off to Bronwyn's tonight,' Mama reminded me. 'You'd better have a bath before you go, and take your new toothbrush and flannel.'

'Are you sure you don't mind me going on Boxing Day?' I asked 'I don't mind *not* going.'

'It'll put paid to Village Life,' grumbled Bob.

'We can always play Scrabble,' Mama said. 'You like that.'

'It'll be a case of having to,' Bob said.

In my room I hugged the camera, and studied the tiny numbers round the dial. I had no idea how to use it. I had no money for film, and I could hardly ask for it now. I stood at my window looking through the aperture in the top of the camera. The garden was reflected and condensed into a tiny sharp image more perfect and satisfactory than the sprawling reality. It looked tidied up and faraway, like a picture already. The icy surface of the pond at the end of the garden glinted, a tiny pewter speck through the frosty branches of the trees. Jacqueline had probably taken pictures of the garden and of Mama and of Bob and of all the things she'd seen. She might have been to the churchyard. She might even have played in the playground before it was overgrown. She had a life here before me and a life leaves traces. Surely it cannot be possible for a person to simply disappear?

I wandered around the house, with the camera strap round my neck, examining the other traces, the silky threads, the sequins.

'If you've nothing to do,' Mama said, 'would you go up into the loft for me? There's a box of bits and bobs I could make use of.'

I went upstairs to the landing and looked at the trap-door in the ceiling. 'All right then,' I called. My interest was caught by the possibility that there would be more of Jacqueline up there, something more tangible.

'Bob's fetching the ladder,' Mama said, coming upstairs to watch.

Bob climbed the ladder and pushed the trapdoor up. 'You'll need a torch,' he said, and handed me his new Christmas torch which he'd had tucked in the waistband of his trousers. 'For goodness' sake don't stand between the rafters though, or you'll come through the ceiling.'

I climbed into the dark place where dust lay thick as fur in the spaces between the rafters.

'Look in the big box,' Mama called; 'near the top there's a chocolate box with kittens on it.' I leant out and looked down at Mama and Bob standing underneath me, their faces turned up like anxious flowers.

'Be careful,' Bob warned, and I crawled away from them into the surprising warmth. The dust sifted and stirred. There were cobwebs clotted with fluff, and a spider ran up its invisible thread in the light of the torch.

'All right?' Mama called, and her voice was muffled. There were chinks of light in places where one roof tile was lapped imperfectly over the next. There was very little up there, as if there had been a deliberate erasing, a jettisoning of a past. I heard, very loudly, the scratching of a bird's feet on the roof, and then its song. The water tank gurgled. 'Can you see the boxes?' Mama called.

'Why don't you go up, Lilian?' Bob suggested.

There were some boxes crowded together. The first one I opened and shone the torch beam into glistened with Mama's beads tangled together with little combs and hair ornaments, miniature scissors, bits of ribbon and the scraps of embroidery silk.

'Found it,' I called. 'What's in the other boxes?'

'Nothing,' Bob said.

'Crockery,' Mama said.

'Fishing stuff,' Bob added.

'Can I look?'

'If you like.'

I opened the lid of a large box. The dust made my fingers feel dry so that I couldn't bear the roughness of the cardboard. The smell of the dust got into my nose and coated my teeth. I shone the torch into the box and saw plates and a bundle of forks and a teapot with a broken spout. Underneath were some old knitting-pattern books of Mama's and an outdated encyclopedia. I was overcome by a great surge of boredom. There was nothing here for me, no great discovery. It was ordinary junk, household flotsam. There was nothing that was particularly to do with Jacqueline. She might have eaten with one of the forks off one of the plates. She might have consulted the encyclopedia while doing her homework. And she might not have done. And even if she had, what then? They were only things. They weren't *Jacqueline*. The traces weren't, after all, important. I crawled along the rafter to the trapdoor and handed Mama's box down to Bob.

'Finished up there?' he asked. I nodded and climbed down. Mama took the box into her room. I washed the dryness off my hands. The end of my plait was grey with dust and cobwebs which I'd dragged away with me. I went into Mama's room. She had tipped the contents of the box onto the bed and was sorting through. She smiled up at me. 'You *ought* to have a bath,' she said and then held me in her gaze and narrowed her eyes as if she fancied herself perceptive. 'I do understand,' she said and there was a husky intimacy in her voice that made me bristle.

'What?'

'You wanting to talk about . . .'

'Jacqueline.' I finished for her. I didn't want her to understand. The moment had passed.

'Yes, Jacqueline.'

'It's all right,' I said.

'No . . . it isn't. There's too much unsaid. We were wrong.'

'No you weren't. It's all right. I'm all right. You've done your job.'

'But surely we can – surely we must – talk.'

I shrugged. 'Don't see why.'

She sighed and ran a string of bright beads through her withered fingers. The backs of her hands were blotched and veined. I picked through the jumble. There was a ring with a dark red stone. 'Is it a ruby?' I asked.

She smiled. 'No, more's the pity. It's a garnet. Try it on.' I slid it onto my finger. 'Have it,' she said. 'My fingers are too thick now.'

I held my hand out and waved it from side to side so that the garnet caught the light with a rubeous gleam. 'All right,' I said. She frowned at my ingratitude, and I got up impatiently.

'Don't you want to know anything about it?' she said.

'It's just a ring,' I said, and of course I wanted to know whether it had ever been on Jacqueline's finger. I wanted to know everything, but I didn't want *her* to tell me. I didn't want her understanding.

'I'm going outside,' I said. And in the garden I stared at the pond, and remembered the digging of the hole. Remembered a different self in a different time. The surface of the pond was partly iced over and twigs and leaves were set into the ice. Deep underneath in the thick green water there was a small orange movement, a glimpse of a lurking fish.

In Bronwyn's house there was a silver artificial tree. 'Since Dad died we haven't bothered with the real thing,' she said. 'He used to go out and get a huge one, right up to the ceiling. But it doesn't seem worth it just for Mum and me.'

'Still, it looks pretty,' I said. And it did. Pretty but slight.

We were standing in the dim hall looking into the sitting room. I noticed a few cards on the mantelpiece. It all looked very orderly, no jostling of angels here.

'What did you get for Christmas?' she asked. 'I got a chainbelt and a nightie and a jigsaw – a thousand pieces –

and some scent, Devon Violets, have a sniff.' She stuck her wrist under my nose and I breathed in a sweetshop smell. 'Like it? It's from my aunt in Torquay. Mum was livid.' I tried to imagine Mrs Broom as livid, and failed. She was too small and papery-thin.

'I got a camera,' I said.

'Really? A real one?' Bronwyn was impressed and deflated.

'Just go in the kitchen and say hello to Mum,' she said, 'then we'll go upstairs.'

Mrs Broom was slicing bread. 'Happy Christmas, dear,' she said, and looked at me anxiously. 'And has it been?'

'Yes, thank you,' I replied and glanced questioningly at Bronwyn, who looked away.

'Chicken sandwiches,' she said, 'and quite an array of pickles. That all right for you?' She wiped her hands on what looked like a brand-new apron.

'And gâteau,' added Bronwyn proudly in a growly accent I took to be French.

'I've never had gâteau before,' I admitted.

'It's divine,' Bronwyn said, rolling her eyes. 'Come upstairs now.'

'Why don't you stay down here in the warm?' Mrs Broom said. 'And keep me company.'

'I want to show Jenny where she's sleeping,' Bronwyn said, pulling me out of the room, although I would have preferred to stay in the warmth of the kitchen.

There was a mattress on the floor in Bronwyn's room, neatly made up as a bed. I noticed that the sheets were nylon. 'Mum wanted to put you in the spare room,' she said, 'but I wanted you in here. So we can talk. It's more fun like that.' She made her eyes go dreamy and stared beyond me into her past. 'I was always having people to stay when I was at Moncrieff. For the whole weekend sometimes.' She flopped down onto her bed and looked up at the ceiling. 'There were always people in and out. Dad's friends. They were always having dinner parties with candles and stuff.'

'What happened to all the people?' I asked.

'Well after Dad – you know – they all dis-app-eared.'

'Why?'

'Oh you know . . . fair-weather friends.' She sniffed.

'You poor thing,' I said.

'I don't care,' she said bravely, lifting her head. It was icy cold in the room. There were frosty ferns on the window and my toes were already growing numb.

'Shall I draw the curtains?' I asked.

She shrugged. 'If you want.' The curtain material was thin and damp, and the curtain rings stuck.

'They won't draw,' I said.

She pulled a face. 'Oh leave them. I never bother.'

'Shall we go downstairs?' I suggested. 'I'm freezing.' Even the dolls looked cold in their light frocks, their limbs bluish in the dim light.

'No. Mum'll keep sticking her nose in. I want you all to myself. It'll be tea-time soon anyway.'

'Do you have a hot-water bottle at bedtime?' I asked, imagining the cold shock of the sheets on my skin, and the draught blowing across the mattress from under the door.

'We might have one somewhere,' she said. 'I'll ask Mum. Oh . . . I like that!' She caught hold of my charm bracelet. I took it off and showed her how to unclasp the little book to see the pictures of Paris spill out.

'I'm getting another charm every birthday and every Christmas until I'm twenty-one,' I said.

'I'm asking Mum if *I* can,' she said. 'Only with all the charms at once. It doesn't look much with only two, does it?' She slipped it on her wrist and looked at it critically before handing it back.

'And I've got a ring,' I said. 'A garnet.'

'What's that?'

'A sort of a ruby.'

'Where?'

'At home in my trinket box.'

'Don't believe you,' she said, and sat down at her dressing table and began to fiddle with her hair.

'I have. I'll show you,' I said.

'When?'

'Next time.'

Bronwyn snorted. She had a saucer full of hairgrips and slides. She lifted her hair over to one side and clipped it there. 'Spanish,' she announced.

'Why did your mum ask me if I'd had a happy Christmas in that way, as if she thought I hadn't?' I asked.

'Because of that fib you told.'

'What fib?'

'When you said your dad was ill. She met your grandparents remember?'

'Oh.' I had forgotten that. 'Well it wasn't really a fib. Bob isn't all that well.'

Bronwyn shrugged and narrowed her eyes at herself in the mirror.

'I'm freezing,' I complained. 'And bored. What shall we do?'

'I've been looking forward to you coming round.' Bronwyn turned to me looking hurt. 'And now you say you're bored. None of my Moncrieff friends were ever bored.'

I sat on her bed and we remained in silence for a while. I could hear the clattering sounds of crockery and cutlery as Bronwyn's mother laid the table.

'This is the first time I've stayed away for the night,' I said, feeling, to my surprise, a longing for my own things and my own room, where at least it was warm.

'Really?' Bronwyn arched her eyebrows at me disbelievingly. 'Haven't you ever been on holiday?'

'I mean the first time without Mama and Bob,' I explained.

'Why do you call them that? Why not Nan and Grandad? That's what I call mine. That's what *most* people call them.'

'I don't know,' I said. 'It's what I've always called them.'

Bronwyn licked her lips and shivered. 'I know what we

can do,' she said, becoming suddenly animated. 'We can have a beauty salon.'

'A what?'

'I'll do your hair for you shall I? Make you look gla-mor-ous. Would you like some scent? Go on, you'll smell lovely.' She tipped the little purple bottle and dabbed the perfume behind my ears. 'There. Now, sit down.' I sat on the stool before the dressing table and winced as she ripped the rubber band off the end of my plait. She unravelled my hair until it lay in pale wispy snakes down my back. 'It reaches past your bum,' she said.

'I can sit on it,' I said, and demonstrated.

'It's pretty. My hair just gets bushier and bushier if I try to grow it.'

I got off my hair and began to brush it. The fine strands jumped up to meet the brush.

'Electric,' she observed.

'I hate it,' I said. 'I really want to have it cut. Mama said I can have it cut.'

'I'll do it,' she offered, lifting a long strand out sideways and making scissoring motions with her fingers.

'You'd better not.'

'Oh go on . . . let me.' Bronwyn leant over my shoulder so that our faces were reflected together in the mirror. 'I'm good at it,' she urged. 'I always do Mum's. I'm going to be a hairdresser when I leave school. An app-ren-tice. I've got the knack, Mum says.'

I thought suddenly of Susan's short hair which lay in such pretty wisps around her ears. 'Oh go on then,' I said. It was only hair anyway, only dead stuff seeping endlessly from my follicles. It would grow again. And anyway, Susan might like it short. All the popular girls wore their hair short.

She was surprised. 'Oh . . . I don't know . . .'

'Go on! You said you would. I want it all chopped off. Now!'

'Well, if you're sure . . .' Bronwyn went to find the scissors. I ran my fingers through the cold baby-fine stuff.

It was my childhood, dead silk between my fingers, nothing to do with me any more.

Bronwyn came back with a pair of pointed scissors with a curl extending from one of the loops. 'They're special hairdresser's scissors,' she explained, demonstrating how she rested her little finger on the loop. 'Mum bought them for me. That shows how good I am. I do her hair, a perm and a trim every three months. They all like it at work. They ask her which salon she uses.'

'Where does she work?'

'Not work really,' she said hurriedly. 'She just helps out at my uncle's club. Cleaning. But she's not a cleaner. She just helps out as a favour. Anyway, I could do you a perm.'

'No,' I said. 'No curls. I just want it short and straight. Dead short, with a fringe. And it wouldn't matter if she was a cleaner.'

'Well she isn't. Sure you want it done?'

'Go on.' I closed my eyes and held my breath as she took the first few snips. She began to hum tunelessly as she warmed to the task. I breathed in her smell, a mixture of violets and sweat, as she moved around me, her fingers against my scalp as cold as the scissors. I felt a lightness as the hair fell away. She cut it so that it fell straight all round to just below my ears.

'Now I can start styling,' she said, and we both took comfort from the professional-sounding word. She cut a fringe straight across my eyebrows. I blinked at my reflection through the falling hair. It made me look younger, which had not been my intention. I knew Mama would be hurt that I hadn't let her take me to the hairdresser and that Bob would mumble and moan at her behind closed doors.

'Very short?' Bronwyn asked. 'Sure you don't want to go shorter in stages?'

'*Dead* short,' I confirmed.

'Well, if you're sure.' She began to lift sections of the hair on the crown of my head up and snip them off an inch or so from the roots. 'Do you know where your real mum and dad are?' she asked. 'Go on, you can tell me. I can keep a secret. I'm your best friend, aren't I?' I nodded half-heartedly. 'And I told you *my* secret. About my dad. Hardly anybody knows about that.'

'Wasn't it in the papers then?'

'No, it was all hushed up.'

'Why?'

Bronwyn shrugged and began to snip busily at the nape of my neck. 'Here goes,' she said. '*Dead* short. Tell me.'

'Well . . .' I hesitated. Bronwyn *was* supposed to be my friend. For now she was my friend. I needed to practise friendship. And this was what I imagined friends were supposed to do – whisper secrets in each other's bedrooms. I wasn't a confiding person. Mama always complained about my secretiveness. 'Not an open child,' she'd often said, for I was the type who liked to curl up and nurse my grief, an awkward hedgehog thing, against my breast. But every snip and snap of Bronwyn's scissors left a little question mark in the air.

'Or don't you know?' she prompted.

'All right then,' I said. 'My mother is called Jacqueline. She was young when I was born, she left me with her parents and went away. I don't know where she is. I've never seen her. But she sent me a present. She sent me the camera.'

'Ah . . .' I felt the scissor points closing against my ear.

'Careful!'

'Sorry . . . and what about your father?'

'I don't know.'

'Il-le-git-i-mate,' she said and her sigh was long and plumy enough to cloud the mirror. 'I've always wanted to be il-le-git-i-mate. Don't you wonder though?'

'No,' I said, quite truthfully, for it had not occurred to me until that moment to wonder about my father.

'Nearly finished,' she said. 'What am I supposed to do about the hairs on your neck, do you think? I've never cut *really* short before. Who would you like him to be if you could choose?'

'I don't know, that's stupid. I haven't got a father.'

'But you must have one somewhere.'

'Well I don't care who he is. I can't see the point of pretending I can choose.' Irritably I shrugged Bronwyn's hand off my shoulder where it was resting. She wiped her nose which was pink and runny from the cold.

'Well, it's finished,' she said. 'Do you like it?'

'I think so,' I said, turning my head from side to side. I looked ordinary and I liked that.

'It's much darker,' she said, 'and it's not *quite* right at the back.'

'Well it's done,' I said, turning away from the mirror. Bronwyn looked crestfallen. 'Thank you,' I added. I felt even colder with my neck all bare. I ran my hand up the back of my head over the peculiar stubbly hairs. Susan's didn't look as if it was prickly like that, it looked soft and downy. On the dark carpet was the pale glistening pool of my hair. I scooped it up, and rubbed it between my fingers. It was my baby hair and my childhood. I held onto it for a moment and then I let it fall. 'What shall we do with it?' I asked. Bronwyn took it and stuffed it into her drawer.

'I'll burn it,' she said. 'When Mum's out.'

'It'll stink,' I said. She took the nugget of sugar pig from her drawer and gnawed at it.

'It must be nearly tea-time,' I said hopefully.

'I don't know what Mum'll say,' Bronwyn said. 'You look so different.'

I shrugged. 'What shall we do now?' I asked.

'Talk,' Bronwyn said. 'My Moncrieff friends always wanted to talk. We used to talk for hours.'

'About what? Anyway, where are your Moncrieff friends?' I asked, meanly, because I was beginning not to believe in them.

'After Daddy . . .'

'I don't see what difference that makes.'

'Oh don't you! That shows how much *you* know. I don't know why you're being so horrible *and* after I did your

· 143 ·

hair for you. I'm beginning to wish you hadn't come now. I *did* have something to tell you.' She bent down and pulled up her socks. Her legs were purple and mottled.

'What?'

'I was going to tell you after tea.'

'Why can't you tell me now?'

Bronwyn's face was losing its anxious look. She thought I wanted to know.

'Tea's ready, girls,' Mrs Broom called up the stairs. 'Wash your hands now.'

We stood in the bathroom waiting for the water flowing through the creaking pipes to warm a little. '*Wait* till you taste the gâteau,' Bronwyn said. 'My dad had French blood you know. Garlic charm. That's why we have gâteau. A family tra-di-tion. But don't, don't you *dare* mention him.' She lowered her eyebrows fiercely at me.

I remembered what Mama had said about family skeletons and felt sorry for Bronwyn, even though I didn't like her much.

'You won't will you?' I shook my head. 'Anyway, we're both sort of the same, aren't we?' she said. 'Sort of orphans. And your hair will soon grow back.'

'*Sort* of orphans,' I agreed, but as I followed her downstairs, I knew that she was wrong. I was no orphan, and nor was she. We both had mothers. Mrs Broom was a good mother, but when I saw her fussing over the table, faded and anxious in the apron, and then thought of Jacqueline with her cheekbones and her photography and her fine green ink I knew which mother I preferred.

'Jennifer?' Mrs Broom looked at me, puzzled. 'You look as if . . . oh surely not . . .' She looked accusingly at Bronwyn. 'Oh you haven't! You naughty girl!'

'She wanted it. She asked me to,' Bronwyn wailed.

'What a thing to do. Oh Bronwyn . . . and on Boxing Day of all days.'

I couldn't see what difference that made. 'It's all right,' I said, 'honestly. I like it. And Mama said I could have it cut.'

She stood looking at me, plucking anxiously at her apron. 'It's *all right*,' I insisted.

She frowned at Bronwyn and shook her head. 'You really are the limit. I don't know what to do with you. If your dad was here now . . .'

Bronwyn recoiled as if she had been hit. I shuffled my feet nervously. Mrs Broom's eyes went pink as if she was about to cry. 'I suppose I'll have to ring your grandparents and explain . . . oh they'll wish they'd never let you come.' She began to sniff. 'I've a good mind to make you go without . . .' She looked from the laden table to Bronwyn and back again. But she couldn't bear the thought of it all being wasted, I could see from her face, all the food and the scarlet serviettes and the crackers.

'They haven't got a telephone,' Bronwyn reminded her.

'It's all right, honestly,' I soothed. 'It'll save Mama paying for a hairdresser. I shifted my eyes to the table again. 'It does look a lovely spread,' I said.

'Yes.' Mrs Broom sniffed back her tears. 'Well we might as well enjoy it now I've gone to all the trouble.'

Bronwyn sat down. I watched her as we said our grace. There was a dark red flush on her face and neck and I thought she might cry too. It was the mention of her dad that had done it. But we pulled the crackers and put on our paper hats and read the silly jokes. They were the same crackers we'd had at home and I got the same joke: *Why did the lobster blush? Because it saw the salad dressing*. There were beautifully thick chicken-and-stuffing sandwiches and several different kinds of pickle: beetroot, red cabbage, large and small onions, gherkins and walnuts and a violently yellow picalilli.

'We always like our pickles at Christmas,' Mrs Broom said, cheering up. 'It's a traditional craft you know, pickling, a way of preserving food for the winter.' I munched my way politely through a plateful until the vinegar wrinkled the inside of my cheeks. We compared our Christmases. I told them about Auntie May and the origami decorations and they told me about the cousins and their loud voices and the amount they ate.

Mrs Broom told me how much my help had been appreciated at the church bazaar. 'You made quite a hit,' she said. 'You'd be very welcome if you ever felt you wanted to . . .'

'Oh no thank you,' I interrupted. She shook her head resignedly at me. 'Oh well, never mind. If Jesus ever comes a-knocking . . .'

Bronwyn choked on her sandwich. I couldn't look at her. I felt the giggle growing in the back of my throat like an awful swelling toad, and I frowned and kept my eyes on my plate, thinking of possible tragedies until the amusement died. I didn't want to laugh at Mrs Broom. She was kind, good, a poor widow doing her best. I liked her better than I liked Bronwyn, and I refused to meet Bronwyn's eyes until the laugh had gone.

'Time for the gâteau,' Bronwyn announced. 'Shall I fetch it?'

'No, I'll do it,' Mrs Broom said, getting up from the table. 'More tea, Jenny? I'll make another pot.' As soon as she had turned her back, Bronwyn looked at me and knocked solemnly on the table and the toad leapt unexpectedly up and out of my mouth, a loud laugh, and an ugly one.

Mrs Broom looked round smiling, ready to be included in the joke. Bronwyn was sitting with her back to her mother and she crossed her eyes at me, while Mrs Broom looked expectant, the smile dying on her lips. And I hated myself but my nervousness made me giggle all the more at her watery anxious eyes and her little twitchy rabbit nose under the green paper crown. She turned her back again as the kettle boiled and I noticed that the label was sticking out of the back of her blouse collar and that her bra strap had slipped down over her shoulder and was visible through the thin stuff of her blouse.

Bronwyn crossed her eyes at me and knocked again and I was clutched by a terrible fear. My shoulders shook and my face contorted with hilarity. My face was like a gargoyle face, a rictus of hideous mirth. Tears came into my eyes and a pain in my belly and I had to leave the room and run up to the bathroom before I wet myself. I locked the bathroom door and leant against the smooth tiled wall, shuddering and shivering. My teeth chattered and a terrible vinegary taste fill my mouth and stung the back of my nose. I waited until the fit had passed – for it was like a fit, terrible paroxysms of the body, the conscious mind unwilling, unamused. I hated myself for hurting Mrs Broom's feelings, for being so terribly rude. And I hated Bronwyn too, for making me so cruel.

Eventually I went downstairs. The gâteau was on the table, a tall chocolate-and-cream confection topped with flaked almonds and sticky cherries.

'Sorry,' I said to Mrs Broom, and I did not look at Bronwyn.

'That's all right, dear.' She looked quite ordinary, as if nothing much had happened. I drank the tea and exclaimed over the lightness and creaminess of the gâteau and all the time there was a dullness deep inside me. Not a pain, more a kind of absence, as if something had been wrenched out of me.

Bronwyn ate three enormous slices of the gâteau. A rim of cream clung to the dark fluff on her upper lip.

'Bronwyn tells me you're something of a poet,' Mrs Broom said. 'I used to like poetry as a girl. We had to learn something off by heart when I was at school. What was it?' She screwed up her face with the effort of concentration. 'Mind like a sieve . . .' I could feel Bronwyn looking at me again but I was full of dullness and I did not look back. The grey film had descended.

'De-da de-da de-da de-da the Lady of Shallott!' Mrs Broom said triumphantly. I took off my paper hat.

After tea Bronwyn washed the dishes and I dried them. When we'd finished she looked at me slyly and said, 'Come upstairs now, I've got something to tell you, remember.'

'Oh, I thought we could all play cards,' Mrs Broom said. 'Don't go upstairs into the cold just yet.'

'It *is* cold up there,' I agreed, ignoring Bronwyn's meaningful looks.

Mrs Broom smiled at me. 'Good girl. We could put a record on, some carols perhaps. Or are you fed up with the carols, dear? What about a musical? *Carousel*. That's Bronwyn's daddy's favourite.'

'Oh?' I said, carefully.

'Let's go,' Bronwyn insisted.

'Or *The King and I*? Or *West Side Story*? Roll on next Christmas,' Mrs Broom said, 'then we'll be all back together again. Did Bronwyn say? Her daddy will be home again, God willing, by then.'

I looked at Bronwyn, but she stared fixedly at the floor. Mrs Broom ran a cloth round the sink and the taps. 'That's that,' she said, 'Thanks for helping, Jenny.' She took off her apron, the first time I had seen her without it. 'Put a scuttle of coke on the fire, Bron, and switch the tree lights on. I'll just powder my nose, then I'll be with you.' She hurried upstairs.

Bronwyn and I remained in silence for a moment. Then she looked at me defiantly. 'He's in prison,' she said. 'He's not dead at all. All right?'

'And I bet your mother *is* a cleaner.' She didn't answer. 'A pack of lies,' I said, hearing Bob in my voice.

'So what?'

'What's the point?' I asked. She grimaced and shrugged. 'Well what did he do?' I asked.

'Fraud.'

'Oh.' I almost felt sorry for her, standing there so awkward and embarrassed with her chest straining against the fabric of her childish dress, and her big blotchy legs.

'I don't think I'll stay,' I said, looking away from her, feeling cruel, seeing my new shorn reflection in the dark glass of the kitchen window.

'Why not?' Bronwyn said. 'Can't you take a joke?'

'Your hair does look rather nice you know,' Mrs Broom said, coming back into the kitchen. She had combed her hair and put a new-looking cardigan on.

'I'm feeling poorly,' I said. 'It's my tummy. I want to go home.'

'Oh dear . . . I do hope it wasn't the chicken. Why not lie down, dear? What about an Alka Seltzer?'

'No really.'

'Oh dear.' She wrung her hands. 'Well we'll walk with you then, so I can explain. And explain about your hair.'

'No really.'

'But I can't let you walk alone. Not in the dark. Not on Boxing Day.'

'Mama lets me walk in the dark. It's only seven o'clock. I like walking. I'll be perfectly all right. Honestly.'

'Well. If you're sure,' she said dubiously. 'Is everything all right? You girls haven't quarrelled?'

'No,' I said.

'Don't go,' Bronwyn said suddenly. She put on her most beseeching expression, but I wouldn't be moved.

She followed me to the door after I'd bidden her mother goodbye and thanked her for having me and accepted a soft slab of gâteau as a gift for Mama and Bob. 'Don't you even want to know what I was saving to tell you?' she asked. I stepped outside into the sharp icy air. 'I've started,' she hissed after me as I went off down the path.

I paused and turned. 'Oh really? I started ages ago,' I lied, for I felt perfectly at liberty to lie to her now. 'Cheerio,' and I went off, my bag over one shoulder and the squashy portion of gâteau wrapped in paper serviettes balanced on the palm of my other hand.

I felt I'd been tricked. 'I told you *my* secret,' she'd said, but it hadn't been a secret at all, it had been a lie, a *huge* lie, almost impressive. 'A whopper,' Bob would have called it. And she'd said she was my best friend and I'd told her about Jacqueline, stupidly. It was not Bronwyn but myself I felt angry with, for being gullible enough to let her trick me out of my own secret.

· Nineteen ·

I walked slowly home. I was in no particular hurry. Here and there where curtains had not been drawn I caught glimpses of the warm and glowing Boxing Days of strangers. There was a smoky smell and coloured lights dazzled. Someone was playing a piano, badly. It was the tune from my trinket box – 'The Dance of the Sugar-Plum Fairy'. I quickened my pace. The air was cold in my lungs and issued from my mouth in long clouds illuminated by the street-lamps. My body was warm. My blood, which had become sluggish in Bronwyn's house, first in the coldness of her room and then in the stuffy warmth of the kitchen, began to flow quickly in my veins and I was invigorated. I started to trot and a little dog appeared at my heels and ran with me, its claws pittering on the frosty pavement. I stopped and patted it and then gave it the slice of gâteau which I had become fed up with the carrying. The dog attacked the creamy mess as ferociously as if it had been alive and I ran off, faster now, my bag bumping against my hip, my heart bumping in my chest, until I reached home.

I approached the front door quietly and lifted my hand to turn the handle – and then stopped. I could just imagine their reaction to my unexpected return: surprise, consternation, acceptance, welcome. Mama would be at work on her macramé, her glasses balanced on the end of her nose, the tip of her tongue between her teeth. Bob would be frowning over a crossword, occasionally throwing a question to Mama. I could hear the wireless through the open top window of the sitting room, there was something funny on, a tinny voice was punctuated by sporadic bursts of audience laughter. I moved away from the door to the window. The curtains were drawn, but they had got caught up on a Christmas-tree branch at one corner and there was a small triangular gap. I crouched down and peered through this into the room. I had to force my eyes to focus past the prickly speckle of the fir tree's needles, and then I saw Bob's leg and foot extended. Bare. He'd left his clothes off since they had their privacy, since I wasn't there to frown and flounce. Mama's skirt moved past and I heard the mumble of their voices, the clink of teacups. 'Another slice?' Mama asked. The glass misted with my breath. I straightened up, feeling dizzy. I went back to the door and once again lifted my hand to the handle, but I could not make myself open the door. I could not bear to be in there in the warmth, sipping tea and eating Christmas cake which is what they – we – always did on Boxing Day evening. Soon there would be the game and I couldn't bear the thought of another game.

I wandered back out of the garden and onto the pavement, and hesitated for a moment wondering which way to go. But there was only one place to go, one person I wanted to see, and that was Johnny. Even if he wasn't there, even if he'd gone off with Mary, I wanted to be in his place among his things. I felt peculiar walking away from home along the road. It was odd to be out at night with no one knowing where I was. I thought about the cosy scene behind the curtains at home. I had been wrong. I wouldn't have been *quite* welcome if I'd turned up unexpectedly once they'd settled down for an evening without me. And when I came to think of it they had been surprisingly willing, eager even, for me to go. Privacy didn't include me any more, not for Bob. And that was my own choice. Without me there, he could sit naked, squelching his bottom against his chair for all he was worth, and they could relax and enjoy themselves without my sullen, critical presence. I wondered whether Jacqueline had felt the same as me and I ached to ask her. I almost felt that she was beside me, pacing the street, deliberately excluded. I didn't *want* to be there with them but I was dismayed to find that they were content that I was not.

I crossed the main road, which was oddly quiet, no cars tonight, no buses. It was a night to be tucked in behind curtains and evergreen boughs, to be in company. The moon was almost full. It appeared from behind a shred of cloud and cast its icy light on the church spire. A car, racing far too fast on the deserted road, burst out of the distance and snarled past, leaving a silence more impenetrable than the previous quiet. I went through the stone arch into the cemetery. I felt not frightened but experimental. Every step I took was careful and measured. I walked beyond the reach of the street lights. I knew the path well by now, but still I stumbled. The moonlight was thin and grainy. It brushed the tops of the gravestones and eerily lit the bowed heads of dead flowers and branches. The tips of the angel's wings gleamed frostily though its face was in shadow. I trod on something that crunched under my foot, I could not tell what, but it was something that reflected back a glimmer of the sparse light. The church wall beside me reared blackly into the sky. My heart bundled itself up and a bolt of fear brought me close to panic, to flight. The church seemed suddenly a live crouching thing. I put my hand out and touched the lifeless stone of the wall and I remembered the boy in 'The Prelude' with the cliff rising between him and the stars. Imagination was all it was.

I looked up to the moon but it turned and hid its face, bestowing the cloud with a ragged glittering edge. I walked forward with tiny steps as if a hole might open up in the ground before me. I kept my hand against the church wall and made my slow way to the side door. I could hear nothing and see no light under the door. I turned the handle and it opened with a gradual stuttering creak. It was more densely dark than ever inside, and I hesitated before stepping in. I called out Johnny's name – although I could sense that he was not there – and the darkness swallowed my voice. I worked my way along the wall to the place where Johnny kept his things. My back prickled as if there were eyes on it, although no eyes could have penetrated the darkness even if eyes were there. I said Johnny's name again and there was nothing in response. I needed to see. My need for light became urgent, like an ache, a physical need. It was as if I was breathing in darkness, as if I would suffocate.

Eventually I found Johnny's corner and fell to my knees. I gasped with relief when I felt the square edge of the suitcase. I had been afraid that Johnny had really gone, bags and all. I opened the suitcase and fumbled until I found his matches. My hand shook as I opened the box and scraped one against the wall. It made a ridiculously loud ripping sound as if slitting the darkness to let in a little waver of light that got me nowhere, illuminating only my fingers, illuminating only *me* if anyone was there to see. I held the match until it threatened to burn my finger and thumb and then dropped it on the floor. I felt in the suitcase for a candle and I drew the ball of my thumb over something that felt silver and fine. It was not until I felt the thick warmth running down my hand that I knew it had been a blade. I squeezed my thumb tight inside my fist. I knew there were candles in the case, a thick white bundle of them. Gingerly now I continued to search with one hand, and at last found them. With difficulty, with my thumb throbbing and aching now that it knew it had been cut, I lit one and then another and another, melting their bases and sticking them onto the box that Johnny used as a table and a seat.

There was a frail ball of light around me now and I huddled inside it, the old damp blanket round my shoulders. My fingers searched for the end of my plait to twiddle with, but of course it had gone. I kept my cut thumb cramped inside my hand, not liking to look. There were dark splashes on the box and a drop of my blood crawled down the side of one of the candles. When I dared to open my hand and look, I saw a curved cut, gaping like a little mouth to show the darkness inside me.

It was the sort of cut that could do with a stitch. If I'd been at home Bob would have gone to telephone for a taxi, and then Mama would have taken me to hospital, and made a fuss of me. But then it wouldn't have happened if I'd been at home. I wrapped my handkerchief tightly around it and held my hand high above my head for several minutes in order to drain the blood from my arm. I felt foolish sitting there with my arm up as if I was in class, daring, for once, to answer a question.

The Christmas branch I'd given Johnny had gone, and I realised what it must have been that I'd crushed underfoot – one of the glass baubles – and I frowned to squeeze away the guilt that I'd taken away part of Mama and Bob's precious innocent Christmas to be crushed underfoot in the darkness of this secret place.

No one in the world knew where I was. That thought gave me a thrill of freedom like a flash of light that was immediately chased away by fear. It was stupid of me to be here all alone. Foolhardy. Any madman might burst in. Anyone could, or anything. There are no such things as ghosts, I reminded myself, though nothing seemed quite as certain as it had before, but there are bad and mad people. There had been murders in our town, murders and vanishings, and of course, I'd been warned, everybody was warned all the time, but the warnings had never crept inside my skin before, never led me to imagine what there was to fear. But now, in the dark of the unholy church, I shuddered. I wished Johnny would come back so that we could fry sausages and brew tea. I wanted to go home, but now that I was in the church in the little bubble of light I was afraid to leave. Johnny's grandfather looked coldly at me and his weak and peevish lips trembled with a spiteful impulse and he seemed more likely to spit and cry. I turned so that I could not see him, so that my back was against the wall. I pulled a book from Johnny's bookcase and in desperation, in an attempt to force my mind away from the present and into some fiction, I began to read. I don't know what I read. It got no further than my eyes, although I turned the pages, for my mind was too crowded with fear to take it in. I got a fit of ragged hiccups and the acidic taste of pickle kept returning to my throat. I found a packet of cream crackers in the suitcase and nibbled one. It was as cold as if the winter had got inside it and it tasted of stone.

I longed for my own bed, my hot-water bottle, my bedside lamp, even the murmur of Mama and Bob downstairs. I had no idea of the time. It wasn't late. Probably not later than ten o'clock. I longed even for the mattress on the floor beside Bronwyn's bed. The longing tired me out. I foraged in the shadows, averting my eyes from Johnny's grandfather, and found some of Johnny's clothes, a woollen jumper and some socks. I took off my coat and put the jumper on underneath and then put my coat over the top. I pulled the socks on over my shoes, wrapped the blanket around me and lay down, my head on another folded cloth.

Surprisingly, I slept, although I kept jerking awake at every real or imagined sound, and every time I did it was like waking from reality to find myself in a ghastly dream. The night dragged on, the unmeasured hours stretching out so that it could have been days that I lay there, sleeping and waking and watching for first light. Once I had to get up and creep outside to crouch by the gravestones and relieve myself. The street-lights were out on the road and the moon had slipped out again. The ivy on an overgrown stone shivered and appeared to writhe.

I slept more soundly towards dawn, and woke sluggishly, not remembering where I was until I opened my eyes and saw, not so much light, but a thinning of the darkness showing through the curved stone gaps at the tops of the windows. I was thoroughly cold and so stiff I could scarcely move, but I was alive and well and triumphant that I had done it, spent a night as, almost, an outlaw, and survived. I thought then that I understood Johnny's life with its constant escapes. But I didn't understand the wings that loomed above me.

There was water in the bottle and I lit the primus stove and made myself a cup of tea. I drank it black with a couple more of the cream crackers. There was a waxy mottled maroon sausage that I didn't fancy, but that was all right. Soon I could go home and eat a turkey sandwich or a mince pie, eat whatever I liked in the electric light. I went to the door and stood looking out, the blanket round my shoulders, finishing my tea and gazing at the lightening world. The frost had stiffened the grass blades and furred the branches and stones. Here and there a bird twittered, the beginning of the day's awakening. Traffic had started on the road and the street-lamps were lit again. The horrible night lay behind me now like a cast-off skin and I stepped out of it with relief and breathed in the fresh frosty air. I threw the slops from my cup out of the door, as Johnny did, and then I had a look at my thumb. The handkerchief was stuck fast with dried blood, and I left it alone, fearing that to pull it off would start it bleeding again. It hurt, but the rest of me felt strong and fine, and somehow purged.

I remembered my haircut and ran my fingers through my hair. I could feel that it was sticking up all over the place. Bob would be angry but it couldn't be helped. Not now. I thought about Bronwyn and her clever scissors and her needless lies. I should have guessed, when she asked me to choose the kind of father I'd have liked if I *could* choose, that that was just what she'd done. She'd chosen the story she preferred, not a father in prison for some shoddy offence but a father murdered in a gangster-film plot. She had chosen the glamorous over the mundane. I wondered how on earth she would have explained his reappearance if I had not discovered her lie. It seemed a wicked thing to do, pretending that he was dead – almost as if she was wishing him dead. It was also a stupid lie, since it was doomed, eventually, to failure.

I went back inside and took off Johnny's clothes and tidied his things before I left. He would know I or someone had been there. I took the Christmas card and poem – crumpled now – out of my coat pocket and propped them up on the box so that he'd know the visitor had been me. There was the waxy mess where the candles had been and the brown stains of my blood here and there on the things in the case and on the box. I took out his mirror and peered at myself. I looked completely different with the fringe down over my eyes and tufts of hair sticking out behind my ears. I looked tired and grubby. 'Burning the candle at both ends,' Bob was bound to say. I wrapped my scarf around my head to hide my hair.

Although I was ready to leave I felt reluctant to do so at once. Now that it was light and safe I hesitated, examining the wings, walking round them. It made me grin, the idea of Johnny soaring through the air like a cartoon bat or bird. As if he ever could! As if he could ever believe he could! He was as bad as Bronwyn. Worse. At least she was only lying to me – he was deluding himself.

Not looking where I was putting my feet I almost tripped over a clod of hard earth. I looked down to see that a hollow had been made in the floor and there was something in it. It was too gloomy in the shadow of the wings to see properly so I knelt down, and I saw that it was bones. I knew at once that the bones were human. It was a long grave-shaped hollow, though not deep enough for a grave. A grave had to be six feet deep, I knew that because Bob always said 'six feet under' instead of the word *dead*. I used to think about that when I was digging to Australia, when I dipped my head beneath the surface and sniffed the breath of the earth. This grave was scarcely a foot deep. It was an adult-sized skeleton but it was nothing like I thought a skeleton would be. I'd imagined that bones were white, bleached neutral. These bones were brown and viscous. I bent closer, fascination and revulsion quarrelling within me. There was a dull mat of something near the skull, probably hair. There were teeth scattered. I imagined how they must have plopped out over the years, the small sounds muffled by the earth.

The bones were mostly separate, lying splayed as if they'd relaxed apart, not like the skeletons in books that stand upright, complete, as if ready to dance a jig. Although I could see that this was a human skeleton, I could not link it to myself, not this collection of dark remains: the stubby bulb-ended bones, the rib-fans, the knobbles and the tapering shards of finger and toe.

I stood up and left the church as quickly as I could. The sky was pale and lemony. I saw that the path was littered, as I'd guessed, with the Christmas decorations I'd given Johnny, some smashed, some rolled into the grass. I picked up a silver bauble and put it in my pocket. I breathed in the air, sharp enough to sting my lungs, but wonderfully thin and clean.

Once I was clear of the church I walked slowly home. It was too early to arrive back from Bronwyn's but I wanted to be at home. I badly wanted to wash. My appetite had gone. I wanted to be somewhere where I felt safe, where I understood what was going on. An image of Johnny came sharply into my mind, his angry face, his bristles glittering sharply, his eyes pale and blank. I thought of the bones. I kept hearing Mama's voice in my head, in time with my footsteps, saying: skeletons, skeletons, skeletons. But it wasn't Bronwyn at all who had the skeleton, that seemed a kind of unfunny joke now. It wasn't Bronwyn but Johnny.

When I reached the corner of my road I stopped. Outside the house was a police car. I walked nearer to be sure, and I could see through the net curtains dark silhouettes, taller than Mama and Bob. I turned away and walked back round the corner, shivering, dithering, my mind in turmoil. I was tempted to run – but where? I couldn't go back to the church, not now I'd seen the bones, not now I'd felt the danger. I had no money, my thumb hurt, my bladder was full to bursting. Eventually I took a deep breath, turned on my heel and walked back, straight though the gate and into the house.

· *Twenty* ·

'Jennifer!' Mama's voice was a high-pitched wail, and she grasped me to her a way she hadn't done for years, or perhaps had never done. 'Where on earth . . . oh thank God . . . we've been so . . . and the police . . .'

A policeman with a grim face emerged from the sitting room. 'So, the wanderer returns,' he said. Bob's face glowered from behind the policeman's shoulder. A policewoman shook her head at me. 'If you youngsters knew the grief you caused . . . If she was mine she'd be straight across my knee,' the policeman said to Bob.

'We don't know what . . .' began Mama in my defence, loosening me from her clutch.

'I need the toilet,' I blurted, my face burning, on the edge of tears. I dashed up the stairs and locked the bathroom door behind me. I used the toilet and washed my face and hands and unwrapped the scarf from my hair, which looked terrible. I looked despairingly at my reflection. And then I brushed my teeth over and over, spitting pools of froth into the sink to try and rid myself of the horror and the shock of the bones and the lies and the police and the frightening haggard look on Mama's face.

'Jennifer!' Mama called eventually. 'Come back down here, please.' I had no choice now. I had delivered myself back into their hands. There had been a moment when I could have run, but I hadn't had the nerve.

I said that I'd been walking all night. They didn't believe me, but once they'd ascertained that I'd been in no danger, the policeman gave me a lecture about responsibility and danger and all at the taxpayer's expense, and then left. All the time they were talking Mama stared aghast at my hair and Bob stared fixedly at the carpet.

When they had gone we all stood motionless in the hall, like a photograph of a scene from a play, Bob with his hand still on the door handle, and listened to the police car driving away. And then we continued to stand in the silence as if no one knew what the next move was, and the time stretched like a rubber band and I was seized by a terrible urge to laugh just to snap the tension – but that reminded me of Bronwyn's mother and the label of her blouse sticking up against her frail neck and I began to sob instead. And that was probably the best thing that I could have done. Bob pulled his warm and crumpled horsey handkerchief out of his pocket and mumbled something and shuffled off, closing the sitting-room door behind him.

Mama took me into the kitchen and made me a cup of cocoa while she explained that Mrs Broom had been worried about letting me walk home alone and that she and Bronwyn had come round before bedtime to make sure that I'd arrived safely. And of course I hadn't, so they had been up all night, worried half out of their minds, and if anything *had* happened to me . . . and Mrs Broom was worried sick and blamed herself entirely. And all the time Mama was balanced between anger and relief, her voice shaking and coming to the point of breaking over and over again so that she had to keep breathing in deep brave breaths just to keep going.

'And where on earth were you?' she finished, banging my cup of cocoa down in front of me so that it slopped over into the saucer.

'Nowhere,' I said.

She reached out her hand as if to slap me and withdrew it again. 'Nowhere indeed! I don't know whether to laugh or cry. Nowhere indeed!'

'Just walking about.'

'All night!'

'I argued with Bronwyn.'

'Then why didn't you come home?'

'Don't know.'

'Can you *imagine* what was going through our heads? Can you? Look at this.' She held out the local paper, folded open at a page which showed the blurry face of a girl, her hair whipped about by the wind, smiling and squinting at the camera. The girl held a candy floss. Mama's hand shook so much that the paper rattled. She put it on the table in front of me. *'Another local girl missing,'* she read, *'police no further with their enquiries . . . appeals to the public . . .* Jennifer can't you *see* how serious? Can't you see the danger?' She sat down heavily as if her legs had buckled beneath her, and hid her face in her hands. I thought she would cry, but she spoke slowly through her fingers in an even, muffled voice. 'I want you to tell me where you were.'

'I told you. Nowhere.'

The sticky bones came into my mind and mad Johnny with his wings. But safe in the kitchen, even with the grainy mysterious face of the disappeared girl in front of me, I couldn't believe that Johnny was a killer. He'd never harmed me, after all, and he'd had the chance. 'I was just walking about. I even walked past the house.'

'Why didn't you come in? *Why* didn't you?'

'I don't know. I'm sorry.'

Mama raised her flushed face from her hands and looked at me again. 'And your hair! Mrs Broom told us about your hair. What a thing to do! It was so lovely. Of course, we'll have to go to the hairdresser's and get it tidied up. But it's not the last you've heard from Bob on the subject. Oh Jennifer, didn't you think about us at all? About how worried we'd be? Half out of our minds we've been . . . and Mrs Broom too.'

'I didn't know you'd know,' I said lamely.

'And what have you done to your thumb?' she said, noticing the bloodied handkerchief.

'Just cut it,' I said. 'It probably needs a wash.'

'Cut it how?'

'Don't know.'

'What do you mean, "Don't know"!'

'Just cut it on a bit of glass.'

'What bit of glass? Where? How?'

'Don't know.'

Mama jutted out her chin and breathed fiercely, her eyes raised to heaven in exasperation. She turned angrily to get the first-aid box out of a drawer. 'I've never been so tempted to give you a good hiding,' she said. 'You've ruined Christmas, you realise that?' She ran hot water into a bowl and tipped some TCP into it. The antiseptic smell rose in a steamy cloud. I kept my eyes averted while she unwrapped my thumb and washed and dressed it more roughly, I thought, than was absolutely necessary. 'You'll have a scar,' she said. 'And serve you right. "Don't know" indeed! I'll give you "don't know".' She was over the worst of the shock now and was taking it out on me with this grumbling and scolding that sounded like someone else's parent, not like herself at all. She wasn't good at it. I went faint when I saw the blood in the basin, and ended up in bed, which was the best place by far until Mama and Bob had simmered down.

I slept for an hour or so, stretching my toes luxuriously between the clean winceyette sheets, but the day was bright, and the curtains not thick enough to prevent the sunshine from disturbing me. It was strange to be in bed, listening to the birds and the passing cars and the household sounds downstairs, and yet not ill. I felt well and strong. I felt as if some balance had been redressed and that now I could start again. I had not meant to hurt and worry Mama and Bob, just as they had not meant to hurt and worry me – but we had all done it, just the same. They had deceived me for thirteen years, and I still smarted at Mama's insensitivity. There was no cruelty involved, all it was was stupidity, and although I could forgive most things I could not quite forgive that. Still, I had, inadvertently, paid her back, and that would have to do.

I stretched again and wriggled my toes. The radiator creaked its comforting warmth into the room and the curtain stirred in the breeze from the open window behind it. I remembered being ill in bed a long time before, and I remembered Mama reading to me from *Alice in Wonderland*. I climbed out of bed and found the book and snuggled back between the sheets to read about Alice, the Mad Hatter and the March Hare squabbling about words.

'*Then you should say what you mean,*' *the March Hare went on.*

'*I do,*' *Alice hastily replied; 'at least — at least, I mean what I say — that's the same thing, you know.*'

'*Not the same thing a bit!*' *said the Hatter. 'Why you might just as well say that "I see what I eat" is the same thing as "I eat what I see"!*'

'*You might just as well say,*' *added the March Hare, 'that "I like what I get" is the same thing as "I get what I like"!*'

I laughed at that and laid the book down again. I closed my eyes and saw Johnny in a tall hat, bent, with a feather drooping from the brim. I saw him in the dim church, a teacup held to his lips, his little finger elegantly crooked, playing with words, talking his sensible nonsense. I wondered whether he was back yet, and whether he'd read my poem. I might never know what he thought of it now, because I might never go back. Not that I thought he was the killer. The bones in the church were old. They were simply old bones in an old cemetery — nothing sinister. They were nothing to do with Johnny. But Mama's fears had penetrated me at last. Someone was the murderer after all, and I shouldn't be putting myself in danger again, going to dark places alone. I was lucky to have got away with it. I had been like bait on a hook, or fruit arranged in a bowl, asking to be taken. And it couldn't have been Johnny, even if the body had been new. Why would he go off and leave it there like that, for anyone to see? A murderer would be more careful.

I got out of bed again and found paper and a pen. I arranged myself against the pillow with Jacqueline's camera beside me, and began to write her a letter. I found it difficult to write to someone I had never met. I didn't know whether she would ever get the letter – that depended on whether I could find out where she was – and that made it easier to write. I could be freer in what I said. As if, more as if, I was writing to myself. I wrote about how I tried to dig to Australia, about the playground and the church, about Johnny and his wings and about Bronwyn and the bones. It took me ages to write, I copied out my poem for her and told her that I planned to be a poet when I grew up. Although even as I wrote that I wasn't so sure. I told her about my hair. I asked her to send me a photograph. I sent her all my love.

Mama brought me up some lunch on a tray. She sat on the edge of my bed for a moment, looking at me wistfully. Then she picked up *Alice in Wonderland* and smiled. I saw the gap where she was missing a tooth.

'What are we going to do with you?' she asked, and I knew I was half forgiven.

'Mama,' I began. 'I'd like to send a letter to Jacqueline.'

'Oh.' She put her hands together as if in prayer and looked down at her fingertips, compressing her lips.

'Will you give me her address?'

'I don't know it.'

'I don't believe you.' We looked at each other and she did her sigh and she looked terribly tired and worn, an old thing about to become unravelled.

'Don't you think I'd like to get in touch with her if I could?' she asked quietly. 'She is my child. Sometimes I can't believe that she can have gone like that. Just gone and left you. Us. I used to think she'd be back. My own flesh and blood. So little feeling.'

I went cold. I pulled the blankets up over my chest. The curtain shivered. 'What do you mean? You made her go.'

'What nonsense!'

'You made her go because of the shame. Because I'm illegitimate.'

Mama gave a humourless laugh. 'Shame. Whose shame? Can you imagine Bob being ashamed? Or me?'

· 164 ·

I closed my mind quickly, a curtain whisked across before I saw too much. 'I don't believe you.'

Mama sighed. 'Well, of course, that's up to you.'

'Why would she?'

'She had her own life to live . . .'

'But why would she lie about it? Anyway, I don't believe you.'

'We all have our own version of the truth.'

I put my head back and looked at the ceiling. It was papered in nubbly paper and painted the palest pink. I remembered Bob painting it. I remembered the splashes of paint on his shoulders and back.

'She had her life to be getting on with,' Mama said quietly. 'She wanted you adopted. We persuaded her to let us keep you, but her condition was that she would never come back. Not see you. Not until she felt ready. She said we could tell you when you were thirteen, if she hadn't been in touch by then.'

'Oh,' I said. That wasn't how it was, not how it was supposed to have been. That wasn't it.

'Anyway,' Mama continued. 'There's been nothing until now. And now . . . a Christmas present for you. No address nor any message. But an Australian postmark.'

'Australia!'

'Couldn't get much further away, could she?'

'Like Peggy.'

'Mmm?'

'The ancestor!'

'Oh yes . . . rather different circumstances.'

'But still, Australia.' Although, as Mama had said, she couldn't be further away, it made me feel nearer knowing where she was. In the garden, all that time ago and without knowing what I was doing, I had been digging my way to her.

'She may not live there,' Mama pointed out. 'She may only have been visiting. Working, or on holiday or something. Now eat your sandwich.' There was a tomato cut fancily up on top of the bread. 'It's a tomato rose,' Mama explained.

'She lives there all right,' I said. 'I can feel it in my . . .' I stopped and shivered.

'Well you might be right. Eat your lunch, then have a bath and come downstairs.'

'Maybe,' I said. I waited until she was out of the room before I got the letter out from under my pillow and read it through. And then I hid it in my trinket box. I didn't believe Mama. It was her way of making it right, putting herself and Bob in the right. Her version of the truth. Only *her* version.

I bathed and washed my hair and brushed it flat. It made my head look small, the wet hair clinging darkly where it had been so fair before. Mama went out to telephone Mrs Broom and put her mind at rest.

'I've invited Bronwyn to tea,' she said when she returned.

'But I don't want her,' I said. 'I can't stand her.'

'Don't be silly,' Mama said. 'She's your friend. And it's the least I can do after all the worry you caused her poor mother.' Bob rattled his paper and I shut up. He hadn't directed one word or glance at me since I'd been down. He was dressed respectably, but oddly, in trousers and a purple blouse of Mama's which was softer round the neck than any of his shirts. He had lost weight over Christmas, and he and Mama were only waiting for the January sales to buy him some new shirts.

'What shall we have for tea?' Mama asked. 'What does she like?'

I shrugged. I didn't want Bronwyn in my home, or in my room. She was a liar and I didn't trust her. I hated the thought that she knew about Jacqueline. I wished there was a way that I could stop her knowing.

'I don't know why you're sitting there frowning like that,' Mama said; 'you'll age dreadfully if you don't watch your expression. What about corned beef and bubble and squeak? Give the turkey a night off?'

Bob grunted approvingly and waggled his foot so that his slipper fell off.

'Where's your charm bracelet?' Mama asked. She sat down on a low stool in front of her macramé – which was growing in a long lumpy swathe from the back of a kitchen chair -- and began knotting.

I paused and then felt a dull shock like the sound of a very distant bomb. I had worn the bracelet to Bronwyn's house and I hadn't seen it since. I certainly hadn't had it on when I arrived home. I forced my mind back to the night before. I remembered it being there as I ran along the road with the dog at my heels, I recalled the way it clashed against my wrist. The memory of a sensation bothered me. There was the cold feeling as I cut my thumb, and it came to me that the bracelet had slid off at that moment, had fallen into the suitcase with Johnny's belongings. I even remembered the clink of it, heard but not comprehended at that moment in the dark and the panic.

'And baked Alaska,' Mama said. 'No. Too fussy. What about a good old apple tart?'

'And a drop of your nice custard, Lilian,' Bob added. He folded the paper onto his lap to tackle the crossword.

'Jennifer can make the tart,' Mama said, and I got up immediately since there was a certain prickle in the air, a certain behave-yourself-or-elseness.

I switched on the transistor radio that Mama kept on the kitchen windowsill. *Hancock's Half Hour* was on and I half listened, and even chuckled obediently as I rubbed fat into flour, my wounded thumb held clear, and rolled out the pale pastry to line the pie plate. All the time I knew that I was going to have to go back to the church and retrieve my charm bracelet. I didn't want to. I didn't *think* I wanted to. I was confused. I didn't even know whether or not I was frightened of Johnny. He wasn't a killer, I knew that much. So there was no need to be afraid. He was a friend, supposed to be a friend. He was a better friend than Bronwyn. Bronwyn only wanted me because she had no real friends. She made me do things, go to tea at her house, tell her my secrets, laugh at her mother – and now she was worming her way into my house so that she could mock Bob in Mama's blouse. I sliced the apples fiercely and made a good apple tart with cinnamon and brown sugar and a handful of sultanas, and I put it in the oven to bake. I switched off the radio.

'Bits of wondrous rarity in old English, Lilian? Four letters. What do you think?' I heard Bob say, and I was stirred by an exasperated fondness.

It was mid-afternoon, still light. There was time before dark to get to the church and retrieve my bracelet. If I ran I could be back before the apple tart was cooked. With any luck Johnny would not have returned yet and that would be good. It would be best, after all, not to see him again. Or not for a while anyway, not until the queasy feeling I had about the bones faded away.

I put my head round the sitting-room door. 'I'm just going out for a few minutes,' I said.

'Oh no you don't,' Bob said. He scribbled viciously in the margin of the newspaper.

'What?'

'You're not going anywhere, young lady. After your performance I'm surprised you've got the face to suggest it! You're staying put.' He sounded like a bad actor laying down the law, not like Bob at all.

Mama pushed her glasses up her nose and looked at him with surprise.

'Understood?' he insisted. I nodded.

'Where were you going, dear?' Mama asked.

'Just for a walk.'

'Well not now,' she said, nodding towards Bob, who had bent his head over his paper once more.

'All right then,' I said. 'I don't care.'

'Bronwyn will be here soon, anyway,' she soothed. I paced around the house like a prisoner, thinking furiously. I must get the charm bracelet back before Mama realised it was missing. 'Eighteen-carat, that is,' Bob had said, and I had promised to care for it, and there were all the charms to come. I knew I must get it back, but there was some relief in the knowledge that I couldn't go now. I couldn't go alone.

I went into my room and squinted out at the garden through the camera. Mama tapped at my bedroom door and came in. She stood awkwardly.

'Well?' I said.

'Are you all right, dear?'

'Yes, why shouldn't I be?'

'Well . . . Bob . . . you know. He's cross. He was *so* worried. And he's upset about your hair.'

'I don't see why. It's my hair. I don't see why I shouldn't cut it.'

Mama sat down on my bed. 'It's just one of his little foibles – women and hair. You know what he's like.' I shrugged. 'I've wanted to have mine cut for years. I nice tidy perm. I look a sight, I know I do.' Her hand went up to her thin hair, and she tucked a loose wisp behind her ear.

I looked at her critically. 'It would look better,' I said. 'Why don't you ask Bronwyn? She does her mum's.'

'How you dare even suggest it!' Mama exclaimed, and then added wistfully, 'It'd be more than my life's worth.' The resignation on her face made me crawly in my stomach. 'I think yours is rather nice, actually,' Mama admitted. I let her stroke it. 'It suits you short. Why don't you let me put a couple of rollers in for you? Give it a bit of a lift. Bob'll come round in time, you'll see.'

'If you want,' I said.

Bronwyn's mother walked her to the door. 'Praise the Lord that you're back safe and sound,' she said to me. 'You did give us a turn, disappearing like that. And I would have blamed myself if anything – you know – had happened.' She looked tired and her eyes and her nose were twitchy and pink.

Bronwyn raised her eyebrows at me and I looked away.

· 169 ·

'I'm sorry,' I said. 'It was very stupid.'

'Where were you?' Bronwyn asked.

'She was just walking,' Mama said quickly. 'Won't you come in for a cup of tea, Mrs Broom?'

'Betty. No, I mustn't stop thanks all the same. I'm off to a meeting. I'll call for Bronwyn at . . .?'

'Eight o'clock?' Mama suggested.

We went into the kitchen with Mama to look at my apple tart which was cooling fragrantly on the table, but Bronwyn fidgeted and fretted. She wanted to get me alone. 'Can I see your bedroom?' she asked, and Mama said, 'Go on, Jenny,' and I had no choice but to lead her up the stairs. Hardly anybody from outside ever came into our house and it felt strange. I saw it all afresh and was quite proud because it was so much brighter and warmer than Bronwyn's house. A window was open in every room, as always, but it wasn't damp and cold. The radiators, Bob's pride and joy, pumped heat around the house, compensating for the draughts. Bob was always bleeding them and listening intently, his head cocked to one side, judging the health of the system by its gurgles and groans. I had never seen it as something to be proud of before, but Bronwyn was obviously impressed. She stood with her bottom against the radiator in my bedroom, looking round at my things.

'This is my camera,' I offered.

She took it from me and turned it over in her hands. 'Not new,' she sniffed. 'Where's your ring?' I opened my trinket box, and we watched the pirouetting ballerina for a moment before I opened the secret compartment and took it out. 'Pretty,' she said grudgingly. She tried it on all her fingers but it would only fit her little one. She handed it back. She picked the lipstick up from my dressing table.

'You can have that if you like,' I said.

'Really?' She wound it up.

'I don't like the colour,' I said.

'Really? I think it's fab.' She put it in her pocket quickly. 'Thanks.'

She opened my wardrobe and looked through my clothes, then, satisfied with her investigation, she took off her shoes and curled up on my bed with her feet underneath her. 'Go on then,' she said.

'What?'

'Where were you?'

'Mama told you. I was walking.'

She looked enormous and mottly in my bright painted bedroom. Her eyebrows were heavy and dark and she was wearing a too-tight dress that emphasised her chest. It had big orange flowers splattered all over it, there was one on each side just where her nipples must be.

'Pull the other one,' she said. 'I know you. You had some plan didn't you? That's why you left.'

'I left because you're such a liar.'

'Am not. Im-ag-in-ation, that's all it is. Vivid, Mum says.'

'What's a lie then, if it isn't imagination?'

'What's this then?' She picked up *Alice in Wonderland*.

'A story,' I said.

'Lies.'

I paused, considering this. I thought it quite a good point, for Bronwyn. 'Don't be daft. It's not *pretending* to be true. That's the point.'

'Nor was I.'

'You were!' I exclaimed.

'Was not.'

'Were.'

'I never thought you'd believe me! A big twerp, that's what you are.'

I opened my mouth to reply and then closed it again. It was no good. She had it all worked out so that she was in the right. I picked the book up and put it in its place on my shelf.

'So where were you?' she insisted.

'I could tell you anything,' I said, 'I could make up any

story I like. How would you know if I was telling the truth?'

'Go on,' she said.

'I have a friend who is building a huge pair of wings so that he can fly. He lives in an unholy church. I slept there all night, and in the morning I found human bones buried in the floor.'

Bronwyn pulled a face. 'Stop mucking about,' she said.

'It's true,' I said. 'Truer than gangsters and America and all that.'

'I didn't want to come here,' Bronwyn said, looking away from me and chewing viciously on a fingernail. 'Mum made me. She wanted us to make it all up. Be friends again. *She* likes you, for some reason.'

'I didn't want you to come,' I said. 'It was Mama who invited you, not me.' I went to the window and stood looking out at the damp garden.

'Don't care,' she replied, and we were silent for some time. I could hear her swallowing and shifting her weight about. Cooking smells drifted upstairs.

'Where's the toilet?' she said at last. I told her and she went out. I heard the lavatory flushing and then her exchanging a couple of words with Bob on the landing. She came back into my room with a scarlet face. 'He's naked,' she squeaked. 'I just saw your grandad, starkers!' and looked at me as if she expected shrieks of glee.

'Oh,' I said. 'So what?'

'I saw his, you know . . .'

'So?'

'It's my first *real* one.' I heard Bob padding across the landing and closing his door.

Bronwyn flopped down onto my bed. Her stomach rumbled. I knew she'd tell someone at school. If she could find anyone to talk to. Such information was hard currency in the playground.

'Have you really started?' she asked.

'Started what?'

'*Periods*, of course.'

'No. That *was* a lie,' I said.

'Well I *have*, really,' she said. 'Shall I prove it?'

'Tea's ready, girls,' Mama called gaily up the stairs.

'Come on,' I said. Bronwyn followed me out onto the landing and put her hand on my arm.

'I'm sorry,' she said.

'What for?'

'Lying. I won't do it again.'

'Don't care if you do.'

'I won't though.' I looked at her sceptically. How could I possibly believe that? It was probably a lie itself. 'Honest.'

'All right,' I said.

'Friends again then?'

'S'pose so.'

Bob wasn't at the table. 'He's off-colour,' Mama explained. 'He's gone to bed.' She didn't look at me. Bob was never ill, it was one of his boasts. He hadn't seen a doctor for years, had never in his whole working life had a day off sick. Bronwyn didn't know that, of course. She munched her way stolidly through heaps of bubble and squeak, and three helpings of apple tart. I was glad Bob wasn't there to be embarrassing, although he'd done his bit just by plodding naked from the bedroom to bathroom, but Mama was bad enough on her own, chattering away in an animated girlish way that made me curl up inside. I wouldn't look at Bronwyn in case she was aiming to set me off again. But she showed no sign of it. She behaved properly, listening to and answering Mama and taking her seriously in a way I had never seen her take her own mother. Mama was impressed, I could tell.

We helped Mama wash up and then there were still two hours to go before Bronwyn could go home. We went back upstairs to my room but there was nothing to do.

'What *did* you do last night?' Bronwyn began again. 'Honestly. I'll never tell.' She licked her finger and held it up. 'See it wet. See it dry. Cross my heart and hope to die. You haven't got a boyfriend, have you?'

'Of course I haven't. I *told* you what I did.'

She hugged herself voluptuously and moaned. 'I can't wait to have a boyfriend. I can't wait to do it. I'm a nympho-man-i-ac.'

'I know. You told me. Actually I haven't got a boyfriend, but I have got a *man*friend – Johnny – the one I told you about, the one in the church where I spent the night.'

'You spent the night with him?'

'No, he wasn't there.'

'Oh.' She leant forward. 'Have you ever . . . you *haven't* ever . . .'

'Not yet,' I said. 'I could though, any time I wanted to with Johnny.'

'Really?' She looked at me wide-eyed, and I had an idea.

'Shall I prove it, about Johnny and the church?'

'And the wings and the bones? All right then, prove it.'

'Now?'

'Yes.'

I went downstairs and persuaded Mama to let us walk round to the newsagent's for a bar of chocolate. She looked uneasily upstairs at the door behind which Bob was either ill or skulking.

'Well all right,' she said. 'Straight there and back. Promise?'

'We won't be long at all.'

'Where are we going?' Bronwyn asked breathlessly, buttoning her coat as she hurried to keep up with me.

'To the church, of course.'

'How are you going to prove you were there?'

'I had my charm bracelet on yesterday, remember?'

'Yes.'

'Well I think I dropped it in the church last night. We're going to look.'

It was busy and light on the main road and Bronwyn hurried quite happily along beside me. It wasn't until we were off the road and through the archway into the cemetery that she began to hesitate.

'I believe you,' she said. 'It's all right.'

'Not scared are you?' I walked boldly between the graves.

'It's a bit dark . . .'

'It's all right. I know my way about.'

'But it's not safe . . . what if a murderer . . .'

'There's no murderer here.'

'What about the man?'

'Johnny? He wouldn't harm a fly.' My voice sounded foolishly loud and bright. I wished I knew whether Johnny was there. If he wasn't, it would be simple. All I had to do was find the suitcase and my bracelet and run home. If not . . . well, it depended on Johnny.

'Jenny, I . . .' began Bronwyn.

'Shhh,' I hissed. We reached the side door and I knocked, but my knuckles against the thick old wood made scarcely a sound. We waited for a moment. I was frightened, but Bronwyn's panicky breathing behind me made me stubborn. I pushed the door and it opened with an alarming creak.

'I'm going,' Bronwyn said and retreated a bit but then jumped forward again. 'Jenny! I saw a ghost . . .' She started to cry.

'Don't be daft,' I said, looking round anxiously.

'There!' And there was a faint wisp of something pale and moving. I blinked hard and my heart stuttered. And then I saw what it was.

'Puss, puss,' I whispered, and I crouched down and held out my hand towards the cat. I knew it was the cat that had led me to the playground, bigger now and as grey as a moonshadow, its fur cold under my fingers. It rubbed against my legs and purred, but when I bent to scoop it up, it slunk away and melted into the night.

'Ghost!' I scoffed.

'Let's go back,' she pleaded, grabbing my arm.

'Shut up,' I said, and wrenched myself free. 'Follow

me. It's all right.' I edged along the wall with increasing confidence. It was perfectly dark and silent. It seemed that Johnny was not there. We could hear the traffic growling on the road and as our eyes grew accustomed to the dark we could see the looming edge of Johnny's construction.

'That's the wings,' I whispered.

Bronwyn said nothing. She was sniffing and snivelling. We reached the place where I judged Johnny's things to be and I felt for the suitcase. And I touched skin.

'What the!' A figure jumped up. It was Johnny.

Bronwyn shrieked and tried to run but tripped over the stretching tip of a wing.

'It's all right,' I said, struggling to keep my voice even. 'It's only Johnny.'

Johnny lit a candle and held it up. 'You,' he breathed. 'What the hell do you think you're doing?'

'There's something I need. Something I dropped.'

Johnny examined me for a moment, held me with his eyes, and I felt like a butterfly on a pin. His eyes were cold, sharp points.

'Who's this?' Johnny approached Bronwyn with the candle. She cringed on the floor, her back against the wall, whimpering.

'It's Bronwyn,' I explained. 'She didn't believe in you. I'm proving that you exist.'

'Ignorant bloody kids,' he said slowly. 'Are you trying to get yourselves killed?'

'I just want my bracelet. I dropped it in your suitcase.'

'You what?'

'Last night. You weren't here.'

'But *you* were.' The candle lit his face underneath and flickered eery shadows on the wall behind him. There was a smell of whiskey. I noticed that he needed a shave, his bristles glistened like sparks.

'Where's Mary?' I asked.

'Gone,' he replied shortly. He turned back to Bronwyn. 'Get up. Don't be scared.' He helped her up and gave her something to wipe her eyes with. He watched her for a moment and then put his arm round her shoulders in a way he'd never done with me, in a man-and-woman way, and she soon stopped crying and shot a smug look at me through her wet eyelashes. 'What you need is a drop of this. For the shock,' he explained, unscrewing the top of his flask and handing it to Bronwyn. He didn't offer it to me. She gave a little gasp as the whiskey hit the back of her throat. 'All right now?' he asked

'Yes, thank you,' she sniffed, almost snuggling up against him.

'You'd better find your bracelet,' he said, turning to me, his voice hard. 'I credited you with more sense than to come here at night. Or to bring friends.' I knelt down and moved my hand cautiously around inside the suitcase, fearful of the blade. I was close to tears now, but wasn't going to let Bronwyn see. I found my bracelet, which had fallen into a cup, and when I turned back I saw the way they were looking at each other, as if there was heat flowing between them. Bronwyn's face had the look it had when she gazed at her reflection, when she pushed her breasts together with her elbows, and wriggled and sighed. I looked away into the framework of Johnny's wings, and now, looming above me, it looked more like the wreck of a wooden ship.

'Were you asleep when we came in?' Bronwyn asked.

'Just having forty winks,' he said.

'Sorry we disturbed you. It was Jenny's idea. She said you wouldn't be here.'

'I did not,' I said.

'Jenny eh?' he said, holding the candle out to see me better. 'Well *Jenny* should have known better,' and I remembered that he knew me as Jacqueline. I shrugged and looked away.

'*She* says you're going to fly,' Bronwyn said, nodding towards me, her voice making it – me – sound ridiculous.

'Do you think that's possible?' he asked.

'Of course not!'

'Well then,' Johnny said. My face burned, but all the same I felt a sort of pride. I knew *he* thought it was possible. He had shown me the beauty of the rippling silk. He was only humouring Bronwyn, and she was lapping it up, blinking besottedly at him in the candlelight.

'We'd better go,' I muttered.

She tore her eyes away from Johnny and looked at me as if I was a tiresome child. 'Oh I suppose so,' she said. 'Jenny's nan will be worrying,' she explained.

'Off you go then,' Johnny said, turning away. 'Mind your step. And Ja . . . Jenny, don't come back again.'

'But . . .' I wanted to ask him whether he liked my poem. I wanted to ask him when he would fly. 'I've still got your book,' I objected.

'Which book would that be?' he asked, and I wanted to hit him. He must have known which book it was. We'd talked about it. He had shown it to me specially, because of our conversation. He had talked to me about epiphany.

'*Portrait of* . . .'

'Keep it. Compliments of the season,' he said, smiling past me at Bronwyn.

'Don't want it,' I said.

'Bye-bye,' Bronwyn said as we left. Johnny grinned, and as soon as we'd opened the door he blew out his candle.

'See?' I said, when we were well clear. 'It was the truth.'

'I didn't see any bones,' was all she said, and then she was quiet. Her eyes were bright and glazed, from the whiskey I guessed. Her face was tight and smug.

I wouldn't take Bronwyn upstairs to my room when we got back. I wouldn't give her the chance to gloat. Instead we sat downstairs with Mama and played Scrabble until it was time for her to leave. I chose Scrabble because I knew Bronwyn would be useless – which she was. She couldn't spell at all, or think of any words with more than four letters, but she didn't care. There was a bright flush on her cheeks, and she laughed at everything. I half wished Bob was there to emanate scorn. When her mother rang the doorbell, she came out into the hall with me to fetch her coat. 'He didn't say *I* couldn't go again,' she murmured. I wanted to kill her then. I knew just what she wanted to happen. She wanted to do it with him. And he might, too. There was never that sort of tense heat in the air when he looked at me. No, that's not true. There had been the day he'd scrubbed the lipstick from my lips and drawn it back on again. Slippery lips. That day I had felt a tremble in my belly, and that night I had slept with my long plait wedged between my legs as a sort of comfort. But I didn't want to do it with him. I didn't want to do it at all, not yet, perhaps never. I didn't think I did. But it wasn't fair that Bronwyn should have him. I had *found* him. He was mine. I wanted him to be mine. I wanted to talk to him about flying and to know what he thought of my poems. I didn't want him to be Bronwyn's.

In the morning I returned to the church to see Johnny. I took back his book, despite his having told me to keep it, as an excuse, although I had never finished it. I couldn't believe that he had really sent me away. I wanted him to be mine. I would have done whatever it had taken to make him mine. I went filled with a strange resolve. I saw my body moving forward as if it was something separate from me, something that could be used like a piece of equipment. I went with a womanly smile upon my face. But Johnny was strange, that day. There was a rank foxy smell surrounding him. I saw myself walk up to him and saw him flinch. I stood very close to him. I willed him to kiss me. His teeth were greenish. There were scraps of dried sleep in the corners of his eyes.

'You don't know what you're playing with,' he said.

And I said, 'Fire.'

It seemed in the gloom that his breath was yellow. He didn't kiss me. He wrenched his head round and pushed me, roughly, away. I sat down. And then I was myself again, surprised at myself.

'I'm sorry,' I said.

'What do you want?'

'I . . . I suppose I wanted you to kiss me.' I was mortified to hear myself say this and my face burned. But Johnny didn't seem surprised.

'I only kiss Mary,' he said.

'Only ever?'

'Mary is the only one who understands.'

'Wouldn't you kiss Bronwyn?'

'You tell that bitch to stay away.'

'I thought you liked her.'

'I like no one. Now go.'

'Bronwyn says she's coming back.'

'Tell her no. Please.' He sounded suddenly weak as he said that, almost as if he was afraid.

'All right,' I said. I kept my eyes very carefully focused on Johnny and on a small area of space around him. I did not let them wander towards the place where I'd stumbled upon the bones. I did not ask Johnny about them.

'I'm on the brink of departure,' he said, and I laughed, relieved by his pomposity. He sounded for a moment as if he was about to revert to the Johnny I knew, who played with words and sang.

'Flying?'

He jumped then as if he had been lashed by the end of a whip. He put his hands over his face, so that instead of his features I could only see the sinewy length of his fingers with the strangely sharp nails. I had the feeling that he might cry and I was interested and repulsed. I thought if I could comfort him, then he might be mine.

'Shall I make some tea?' I suggested. But he made a noise, like a growl, or it may have been the word *go*.

'Did you read my poem?' I asked. But he took his hands away from his face and stepped towards me suddenly and I was frightened by his face. The flesh on his cheeks was drawn back into the bristly folds of a sort of snarl and the upward curve of his open mouth was not a smile.

I tried to laugh but there was no joke, and so I turned and fled. I dropped the book as I went. I dropped it open on the wet ground. He let me go. He could have got me if he'd wanted. He *let* me go.

· *Twenty-One* ·

'Hi Jenny, have a good Christmas?' It was Susan who spoke to me, came up to me in the playground on the first frosty morning of term.

'Yes, did you?' I replied and a warmth swept through me, lighting my cheeks.

'OK. I love your hair. It looks tons better short. Suits you.' I looked around for the popular girls who would surely claim her, who might even be laughing at me now, laughing at my credulity. But there was nobody there. There was no joke. She was simply being friendly. 'I heard about . . . you know . . .' she said breathily, rolling her eyes and moving her face close to mine. 'What happened?'

'What?' I said.

'*You know*, my uncle's a policeman, he said you'd gone missing and nobody knows where.'

The rumour spread and soon other girls were clustered around us, all the popular girls and me in the centre. All at once I was someone special. I had a sort of glamour even, and I had become part of a crowd. And from outside the crowd I was watched by Bronwyn. Whenever she got the chance, she clung to me like ivy, a terrified lonely look in her eyes. And there was nothing I could do but turn my face away. After school I walked past Bronwyn and went home with Susan and watched *Blue Peter* on their television – a colour television – curled up on the sofa. We were allowed to drink Ribena and eat chocolate biscuits while we watched. Her mother was young and ordinary and wore slacks and carried a dribbling baby on her hip. She accepted me as a friend of Susan's without a second glance. And when I looked at myself in the mirror in

Susan's bathroom – a bathroom with talcum-powder footprints on the floor – I saw a normal girl with bright eyes under a straight fringe, the sort of girl the world is full of, neither beautiful nor hideous, neither brilliant nor stupid. A satisfactory kind of girl.

And it wasn't just for that day, not a fleeting change. Only gradually did I learn to trust the change, to take it for granted. At first I was afraid hour by hour and then day by day and then week by week that it would change back, that I would put a foot wrong, say the wrong thing and slide back to aloneness – or to Bronwyn. She was always there, just in case, near. For she didn't believe in me either. I was never cruel to her, but still she was left behind, left out. I still talked to her and sat beside her in class, and accepted her peppermints under the desk. But it was Susan I met afterwards, Susan I linked arms with in the playground. And Bronwyn was left lumpish and alone, but it was not my fault. I couldn't help it if the miracle – the sudden transformation into a popular girl – had happened to me and not to Bronwyn. Her presence was a snag in the smoothness of my new life. She was a reminder of things I might otherwise almost have succeeded in forgetting. She was the only one who knew how frail my new-found popularity was, the only one who expected it to end.

I turned my face away from the church when I had to walk that way. I almost forgot about the playground, I had no wish to mope around alone. Susan had claimed me as her best friend and I basked in the honour. It was a tricky business; playground politics were extremely delicate. The web of friendships and enmities and jealousies and tenuous loyalties spread newly before me, a complex revelation, and I trod with caution. I learnt games with mysterious words, skipping and clapping games, and I muttered the words to myself like spells when I was alone to keep me safe and ordinary, to keep me balanced on the frosting. *Empompey polleney, pollenistic, empompey, polleney, academic, so fa me, academic, poof, poof.* Everything was clever and mysterious and belonged to me and my friends and nobody else and it kept me from falling through. And I knew without having to learn it that I must never fall through, for there was nothing beneath all the thick new frosting but emptiness.

Sometimes I took Susan, or one of the others, home and Bob slunk away and Mama tried too hard to be nice. She was just too old, I could see my new friends thinking that, although nobody said. Because we had no television nobody wanted to stay at my house anyway and so I usually went elsewhere, most often to Susan's. And nobody laughed at Mama, or at Bob. I just told them I lived with my grandparents and it was fine. I couldn't remember where the shame lay. Now that Bob wore clothes and kept out of the way everything was quite ordinary. And ordinariness was all that I had ever craved.

One morning I woke late. I knew that it was late because it was fully light and the birds were chirruping lazily, over the frenzy of their dawn awakening. Something was different. I never usually drifted awake so naturally. I lay puzzling, and then I knew. There had been no lumping and thumping downstairs this morning. There had been no daily dozen.

When I went downstairs, Bob was in his dressing-gown at the table. He didn't look up. Mama put a bowl of porridge on the table in front of me and I sprinkled brown sugar thickly on top, and he didn't make his usual complaint.

'Aren't you well?' I asked. The paper lay still folded beside his plate.

'Leave him be,' Mama advised.

I shrugged. I was late anyway, and impatient with the sorrowful old face. There were deep fuzzy lines from his nose to his chin which his razor had missed. His face looked as if it had been smeared downwards. I got up to go. I had to tread with care. I could not let myself stumble just because an old man took the grumps at breakfast.

'Mama,' I asked, in the evening after Bob had gone early to bed. 'Don't you do the daily dozen any more?'

She was kneeling on the floor in front of a gigantic curtain she was making out of hairy green string and bamboo beads. She shook her head. 'I'm worried about him,' she said. 'More than forty years we've had that palaver, year in, year out. I don't know what's up with him. Not that it isn't a relief for me – I get enough exercise about the house – but I do worry.' Mama executed a complicated knot and then pushed her glasses up her nose to look at me. 'He's only gone and lost heart,' she said sadly. 'That's only what he's gone and done.'

'He's just old,' I said, and I didn't mean to sound cruel, but after all, Mama and Bob were exactly the same age. She hunched her shoulders miserably and threaded a long bead onto the bristly string.

· Twenty-Two ·

My periods started and, at first, I told nobody. It began one morning when I awoke with a dull tolling in my belly like a muffled bell. When I got up I felt the stickiness. The blood was uneven and seeping and dangerous. I had expected a clean crimson flowering every month, not this ragged, aching, brackish leak. I stuffed wads of tissues in my knickers and struggled through the day self-consciously, certain that I would leave a stain behind me wherever I went, certain that it showed on my face, the shameful, sticky, womanish thing.

Mama realised what had happened to me and bought me a pink elastic belt with hooks and a packet of sanitary towels. It was a private event though, every month a succession of packets smuggled, rustling deafeningly, under my cardigan into the toilet. When Susan started, shortly after me, she was proud. She came round early one morning to make her announcement and I didn't admit that I had beaten her to it. It wasn't suffering as far as she was concerned, nor dirty, nor shameful. It was a cause for celebration. Her mother took her out for tea. I was amazed to see that she kept her sanitary towels in the bathroom at home, quite openly, so that even her father could see. I pretended some weeks later that I'd started too, and she linked arms with me in a special way and gave me plenty of advice. Mama never said a thing, but every month a packet of sanitary towels appeared like magic in my underwear drawer.

The worst part was getting rid of the things. I saved them up in a bag under my bed until I had finished, and then crept downstairs late at night when Mama and Bob were asleep and put them in the stove. Bob would have gone mad if he'd seen me. He loved that stove, that heating system, as if it was alive. He tended the stove, regulated the heat, regulated the circulation of warmth around the house as if he was nursing some great greedy temperamental heart. I felt stealthy and mutinous feeding the bloody wads into the stove, and kept well out of the way next morning as he riddled out the clotted ash and cinders.

Just as the first green nubs of spring began to force themselves up through the earth and the tips of the twigs to unfurl, just as the sun became warmer and the evenings light until after tea, Bob took to his bed. I visited him every day and sat in the old straw chair beside him, and tried to help him with his crossword. He was different and it was harder to know quite how to be with him. We had nothing much to talk about; there was no more need for me to sulk and flounce. He withdrew from all corners of the house, as if long roots were withering back to a central corm. As the spring turned to early summer, Mama and I let the stove go out and the pipes go cold. Usually this was a major event, accompanied by much ritual decoking and chimney-sweeping. Mama mentioned to Bob what we had done but he didn't say a word. His concerns had shrunk to the size of the room. Mama and I carried trays of food up to him at mealtimes and then carried them away again, scarcely touched.

Mama was drawn with worry. Every day she urged him to let her call the doctor, but he wouldn't hear of it. One day I found her crying in the kitchen. I stood by, appalled. Something prevented me from putting my arms around her, but I filled the kettle for a cup of tea. Susan was waiting outside for me on her bicycle. I had borrowed another bike and we were going for a ride and a picnic. It was spring, the first warm day of the year. I really wanted to go. With my fingers crossed I asked Mama if I should stay, but she shook her head. I was ashamed of my relief. I went to the door and called to Susan to wait. Mama stopped crying and sat with her hands limp on the table, turned up with the palms open. I had never seen her hands so still before. I thought it meant that Bob would die.

I made her a cup of tea and cut her a slice of cake and then I went off with Susan. We sped along on our bikes, breathing in the warm polleny air. The lanes outside the town were a fervent juicy green, the May flowers as thick as clotted cream in the hedgerows. We raced, and I shouted with laughter and rode downhill with no hands for a dare, and all the time I felt my new knowledge balanced on my head like a solemn hat. Bob would die. It rode with me and only served to make the day more vivid, the cake and ginger beer and sausage rolls more delicious. Susan told me she was going away to spend a few days with her granny in Norfolk, and only that dulled my enjoyment of the day a little. But we rolled down a hill and made daisy chains and tried to paddle in a stream – but the water was icy. We poked at frog-spawn and minnows with sticks, and Susan told me the story of the film she'd watched the night before. She lay on her back, a blade of grass between her lips, her eyes closed, the sun glinting on her short ginger lashes. I lay down beside her and chewed the green taste out of another blade of grass and then I tickled her nose with a feather fallen from the sky and she sneezed and giggled. I never wanted to go home.

I was flushed and silly from the sun when I returned. Mama hovered nervously in the hall as if she was trespassing in a stranger's house. The doctor was upstairs with Bob. 'He's furious,' she whispered as I came in.

'Who?' I could hardly see her, the inside of the house was so dark after the sparkling brightness.

'Bob. I called the doctor against his wishes. I was so frightened. He's not right. I don't like it. He hasn't been right for weeks.'

We waited together in the hall until the doctor, a tall

bent woman, came downstairs. Her face was grave. 'How long has he been like that?' she demanded of Mama, accusingly, almost as if it was her fault.

'I can't say for sure . . . he's got worse. Weeks and weeks . . .'

'Months,' I corrected. 'Since about Christmas. Remember, Mama?' Mama nodded.

'Perhaps you could put the kettle on?' the doctor suggested to me, indicating the kitchen door with her eyes. 'I'd like to have a word with your grandmother.'

Mama darted me a terrified look, and then, with a frozen face, led the doctor into the sitting room. I watched the heavy way she walked, her hands groping in front of her as if reaching for other hands to hold. I splashed my face with cold water from the kitchen tap and put the kettle on to boil. Of course, this was how it would be if Bob *was* to die. It would be sad and terrible, but, I couldn't help it, I couldn't suppress a little leap of excitement. Not that I didn't love him in a dull familial way, not that I wouldn't miss him. But it would be new, a new way of living, and I craved the new and different. And it was awful having an invalid in the house, the smell of illness, a shrunken familiar stranger who looked up at me beseechingly from his bed, as if my youth and strength were things that I could share.

When the doctor had gone we didn't bother with the tea but went and sat outside on the bench beneath the window.

'I'll have to mow the lawn,' Mama said. We looked at the grass that had grown long and ragged. The care of the lawn was another one of Bob's foibles and he was reluctant to let anyone walk on it, let alone tend to it.

'I'll do it,' I offered. She stretched her lips into a smile.

'Well?' I asked.

'She wants him in hospital for tests. But of course he won't go. She's left a prescription for painkillers, that's all she *can* do if he won't co-operate.'

'What is it then?'

'It's something rather delicate – to do with his water-works. He won't tell *me*, let alone the doctor. So we don't know quite what it is. Well how can we if he won't have any tests? But she doesn't think the prospect's good. Not if he lies in bed and doesn't eat and lets himself go.' Her voice tailed off in despair.

We sat quietly in the blatant sunshine and a blackbird thrilled me with its song.

· Twenty-Three ·

Once Susan had gone to her granny's the days were dull. All the other girls had paired off like lovers and I didn't have the nerve to interfere, to upset the balance. Home was a miserable place. A half-finished plant-pot holder dangled from a chair. Mama was too sad to finish it. There was a sickly quietness everywhere and a smell of soaking sheets, for Bob had become incontinent. I sat with him in the mornings after Mama had cleaned him and propped him up against his pillows and folded the paper open at the crossword for him. I sat and watched his bleary eyes strain at the crossword puzzle, the branched yellow bones of his hand clutching his pen.

'Why won't you go to hospital?' I asked him impatiently. 'It might be something simple. They might make you better.'

'No use,' he muttered. 'Happier in my own bed.'

'But you'd be even happier if you were better.'

'I'll not get better.'

'Not if you don't try! Try for Mama at least. She's exhausted.'

'Look after her for me . . .' He reached for my hand but I pulled it away.

'Do you actually want to die?' There was a little shock in the air like a gasp. I had the feeling that Mama was hovering somewhere listening, her hand flying to her mouth. I had spoken the word that had not been spoken. Bob was 'not right' and 'not getting any better', 'there wasn't much hope', but we had not said the word *die* before, or the word *death*.

'Leave me be,' he said and I went out gladly, afraid that

I might throw something at him if I had to stay any longer and listen to his plaintive voice.

One day I arrived home with a bag of groceries for Mama. The house was quiet. I guessed that Mama was upstairs with Bob. It was a warm and sunny day, a picture-book spring day, and the shops were full of Easter eggs. As I had walked I had been thinking about Johnny. I went to the butcher's and I remembered Mary and her warning. I remembered the prickly snarl on Johnny's face and I wondered if Bronwyn had ever gone back. I had not dared, not again, not after I'd seen something in his eyes, something that replaced the blankness.

I never warned Bronwyn. Why not? Was it simply careless-ness, forgetfulness? Or was there intention in this omission? No. It was just that I didn't see the point. She wouldn't go, I knew, for all her talk, she'd never have the nerve to go.

I walked along the main road to the church, and hesitated outside, overcome with curiosity, just wanting to know if he was still there. I didn't want to enter the place. I didn't want to see him. I just wanted to know whether he was there. I certainly didn't really think he would be. I walked softly between the graves where wild flowers were tangling in the long grass. I made no sound. I held my breath. And then I heard whistling. I think I heard whistling. After all this time. It made me cold, despite the sun, as if I'd opened a door onto a landscape recognised from a dream. I ran then, not caring that the eggs were jolted in their box or that a tin of beans was squashing the lettuce.

When I opened the door I was greeted by the depress-ing smell of fried liver. Mama was making yet another nourishing lunch for Bob to leave. I put the shopping on the kitchen table beside an exercise book which I didn't at first recognise. Puzzled, I picked it up. It had Bronwyn's name on the front. There was some of her scrappy work in the front, a story never finished, a spelling test with red crosses beside it. I flicked through to the end, and there were the angels I had drawn for Bronwyn, herm-aphrodite angels with wings and leering faces and breasts and penises jutting like giant thumbs.

'Well?' Mama said. She had come into the kitchen silently and was standing beside me looking over my shoulder. I put the book back on the table. 'Well?' she repeated. 'What have you got to say for yourself?'

'Nothing,' I said.

'Mrs Broom doesn't say "nothing". She says blas-phemy. She says sexual perversion. She came round here trembling like a . . . I don't know what . . . aspen or linden or something . . . and I didn't know where to put myself.'

'It wasn't *just* me,' I objected. 'It's Bronwyn who's sex-mad. I only drew them for her because she can't draw.'

Mama pursed her lips and shook her head as if it was all too far beyond her.

'Did she say it was me?' I demanded.

'Apparently.'

'I'll kill her,' I said. A trickle started inside me like the first inkling of a landslide. I tasted rage.

'What you *will* do,' Mama said, 'is go round and apologise.'

'I will *not*.'

Mama picked up the book and flicked back to the picture. 'If you don't,' she said, 'I'll show this to Bob.'

'I don't think Bob would mind,' I said. 'He thinks the human body's a beautiful thing.'

'Beautiful!' Mama scoffed, waving the crude childish pictures in front of my nose.

'Oh all right then.' I kept my voice even, but something was rushing within me. So much anger for such a small thing, so much anger directed at so dull a target, I was surprised at the force of it. And more surprised still by the way my face and my voice behaved themselves and gave nothing away.

'Anyway,' she said, 'what's happened to Bronwyn these days? I haven't heard much about *her* lately.'

'We're not friends any more,' I said.

'Oh don't be so silly! You were such great friends at Christmas. It's all Susan, Susan, Susan these days. Why not go round and see Bronwyn? Apologise to her mother. Get it out of the way. You've nothing else to do. Unless you want to mow the lawn?'

I went out and walked along the flat, sunny streets. There was the sweet smell of flowering currant in the air, and fat tulips nodded beside the garden paths. My feet carried me to Bronwyn's house. I was threaded through with rage, a cold controllable rage that had little to do with the stupid angels. It was to do with the past. It was to do with Bronwyn knowing things about me, reminding me, by being there, by hanging about looking so lost and lonely, hanging around like a warning, so that I had to keep glimpsing her, I had to keep remembering the things I wanted to forget. I wanted to do something, I did not know what. I wanted her exorcised.

But I did not mean to cause her any harm.

When I knocked at Bronwyn's door there was at first no reply and I turned to go, half relieved, but then the door was opened by Mrs Broom. She peered at me as if puzzled and then drew me inside the dim cabbage-smelling hall. 'Jennifer,' she said, gripping my wrist with her cold fingers and regarding me sadly.

'I *am* sorry about the angels,' I said. 'We were only mucking about.' I was pleased with the way my body behaved, my eyes serious, my face properly contrite.

I heard Bronwyn moving about upstairs and then her face appeared over the banisters at the top. 'Hello,' she said coolly.

'All right,' Mrs Broom said. 'I was surprised at you. I wasn't sure whether it was wise to let Bronwyn play with you again . . . but I've been praying for guidance and I think you deserve another chance.'

'Thank you,' I said, and my other hand squeezed her cold wrist in a play of affection. My lips made a smile. I wondered if she ever looked in her innocent daughter's underwear drawer, if she'd ever seen the playing cards.

'You can go up and see Bronwyn if you like,' she said. 'But please, girls. No lewd talk.' She let me go and I climbed the dreary stairs. It was cold in the house, even on such a warm afternoon, and the landing light bulb glared weakly.

'What do you want?' Bronwyn asked as soon as she had shut the door behind us.

'Nothing.' I looked around. The dolls were grey with dust. There was the lidless stub of my old lipstick on her dressing table and a grubby powder puff. I sat down on Bronwyn's unmade bed. She stood and glowered down at me.

'Where's Susan?' she demanded.

'Don't know,' I lied.

'Fallen out?'

'No.'

'Oh.' She folded her arms across her chest. She looked dirty and tired and smelt of stale perfume and sweat. I felt the cold reptilian quickening of the anger in my belly.

'Why did you tell on me?' I asked.

'Why not?' she said.

'Because it was sneaky.'

'I had to say something,' she said. 'Mum was hys-ter-ic-al. I couldn't say it was me. Anyway, I can't draw.'

'She seems all right now,' I said.

'She's been praying,' she explained. 'That always calms her down.'

Mrs Broom came in with a tray of orange squash and biscuits. She put it on the floor, looked at us both searchingly and shook her head, before she went out.

'What have you been doing then?' I asked, biding my time.

'In what way?'

'Just generally. I haven't seen you for ages.'

She went to the mirror and bent to study her face for a moment. She licked her forefinger and smoothed her eyebrows. Then she picked the tray up and put it on the bed and sat down. She wore her school dress, although it wasn't a school day, and she looked enormous and bloated, over-inflated in the childish dress and the big flat kippers of her sandals. I took a ginger biscuit.

'Wouldn't you like to know,' she said. She swigged her orange squash and wiped her mouth with the back of her hand. The smug look was back.

'Not particularly,' I said, 'I was just wondering.'

She munched a biscuit and brushed the crumbs off her lap onto the floor. Her finger-ends were gnawed right down so that they were ragged and blood-flecked.

'Well, I'd better go then,' I said and hesitated, waiting for her to crack.

'Don't,' she said. 'Not yet. Mum's so pleased that you're here. She thinks you're worth praying for. She still thinks you're my friend. I told her your grandad was ill, that's why we hardly see you.'

'He is,' I said.

'Really? That's a co-in-ci-dence.'

There was a tense crunching quietness while we finished the biscuits.

'Have you seen Johnny lately?' she asked.

'Have you?'

She tapped the side of her nose and smiled complacently. And I hated her in a pure quicksilver way as I remembered just what she was like, with all the little bits of secrets she hoarded, like bait. She was like a fisherwoman teasing a fish. And it wasn't even true, it was another one of her lies. I thought she must have forgotten the difference, that her whole world was woven from untruth – a tissue of lies, Bob would have said.

'Well you probably already know then,' I said, casting my own piece of bait.

'What?' the smugness dropped from her face so swiftly it was almost comical.

'Nothing,' I said, teasing her now. I could almost feel her bite, feel her tug.

'Oh go on,' she pleaded.

'So you haven't seen him?' I asked. 'You never went back to see him?'

'I never dared,' she admitted.

Only I know that this conversation took place. And only I will ever know. No one can wrench it from me. I told Bronwyn lies. I told Bronwyn to go back. She had been unsure in the light of day, she said, whether it was wise. Even stupid Bronwyn who couldn't say long words hesitated in the light of day. She asked me to go with her. But I said no.

'It's you he wants,' I said.

'Don't you mind?'

'There's something he wants to tell you.' She blinked at me with her pale eyes. 'There's nothing to be afraid of,' I said, 'I've been going there for months.'

'All right then,' she said. *But I never thought she would. I never really thought she would.*

Mrs Broom invited me, tried to persuade me, to stay for lunch, but I explained that I had to get back to help Mama. I was sorry. She looked so disappointed. I might have stayed if it had only been Mrs Broom but I wanted to get away from Bronwyn with her smugness and her weakness and the blinking of her deceitful, credulous eyes. I had finished with Bronwyn and all the gloominess of spirit I associated with her. I had to get back out into the sunshine and the fresh air. She called me back as I left the house and handed me a paper bag. 'A present,' she said, smiling oddly. I walked away from the house before putting my hand in the bag. It was full of hair. My own cold, dead, childish hair. I threw it in the gutter.

· Twenty-Four ·

Bronwyn was missing. I knew even before I knew. There was an uneasiness as if the world was holding its breath at my wickedness. A sort of waiting for the worst.

I am not an evil person, not wicked, nobody could call me wicked, I would never harm a fly. It was only wishful thinking that led me to tell Bronwyn to go to Johnny, when I was frightened of him myself. It was only wishful thinking. And is that a sin?

Bronwyn's desk was empty and there were rumours, dark rustlings, and a police car parked outside school. Miss Clarke was preoccupied and ignored the whispering and inattention.

Because I had gone missing myself, and because I was the only person to have been friendly with Bronwyn, I was seen as connected in some way. This time I didn't enjoy the attention, didn't need it. By lunch-time the school was stiff with rumour and speculation and I was surrounded by girls asking questions, or just wanting to be seen with me. Susan held my arm proudly, shielding me from the fray. I was so much the centre of attention I had to force my face not to grin but to look properly grave and concerned. I *was* concerned, and frightened, and the grin wasn't real, it was just a reaction to the excitement, a sort of reflex. All around, girls who had never even spoken to Bronwyn brimmed with tears and muttered 'What if's to each other, thrilled with fear.

I could not get Bronwyn out of my head. Bronwyn and the flying man. I could almost hear the beating of the wings.

'Do you know anything?' Susan said. 'You can tell me, I wouldn't pass it on. Honest.'

I shook my head.

If I screw up my eyes I can see Bronwyn crouching in the church and Johnny holding the candle out so that he can see her, the light glinting in his clear eyes. Johnny wouldn't have hurt her. But if he had . . . I cannot allow that because it was me that sent her. Nobody knows. I lied to her, sweetly, confidingly. I said I had done it with Johnny. But inside I am still sealed. I imagine a closed pink flower. A clean nub. Intact. I said he'd done it with me and he'd like to do it with her. But she may not have gone to Johnny. Probably not. Surely she wouldn't have been so stupid? So stupid and believing. And he may not still have been there. The whistling I heard may not have been him. Someone else might have been there. It might even have been a bird. Or perhaps it was nothing at all.

'What if she is dead?' I whispered to Susan on the way home.

Susan frowned at me. 'She's probably just run off with a boy,' she said.

'Yes,' I said, and I felt relieved. 'Yes, that's probably right.' Susan smiled, her little nose wrinkling up. We linked arms. 'She was sex-mad,' I said, 'that's what she told me.'

'Really?'

'And her dad's in prison.'

'He isn't!'

'He is.' There was something wedged in my throat. Something that was close to painful. Something that made me try and hurt Bronwyn, even now. *Although I didn't really mean her any harm.* Something that made me try and hurt her memory. And, of course, Susan was probably right. Bronwyn had run off with a boy, and it was nothing to do with me, nothing at all.

'Shall we ask if I can move desks and sit next to you?' Susan suggested. 'Just until Bronwyn gets back, of course.'

*

When I got home, Mama was sitting at the kitchen table with her head in her hands. I began to tell her about Bronwyn but she already knew. Mrs Broom had been round, and the police, and they were coming back to interview me. 'Poor woman, poor, poor woman,' she kept saying. 'I can't take much more of this myself, I can't stand the strain.'

'It's all right,' I said, uselessly, 'I'm sure she'll be all right.'

'Are you?' She looked at me hopefully, as if she really thought I knew, but then the hopelessness closed over her face again, like a skin of water. 'And it's not just that, it's Bob too. We've had the doctor in again. He's failing. She didn't say as much but I know. He won't eat, he won't drink. He doesn't care. He's got that look. He's given up.' She began to sob, and it was an awful dry wrenching sound, but there were no tears in her eyes. 'Stupid man,' she gasped. 'Can't he see what he's doing? Doesn't he care about me? About us? Selfish old bugger.'

I had never heard Mama swear before. I didn't even know she knew how. It was awful. I lurked uselessly behind her. There was no comfort I could think of to give. No cup of tea was going to make this better. She made a terrible roaring, teeth-gritting sound and then got herself back under control. I could see her, literally, pulling herself – her face, her limbs, her voice – together, like a puppet I thought, like a puppeteer gathering the strings, but that only made me think of Johnny and something he'd said about bodies being puppets. Borrowed puppets. And I knew there was no way out of it. I'd have to tell them about Johnny.

I went upstairs and peeped round Bob's door. Someone had taken away most of the pillows, so that he lay almost flat, his face a dreadful mustard colour against the white pillowcase. He may have been asleep. His eyes were sealed and his breath was shallow and rattling. There was a frightful smell like that of a dirty animal cage. I closed the door softly and went into my own room. I sat on my bed and composed myself so that I would be ready for Mrs Broom and the police when they arrived.

I told them about Johnny. I told them I had taken Bronwyn to the church, once, a long time ago. I said that I had never been back. And I had no idea whether Bronwyn had. I had no reason to think so. They listened gravely, but the policeman smirked at the policewoman when I had told them about Johnny's wings, and she pressed her lips together to flatten her smile. They thought I had been spun a yarn, and perhaps they were right. But when I told them about the church they said there'd be a search. The land beside the church was due for clearance they said, overdue. They were clearing it to make a park with a lake and trees and swings. A place for children to play.

After they'd left, Mama would not at first speak to me, or even look at me. 'How could you?' she squeezed out eventually. She'd made some sort of food for tea, and we made some sort of pretence of eating it. 'How could you be so deceitful? All those secrets? All those lies?' She raised her eyes from her plate and they met mine, but they were not as I had expected, full of rage. They were like gone-out fires. There was nothing I could say. I thought of her lies, of Jacqueline, of my November birthday, but there was no point in speaking of that. I scraped our tea into the bin and washed the dishes while Mama went upstairs to be with Bob.

The evening paper was still on the mat. I carried it into the kitchen and unfolded it on the table. And there was Bronwyn. The picture was taken when she was younger, before I knew her, when she still wore her hair dragged to the side and tied with a bow. Otherwise she looked just the same, with her dark thick brows and her pale lips pursed upon some secret. The photograph was a blown-up section of a snapshot, enlarged so that the gaps between the tiny dots showed through, giving her the look of someone dispersed, already part of the past. The newspaper report gave her full name. Bronwyn Margaret Rose Broom. I hadn't known she had middle names, and such dignified names too. They made her sound like someone else. Somehow that made it worse.

Later, I looked into Mama and Bob's room. I think Mama was asleep in the chair. At least, her eyes were closed. Bob had stopped breathing. His cold yellow toes with their curved ivory nails stuck out from the end of the bed. I covered them up, and then I crept to my room and shut the door.

That night I dreamt of the church, empty of wings. The bricks had been knocked from the windows and the light flooded in and lay in swathes on the floor, like silk. It was silk. I lifted the edge and flapped it so that it floated and rippled. Under the silk, in the place where I had seen the bones, lay Bronwyn. The silk fluttered down and covered her. I flapped the silk again to see her, to be sure that it was her. She was solidly white and naked in the sun's glare, whiter than the silk. Her nipples were like orange flowers. Her head was to one side and she was dead. I flapped the silk again and again in order to catch quick rippling glimpses. And then all at once she was gone and the silk lay flat on the earthen floor, and it was only light, after all, and impossible to lift.

When I woke I was relieved for an instant that it had been nothing but a dream. I lay basking for an ignorant moment, the real sunshine spilling onto my bed, and then the horror caught up with me. It may have been only a dream, but Bronwyn had really gone, and might really be dead, as white and still as the dream Bronwyn. And Bob *was* dead. He had not been breathing last night, and Mama had screwed her eyes tightly shut against the truth. But it would still be there this morning.

· Part Three ·

· Twenty-Five ·

Susan and I slumped in front of the television. We had
the curtains drawn against the afternoon sun that otherwise blotted the picture from the screen. It was midsummer's day. Last year it had been my birthday. There was
a box of chocolates on the sofa between Susan and me,
Mama's gift, though she hadn't said why. The significance
of the day was unspoken. Mama came in and sat down. I
held out the box and she chose a Montelimar. It was hot
in the room, the people on the screen flickered like
shadows. Susan's mouth was open. I offered her a chocolate but she didn't see. She leant forward, absorbed. I
was proud that she could be content in my house. We
were watching *Crackerjack*, which I thought a stupid programme. Susan liked it though and I liked to watch her
watching. Someone was hit by a custard pie and Susan
giggled. She sat back and took a chocolate. Mama reached
for her knitting. She was making me a school cardigan,
perfectly plain, no cable or fancy stitches, just like Susan's.
A sunbeam inveigled its way through a gap in the curtains
and lit the points of her needles so they flashed like sparks.
My mouth was full of sweet, melting chocolate. I'd been
showing Susan my first set of photographs, and they
remained spread out all over the floor in front of us. Most
of them were unsuccessful, subjects were blurred or
missed altogether, several of them showed nothing but
the bloated smudge of my thumb in front of the lens – but
there was one that was perfect. It was a picture of Mama
on the back doorstep. She was wearing her apron, and
her hair was all windblown wisps, and her hand was a
fuzzy streak on its way to her mouth, for I had caught her
by surprise and her mouth was open in protest. It was a

good picture, a real picture, better than the one Mama had taken of me, perfectly in focus, posed in front of a rose bush with a stiff smile on my face.

The programme ended. 'Fabulous,' Susan said. 'I *love* Crackerjack – especially Leslie Crowther. I *do*,' she protested to Mama, who was shaking her head with amusement.

I took another chocolate and jolted my teeth against a hazelnut. Bob had liked hazelnuts. He would have chosen that one first if he'd been there. My happiness was blunted when I thought – as I often did – of Bob. It had not been my fault that he'd been ill, no one had ever suggested that. It had been his own fault that he hadn't accepted the treatment that might have saved him. I knew that, but all the same a cloud drifted across my happiness now and then, casting a shadow that made me think that he had sulked himself to death because of me. I couldn't enjoy the light fluffiness of my hair without a flicker of guilt. I couldn't slump in front of the television without thinking of the gamma rays. I couldn't drag myself sluggishly from bed without thinking of the daily dozen. And despite all that, I badly missed him. No one bothered with the crossword any more, and the lawn was long and daisy-spattered. In the winter, the heating would be haphazard, because Mama had never got the hang of the system.

I never meant Bronwyn any harm. Her own feet carried her wherever she went. Nobody held her hand. And someone else took her. It wasn't me. People shouldn't believe lies. I wouldn't harm a fly. I wouldn't feel guilt for Bronwyn, I wouldn't and I won't.

Mrs Broom called me over once and invited me in for tea. When I hesitated, not liking to say no, she called at our house and asked Mama if I might go. She wanted someone young in her house, she said. She saw me as innocent. She hadn't linked my visit with what followed. And why should she? Bronwyn was headstrong, always had been. Whatever she'd done it would have been her own decision. And she might come back after all. There was no reason to think – a big strong girl like that. But she would like me there to help her remember, just for a bit of company. Her hands darted nervously about as she spoke, and there was a fluttering at her temple. All the curl had fallen out of her hair.

It was impossible. I had to stay away. I had to look away, even, when I saw her again. She wore her braveness like a coat, imperfectly buttoned over her despair, and I could not bear it. I felt the grey film round the edges of my eyes whenever she was close. I simply could not bear to see her. Mama declined for me. She visited Mrs Broom sometimes and returned home looking squeezed-out, exhausted. I fussed around her then, trying to make amends, bringing her tea and aspirins.

One afternoon I arrived home to find that Mama had tea ready on the special trays with legs she'd bought, so we could eat in front of the television. But the set was not switched on and the room was unnaturally quiet. The sun shone sharply onto our plates of salad. Mama was waiting for me, and she was looking grave. 'Sit down,' she said. 'Bronwyn's clothes have been found. The police came to tell me.' There was a wobble in her voice.

'Just her clothes?'

'Yes. On some wasteland near the old cemetery. Some council workers found them.'

'*Just* her clothes?'

'All of them.'

'Well then, she probably left them there herself. She probably changed and went off, ran off . . .'

Mama shook her head. 'Well, perhaps you're right, but that's not what the police are thinking. They're thinking murder. It's only a matter of time, in cases like this, they say, till they find her.'

I thought what an ugly word *murder* was. It was ridiculous, not related to Bronwyn at all. It was too serious. I thought of her big silliness, of her dolls, of her difficulty with long words. She wouldn't even have been able to spell it. The salad on my plate was brilliantly coloured. I saw it as if magnified: the furled lettuce leaf cradling drops of water, the translucent cucumber slices, the beetroot leaking purple juice into the white of an egg.

'Oh dear,' I said, uselessly. Somewhere far-off I could hear the ice-cream van's jingle.

'Poor, poor Mrs Broom . . . Betty,' Mama whispered.

'It still might not be,' I insisted stubbornly. 'She might not be. We can't be sure, not unless they find the . . .' *Body* I was going to say, remembering the way Bronwyn's body strained against her clothes, the plodding of her feet, her sickly scent of sweat and violets.

'No,' Mama agreed, 'you're right. We must look on the bright side.' She speared a piece of cucumber and put it in her mouth. 'We mustn't dwell on it.'

'No,' I agreed. I switched the television on and we sat side by side, eating our tea, our eyes fixed on the screen.

In the morning there were two red-and-blue-edged airmail letters on the mat. Mama scooped them up and handed one to me. We said nothing. I carried mine upstairs. The writing on the front was sophisticated. The ink was green. The postmark was Adelaide. I was washed over with a wave of confusion. The timing was wrong. I had been awake all night forcing Bronwyn from my mind and now Jacqueline had written. After all my longing. The timing was way out. At this moment, Jacqueline was irrelevant. But I opened the envelope. Inside was a short note and a photograph. I slid my finger over the glossy surface of the photograph before I looked. Jacqueline wasn't the only subject of the photograph. There were four of them: Jacqueline, a tall man with a red beard and two children. Jacqueline smiled out of the distance at me. Her hair was very long and neither light nor dark. It was as long as if it had never been cut. It hung in a tapering plait over one shoulder. I put the photograph on my bed and walked to the window. The children were girls, that made it worse. If they had been boys it might have been all right. One of them was not much younger than me. The girls were tall and golden. I kept glancing back at the photograph, learning it in small glimpses. Jacqueline was wearing a long Indian dress. The man's hair was long and his shirt was open to show his chest. They were in what might have been a vegetable garden. In the distance were some sort of animals. Horses? Cows? Were they farmers then? They looked liked hippies. Jacqueline was much shorter than the man and she was very round. She might have been pregnant. The tiny squinting points of her eyes met mine. She looked like Bob.

Because she looked like Bob I allowed the thought that perhaps Mama *had* told me the truth. The Jacqueline who had been so cruelly banished – who had been forced to rip the threads that bound her to her child – was not this dumpy woman with the tatty rope of a plait, with her bare feet planted squarely in the red earth. *That* Jacqueline had been tall with bone structure and high heels and flashing gems and eyes. *That* Jacqueline would never have done what this Jacqueline did. This Jacqueline was ordinary and did things that were weak and selfish and then tried to make amends. Thirteen years too late.

I read the letter. I had three sisters now. One – Abigail – had been born shortly after the photograph had been taken, at home with her sisters watching. The big girls were called Joanna and Lucy. Would I write to them and say hello? They all wanted me to visit. Jacqueline would pay all our fares. Could we come for Christmas?

Mama came into my room. She looked as if she, too, had had very little sleep. But there was a trembling, precarious brightness about her. She held her letter in her hand. 'A separate envelope!' she said. 'Talk about extravagant!' She fed greedily on the photograph, and read every word of my short letter.

'Well?' Mama said. 'Are you happy? Isn't that what you wanted? Are you going to write?' I shrugged. 'You don't have to, dear, but I shall. I must let her know about Bob. I'll tell her you're fine, shall I? I could send her the nice snap of you in the garden.'

It was slipping out of my hands. I wanted to write myself. I didn't want to be written *about*. 'I'll do it,' I said. 'Let me, please.'

'All right then,' she said. 'We'll both write. And we'll have to think about whether we want to visit, to fly all that way! Can you imagine!'

When she'd gone downstairs I took the long letter I'd written Jacqueline out of the secret compartment of my trinket box and read it through. It was hard to do because it was full of things I wanted to forget. And it made me sound selfish and cruel. And perhaps that was the truth. It also made me sound ridiculous. I considered sending it just as it was. I imagined the effect it might have on her. Quite a surprise, an ugly load to get through the letterbox. Would she let my sisters read it? My golden half-sisters. Eventually I put the letter away and took a fresh sheet of paper and wrote to her from the girl I wanted to be. I was clever and bright and untroubling, a girl made of best handwriting and cheerful words. I said that Bob had 'passed away peacefully' and that Mama and I were 'over it now'. I said I wanted to be a nurse when I grew up, or perhaps a teacher. And that was the truth. I'd abandoned the idea of being a poet now that I felt included in the world. I wanted to be doing something useful. Not reflecting. Not thinking too much, not letting my mind slip into the gaps between the dark and the light. I was happy to be fooled by the surfaces of things – and no poet could be content with that.

I sent her the photograph of me with its silly paper smile. The letter was so innocuous that I let Mama read and approve of it before licking and sticking down the envelope. But I kept the real letter for myself and made myself read it sometimes as a sort of penance to appease the shades of Bob and Bronwyn that hovered in my curtain folds at night.

· Twenty-Six ·

One afternoon after school, weeks later, Susan and I wandered together round the shops and then she went home and I was left near the cemetery. I had avoided it until that day as I tried so hard to avoid thinking about Bronwyn. Nobody mentioned her any more. It was almost as if she had never been. The space she'd left had closed, and it was only from within myself that the bad feelings came. I paused outside the cemetery. The council had started to clear the site and already the whole place looked different. There was a film of dust over all the greenness. There were the rutted tracks of a bulldozer between the graves, and Grace Clover's angel had been knocked down, or had fallen. Its head had broken off, leaving a clean, glistening fracture, and the stone eyes gazed up at the sky. I looked up to where they looked and was dazzled by the sun. With the shimmering sunbursts in my eyes it took me a moment to realise why the cemetery seemed so open and different, and then I saw what they'd done. The briar hedge that separated the playground from the cemetery had been uprooted. It had been piled into a mountain of broken branches and scattered petals. A yellow bulldozer beside it was at rest. No one was there. The workers must have gone for tea. There was a smell of sap and earth, a faint rose scent. Bees still buzzed around the blossoming chaos. Birds did not sing but chirruped indignantly. The playground had gone. The swing frame and the roundabout and the see-saw stump were smashed and piled together, like a giant child's discarded toys. I was dwarfed between them and the mountain of wrecked briars. I could see straight across the strip of wasteland now to the neat back fences of the houses. I could hear a radio playing The Tremeloes, very faintly. I closed my eyes and heard a baby cry. I suppose it was the baby the woman in the house had been expecting the last time I'd seen her, the time she'd seen me. The last time the playground had been my own.

I walked back to the church. Some rose-bay willow-herb had rooted itself in the gutter. Looking up at it and the way it flamed pink against the blue sky, I did not at first see the heap of rubbish outside. It was a stack of old planks, or broken ladders, wormy old stuff, fit only for burning. As I began to turn away something caught my eye, the glint of a brass nail-head. I bent down to look more closely and I saw that there was a streak of red paint where the nail was embedded in the wood. I looked again at the splintery old mess, spotted with worm-holes. I looked fruitlessly for a sign that it had ever been more than the junk it was – that it had ever been wings.

The great arched doors of the church were flung open and for the first time I saw it filled with light. It was smaller than I'd thought, just a space walled in with stone and slate. The floor was perfectly flat. There was no hollow in it and no bones. I walked round and round but it seemed so different in the light that I could hardly remember where Johnny's things had been, and where I had seen the bones. The police had found no sign of them, no sign even that the floor had been disturbed. And it had been so dark that night after all, and I had been tired, half asleep. Perhaps I had dreamt the bones. Or perhaps it was wood that I had seen, just a collection of old sticks that the darkness and my own fear had transmuted into bones. That may have been it. It is strange what sense the mind will make of fragments – especially a frightened mind.

I walked home. The afternoon was hot and tired. Cats lolled in the sunshine, people dawdled, even the yells of children were languid. I imagined Jacqueline walking along this same street, with the same sun shining upon her. And now it shone upon her in another land. Where now it would be winter. The sun was hot on the back of my neck. 'Indian summer,' Bob would have said. And this time last year he would have been out in it, in his deckchair, doing his crossword, brown and naked but for his sunhat, quite secluded behind his tall wooden fences, his trellis screens choked with clematis and honeysuckle. The tarmac path felt sticky under my feet, the smell of sun-baked creosote rose from fences and gates. An ice-cream van blaring a crackly tune drew up in front of me. I fished in my pocket and bought myself a lolly.

'What about Australia then for Christmas?' Mama said, later. We were in the kitchen and she was arranging a potted spiderplant in her latest macramé plant holder. I was polishing my shoes ready for a birthday party.

'Remember Peggy?' I asked.

'Yes, of course. Shall we go, do you think?'

'What about Auntie May? This could be her last . . .'

'It could be,' Mama agreed. 'Poor dear Auntie May.'

'I'm going to have a bath,' I said. 'I'll think about it.'

'That's right. We'll have to make up our minds soon. Like it?' Mama held up her creation.

'Lovely,' I said.

I locked myself in the bathroom and turned on the taps. I crumbled the last of the bath cubes into the water and the faint fragrance of peaches filled the steamy air. There would be no Bob this Christmas and no games. I thought about Peggy, sent to Australia for stealing a peacock. I thought about the hole in the garden, the dirt under my nails, Bob smiling down, encouraging my efforts: 'Put your back into it, girl.' I screwed my eyes up against the sunny steam and tried to remember where I had thought I was going: Wonderland and Australia rolled into one, a place of light and gold and Christmas dinners on the beach. I'd tried to dig my way there once, now I was offered a chance to fly. The bath cube's residue was gritty against my back and bottom. I shifted my weight and thought of Auntie May on Bob's chair beside the Christmas tree, her little feet dangling, and the humorous gleam in her ancient eyes.

I opened my eyes to the ordinariness of my body beneath the soapy film on the surface of the water and I knew that Christmas dinner on the beach would only mean sand in the food, and that I would just be one of many to Jacqueline. I would meet her one day, but there was no urgency. I had seen her now, a small distant woman with a look of Bob.

I relaxed back, breathing in the scented air. It was hot in the bathroom with the sun shining through the frosted glass, and the water warm against my skin. I closed my eyes.

I close my eyes and I put my fingers in my ears and I sing. I sing in the bath with the sun sparkling through the steam and making peacock feathers of my lashes. What happened to Bronwyn I do not know. I do not know whether Johnny was involved, or whether Johnny was ever more than a dreaming fool. There are awful things that run through my mind like trains rattling on their tracks. But I have this way of stopping them reaching their destination, of jolting them off their tracks. I screw up my eyes and I put my fingers in my ears and I sing. I sing

> *Empompey polleney,*
> *pollenistic,*
> *Empompey, polleney,*
> *Academic,*
> *So fa me,*
> *Academic,*
> *Poof, poof.*

Also by Lesley Glaister
available from Minerva

Trick or Treat

'*Honour Thy Father* by Lesley Glaister was one of last year's treats, a first novel with an unmistakable voice, it won the Somerset Maugham Prize and one of the Betty Trask awards. *Trick or Treat*, her second, is even better . . . Three adjoining houses in a northern town. In one, huge Olive and puny Arthur, 17 and 7 stone respectively, still adoring after 50 years of happy, left-wing free love, their antifascist posters still drooping from the walls . . . In the next, pregnant Petra and her brood . . . And in the next, Nell with her mad search for cleanliness and her dirty, middle-aged son, a child-molester . . . Here are lives of dreadful messiness somehow, through love, achieving grace'
Isabel Quigly, *Financial Times*

'As black as molasses, and, in an odd sort of way, as sweet . . . The author has a glorious, flesh-creeping talent for the macabre'
Kate Saunders, *Cosmopolitan*

'Glaister writes extremely well, in the manner of a fledgling Hilary Mantel . . . A superb depiction of an older generation and their ways of coping, and of how festering 50-year grievances can explode into violence'
Tina Ogle, *Time Out*

'Gamey, fetid, squalid old age is a condition that Lesley Glaister writes about with delicate relish . . . Her writing is extraordinary: her tales of scarcely imaginable horror jumbled up with everyday comforts produce an Ortonesque effect that gives rise to shivery laughter'
Penny Perrick, *Sunday Times*

Honour Thy Father

Winner of the 1991 Somerset Maugham Award

'I stayed up into the small hours to read this frightening
yet eerily beautiful book, and later I dreamt about its
strange Fenland landscapes and the sinister but pitiful
people who inhabit them. Lesley Glaister's first novel is
precisely written, with a grim humour; her ear and eye are
exact, and her imagination vivid but controlled. I think
you should buy a Lesley Glaister book now, before
everybody wants one; this new writer is adept, original
and mature'
Hilary Mantel

'Wife battering, incest, murder, madness and monstrosity
seem a lot to pack into a slim volume but Lesley Glaister's
startling short work never gets crowded. This first novel is
a true original. Glaister's writing has an earthy grace that
takes enrichment from sunshine or corpses. The result is
eerie and satisfying – a horror story told with tenderness'
Sunday Times

'Glaister takes a familiar literary scenario – a cantankerous,
ageing crew of maladroit lady relatives holed up in a
remote house (one which can barely withstand the
Fenland winds) – and turns a number of variations on it, to
emerge with not simply a Beryl Bainbridge version of
Waterland but a distinctly individual voice . . . Precise
observation accumulates to form an outrageously plausible
whole, the grotesque modified by the sensitive and
rendered with care'
Times Literary Supplement

A Selected List of Fiction Available from Minerva

While every effort is made to keep prices low, it is sometimes necessary to increase prices at short notice. Mandarin Paperbacks reserves the right to show new retail prices on covers which may differ from those previously advertised in the text or elsewhere.

The prices shown below were correct at the time of going to press.

☐	7493 9145 6	**Love and Death on Long Island**	Gilbert Adair £4.99
☐	7493 9130 8	**The War of Don Emmanuel's Nether Parts**	Louis de Bernieres £5.99
☐	7493 9903 1	**Dirty Faxes**	Andrew Davies £4.99
☐	7493 9056 5	**Nothing Natural**	Jenny Diski £4.99
☐	7493 9173 1	**The Trick is to Keep Breathing**	Janice Galloway £4.99
☐	7493 9124 3	**Honour Thy Father**	Lesley Glaister £4.99
☐	7493 9918 X	**Richard's Feet**	Carey Harrison £6.99
☐	7493 9028 X	**Not Not While the Giro**	James Kelman £4.99
☐	7493 9112 X	**Hopeful Monsters**	Nicholas Mosley £6.99
☐	7493 9029 8	**Head to Toe**	Joe Orton £4.99
☐	7493 9117 0	**The Good Republic**	William Palmer £5.99
☐	7493 9162 6	**Four Bare Legs in a Bed**	Helen Simpson £4.99
☐	7493 9134 0	**Rebuilding Coventry**	Sue Townsend £4.99
☐	7493 9151 0	**Boating for Beginners**	Jeanette Winterson £4.99
☐	7493 9915 5	**Cyrus Cyrus**	Adam Zameenzad £7.99

All these books are available at your bookshop or newsagent, or can be ordered direct from the publisher. Just tick the titles you want and fill in the form below.

Mandarin Paperbacks, Cash Sales Department, PO Box 11, Falmouth, Cornwall TR10 9EN.

Please send cheque or postal order, no currency, for purchase price quoted and allow the following for postage and packing:

UK including BFPO £1.00 for the first book, 50p for the second and 30p for each additional book ordered to a maximum charge of £3.00.

Overseas including Eire £2 for the first book, £1.00 for the second and 50p for each additional book thereafter.

NAME (Block letters) ....

ADDRESS ....

....

☐ I enclose my remittance for ....

☐ I wish to pay by Access/Visa Card Number

Expiry Date